PENGUIN BOOKS

THE *CITY LIFE* BOOK OF MANCHESTER SHO

Ra Page was born in 1972 in Portland and gre
Peak District, hitching every weekend to Manche
the age of thirteen. He claims to be the first person allowed
into the Haçienda with a rucksack. He read Physics and
Philosophy at Balliol College, Oxford, and then did an MA in
English under Michael Schmidt at Manchester University.
He has worked variously as a chain-gang member, farm
hand, landscape gardener, and book reviewer for the
Guardian, *The Times*, the *New Statesman* and, of course, *City
Life*. He has also had his poetry published in a number of
British literary magazines.

The *City Life* Book
of Manchester
Short Stories
Edited by Ra Page

PENGUIN BOOKS

City Life, Jan '00

PENGUIN BOOKS

Published by the Penguin Group
Penguin Books Ltd, 27 Wrights Lane, London W8 5TZ, England
Penguin Putnam Inc., 375 Hudson Street, New York, New York 10014, USA
Penguin Books Australia Ltd, Ringwood, Victoria, Australia
Penguin Books Canada Ltd, 10 Alcorn Avenue, Toronto, Ontario, Canada M4V 3B2
Penguin Books (NZ) Ltd, Private Bag 102902, NSMC, Auckland, New Zealand

Penguin Books Ltd, Registered Offices: Harmondsworth, Middlesex, England

Published in Penguin Books 1999
1 3 5 7 9 10 8 6 4 2

Lyrics quoted on page 46 are from 'This is the Day', words and music by Don van Vliet and
Andy di Martino © 1974, Honeysuckle Music Inc. USA. Reproduced by permission of
EMI Virgin Music Ltd, London WC2H 0EH

Set in 9.75/14 pt PostScript Monotype News Gothic
Typeset by Rowland Phototypesetting Ltd, Bury St Edmunds, Suffolk
Printed in Great Britain by Clays Ltd, St Ives plc

A CIP catalogue record for this book is available from the British Library

For Jackie

Take me back to Manchester when it's raining
I want to wet me feet in Albert Square
I'm all agog
For a good, thick fog.
I don't like the sun
I like it raining cats and dogs!

I want to smell the odours of the Irwell.
I want to feel the soot get in me 'air.
Oh I don't want to roam.
I want to get back 'ome
To rainy
Manchester . . .

Traditional

Contents

Acknowledgements

Ra would especially like to thank Steven Blyth and Chris Hart at *Prop*, Sean Body, Terry Christian, Tibor Fischer, Sophie-dot-Hanson, Russ Hickman, Sue Jones and Brian Harrison at Manchester Airport, Michelle Kass, Ric Michael, Erne Naughton, Simon Prosser, Lesley Shaw, Adrian Slatcher, Lin and Jon Shaffer, Bron Williams at North West Arts Board, everyone at Waterstone's Deansgate, and of course everyone at *City Life* magazine.

Introduction

What is it with Manchester? Not content with having the country's most talented football team for the last decade (Man City, that is). Not satisfied with being home to the nation's most influential music for arguably the last twenty years. Not sated with being the birthplace of the world's first computer, the shooting ground where Man first split the atom, the sociological model on which Friedrich Engels helped found Communism, and the world's first industrial city ('the oldest modern city'), here it is challenging London, New York and Paris for the title of literary epicentre.

Am I serious? Kind of.

Though this burgeoning city of ours boasts no nationally distributing fiction publisher, not a single literary agent and nowhere that remotely resembles the Groucho Club, it is, as this anthology hopes to demonstrate, producing some of the most daring and innovative writing of the moment.

Of course it wasn't always this way. At the turn of the eighties, when John Cooper Clarke wrote of the Beasley Street kids 'their only common problem / is that they're not someone else', he might well have been speaking of all Mancunians. Such was the lack of what fat councillors might call 'civic pride', almost anyone with an inkling of creative ambition inevitably joined the steady exodus south, shedding everything that constituted their 'regional' identity on the train down. Writers in particular felt they had to ascend from the parochial into the locationless concerns of the English literary elite. And in a tradition started by Thomas De Quincey, who ran away from Manchester Grammar in 1802 for the backstreets of Soho, Manchester writers from Anthony Burgess to Howard Jacobson and Nicholas Royle have treated the capital as an opportunity to reinvent themselves, shed their roots. Even a writer like Bill Naughton, whose forte lay precisely in capturing regional idioms, broke through into the wider public consciousness only when he turned to the capital's cockney in his play, book and film *Alfie*.

The few strong writers who stayed in Manchester, continuing the tradition of Harold Brighouse and Walter Greenwood, saw their work read as socio-political arguments rather than evocations of the Manchester experience. Even the classics of social realism were stretched, bullied and generally manipulated into the social realities beyond their texts, and Manchester as a setting faded with all the other kitchen-sink dramas into just another bleak urban province. The film of *A Taste of Honey* seemed to come from pretty much the same place as the film versions of Stan Barstow's *A Kind of Loving* (West Riding), John Braine's *Room at the Top* (Bradford) and Alan Sillitoe's *Saturday Night and Sunday Morning* (Nottingham). Indeed the most successful provincial realist drama of the fifties and sixties, *Billy Liar*, was set in no particular city at all, just a fictional and diluted amalgamation of all of them, Stradhaughton.

What happened to transform Manchester into a town that stood proudly above the provincial crowd, a place where artists flocked to rather than ran from, was quite simply music.

After Manchester's visceral, independent punk scene in the late seventies, and the diametrically opposed trail-blazing of New Order and of The Smiths in the mid-eighties, the gathering cultural might of Factory Records with its Situationist super-club, the Haçienda, lit a fuse for an eventual explosion of music at the end of the eighties. 'Madchester', as the music press tagged it, saw a two-pronged revival in dance and guitar music which Manchester bands and British music in general have built on ever since. In the space of ten years Manchester became the place to be. The city's night-time economy featured on the cover of *Newsweek* and the *LA Times* and became the yardstick against which all other British club scenes were measured. Unlike the Mersey scene which came and went in the twinkling of a decade, Manchester is still, ten years later, firmly stamped on the nation's musical imagination, with Oasis still ringing in our ears, a new crop of independent record labels and various reformations.

What does this have to do with the city's writing, or the experience they are writing out of? Why am I mentioning it and including music industry figures as authors, if this *isn't* supposed to be just another *Zeitgeist* companion/nostalgia trip? Why? Because the natural voice of the city, its language, perspective and character are, I believe, intrinsically wrapped up with its musical lyricism: 'the ready-made poetry of Mancunian conversation', as Michael Bracewell put it (in *England is Mine*, 1997); the song-infused speech that laced the early plays of Shelagh Delaney with obscure ballads and nursery rhymes (though they were expunged from Tony Richardson's

1961 film *A Taste of Honey*), and which bubbled back into the magpie lyrics of The Smiths. It was to this sing-song tradition that Manchester's greatest film director, Mike Leigh, paid tribute in the climactic bathroom scene in *Naked*, and which is evident in the rich rhythms of Jeff Noon or in the career trajectory of Factory-signed rapper turned bestselling novelist Nicholas Blincoe.

As the outside world became more attuned to the musical Manchester tongue, through the lovable rogues of its music and the brief opening for regional accents in the national media (before the Beryl Bainbridge prejudice reasserted itself), so the city's writers grew more confident in their own voice. Of course other factors have contributed to the city's literary ascendancy: the creative writing schools pioneered by Richard Francis and Michael Schmidt at the Victoria and Metropolitan universities, the presence of community publisher Commonword and Carcanet's poetry press in the heart of the city, to name but two. But it was the city's musical revolution that awoke the real lyricism in the Mancunian voice: that buried Irish lilt, mixed with bluff Lancashire obstinacy, with more than a pinch of Afro-Caribbean swagger, Jewish argot and Asian colour (left in a pre-heated post-industrial oven for two to three generations).

As Manchester is an immigrant city and composed right to its very core of diversity, the 'Manchester Story' can never realistically be told by one author. My abiding criterion then was simply to represent this diversity: some writers address the tensions between the city's diverging and converging social groups, others stay safely within their own. The experiences and perspectives of four members of Manchester's music industry are also represented, though the author of 'The Lightweight Trigger' wishes to remain anonymous. I have also included one story not set in Manchester, because, being part of a heavily autobiographical novel in progress, it provides an insight into one of Manchester's central literary figures, Michael Schmidt.

The closing couplet of stories (including an unpublished one by the late Bill Naughton) question the very idea of trying to understand a community's experience from outside. Although these talk of infiltration at a personal and sociological level, they also raise questions about the aim of this kind of anthology and the feasibility of ever sharing the Manchester experience with outside readers. As with all lofty endeavours, though, the mere fact that it's impossible shouldn't put us off trying.

Ra Page
April 99, Manchester

How It Came to Pass

This anthology began as a germ of an idea that could only grow into something much bigger: a desire to reflect the city's contemporary literary scene and promote that most undervalued of literary forms, the short story. And it began in Manchester, at *City Life* magazine, the city's fortnightly guide to all that's happening in arts and entertainment in the area.

After a number of increasingly enthusiastic conversations between myself and Ra Page, *City Life*'s Books Editor, the idea began to take shape for two collections of six short stories featuring twelve of Manchester's finest contemporary writers, to be distributed free with *City Life*. With the support of the North West Arts Board and Manchester Airport, these were published in September 1998 and February 1999.

It was always our intention that this would be more than just a Manchester thing, and it's thanks to Penguin's enthusiasm for the project that we've been able to take such a unique collection of fiction to an international audience. A number of the stories included here were first published in those *City Life* collections, and I'm immensely proud of the magazine's role in making this unique book happen. I hope you enjoy reading the stories set down here as much as I have enjoyed seeing this project grow, develop and finally come to fruition.

Chris Sharratt
Editor of *City Life*
April 1999

The Beautiful Beaten-up Irish Boy of the Arndale Centre
Nicholas Blincoe

Me and Maureen are a double act. She takes the money, three pounds on the door or two-fifty with a flyer. I do the heavy work, all padded up as usual, wearing a puffa jacket so I look about twice my normal size. Even naked, I'm six foot four and weigh sixteen stone. You can imagine. There's never much trouble.

So Maureen is sitting, I'm standing. We're practically shoulder-to-pelvic bone, blocking the whole of the entrance, when this blur, this streak of blue-black lightning, comes whizzing between us. I could have said like stuff off a shovel but I didn't see any shovel, it was more space-age than that. Like a sci-fi whoosh: Ground Control to Great Ancoats Street, you want to beam me up or what? Maureen pokes me in the side, says, 'The frig was that?'

I tell her, 'Got to be some beggar thinks he can get in without paying. Though he's light on his feet, that's all I can say.'

Every other Thursday, there's a bit of an Irish night upstairs at the Volunteer. The same every week, it's always Barry's

Showband; basically Barry, his pal Steve and a couple of kids who are in it for beer money. They never practise, so they aren't much good, but they can play 'Whiskey in the Jar' which is the important thing. Anyway, the top room at the Volunteer is up this narrow flight of stairs. So I take a look over the rail, see everything looks quiet and tell Maureen I'll go see. Got to find the monkey first, then he's out on his ear.

I never know why but Barry can pull a crowd. Not a big crowd but Thursday night has always been competitive. As I walk into the main room, Barry's starting in on 'Dirty Old Town' and people are lifting their heads out of their glasses and shifting position slightly so they can catch his eye and nod, showing they like his choice. As I push between them, it's like I'm squeezing through almost-set jelly: it's all just wobbling slightly but still quite wet. Then I see this kid and I know he's the one. The way he's buzzing round the crowd, he has to be. He's so quick, all the jelly in the world couldn't slow him down.

I see immediately he's Irish. He's got black curly hair like he's one of those descended from the Spanish sailors the time the Armada went down. He's totally hyperactive, I would say about one-twenty-five pounds, maybe one-twenty-eight. I reckon he could choose his weight, he would do okay fighting in two or three different divisions. If he could fight, that is. The reason I'm thinking he'll never be a contender, he has both eyes blacked and a broken nose besides.

I go after him.

The puffa jacket makes me look impressive but you don't want to be doing anything too strenuous if you're in a semi-busy bar with the heating turned up high and a humid haze coming off the punters' damp clothes. As I move towards him, I'm hoping he doesn't make me work because I don't want to be chasing all over the show. He looks over, our eyes lock. I'm doing a Schmeichel, trying to guess if he's going for my left or my right. But he just breaks into this smile and it doesn't matter that the flesh around his eyes is swollen like red onions and his nose is like dirty putty, he just looks so bloody beautiful. His eyes are a clear and sparkling blue, bright enough to shine through the purple bruising. His dimples set off his smile, so you don't care about the misshapen mess of the rest of his face. Then he's got these teeth, baby-like little pegs that could be individually back-lit, they look so radiant. He's got curls falling around his forehead and twisting about the rose-petal flesh of his ears. He's about half my weight and more than a foot shorter, and when he juts out his chin and stares up at me, it's like he's got the lighting situation completely sussed. He is the picture of a bruised angel.

He says, 'How about you? You alright?'

I nod. 'You're not going to tell me you paid, are you, son?'

'You have to pay? But I thought I'd be fine, I'm a mate of Barry's.'

'Everyone's mates with Barry,' I say. 'And they all paid for the pleasure.'

Barry is starting on his version of Steve Earle's 'Guitar Town'. Following on from 'Dirty Old Town', it's part of the Barry Town trilogy which always ends with 'Downtown', the old Petula Clark number. Though Barry only knows the words as far as the second line. If the audience wants any more, they have to sing it themselves.

I have my hand on the Irish boy's shoulder, his smile growing even wider.

'Will you give me a second? I'm just looking for someone, five minutes and I'll be gone.'

I can feel the bony knob of his shoulder under the thin

plastic of his anorak. I could pick him up one-handed and swing him out the door. But looking down at him, he is already so beaten-up, I couldn't do it. I know he's a liar, that he is taking the piss. But it's my choice. I tell him, 'Okay. Just keep out of trouble.'

Back at the door, Maureen asks, 'Couldn't you find him?'

'He'll be okay,' I say. 'Little twat.'

I'm right, everything is fine. For five minutes.

The disturbance starts over at the far end of the bar. It's the only real problem with the Volunteer, the way the bar runs off the main room down a kind of blind corridor. It's a design flaw, always leads to bottlenecks. If there's ever any trouble, it's going to kick off down there.

I hear the screaming and the shouting and I get stuck in, hauling bodies out the way. I have to go in both arms swinging, how else am I going to get to the trouble? The bar area is so crowded, it's rammed. Looking over everyone's head, I see this guy taking a punch at someone. I know I'm too slow to stop him, I just want to make sure it goes no further. By the time I grab hold of his arm, he's already pasted the other guy's nose. There's a line of blood filling the space between the two halves of his 'tash but, even so, he's not even trying to fight back. He is too outraged. He's shouting, 'The hell you playing at? You bloody lunatic.'

The guy I'm holding is yelling, 'Bugger took my shot. I just turned to pay for it.'

I look to the bar. There's a full pint glass and a shot glass next to it, empty. The guy with the bloody nose is saying, 'Well, it wasn't me, you psycho. You saw the lad do it.'

'He was your mate.'

'I never saw the bugger before. You want to tell me, what's your fucking problem?'

I decide the guy threw the punch has to go. Though I know him and he's never once given me bother before. I tell him, 'Come on, son. Let's be having you.' He lets me guide him out.

We're out of the bar area when I ask, 'Why'd you hit him?'

'I couldn't hit the lad who'd done it. The state of his face, someone had already given him a real hiding.'

I knew it was the beaten-up Irish boy, I didn't have to ask.

We are halfway across the room when the next thing flares up, a woman this time. My problem is, I don't know whether to leave hold of my guy or not. My brain goes static on me for a second, trying to make that decision. By the time I've dropped him and run across the room, Maureen is handling the situation.

She's yelling, 'Has anyone seen this lady's purse?'

The band has stopped playing. They're just standing at the edge of the dais, seeing what's happening. Steve the bassist shouts out, he's seen the lad throw something under the next table.

A bystander gets on his knees under the table. I wouldn't go down there, that's all I can say. I have nightmares about the carpets in the Volunteer, I'm not joking. But he scrabbles around and he comes up with the woman's purse. It's been opened and emptied, of course.

Maureen takes it, hands it to the woman, saying, 'You saw him do it? Why didn't you stop him?'

'I told him to leave it alone.' The woman is standing with her big mitts balled up, stuck in her sides. She has a dazed look on her face that is not just down to the shandies and when she speaks she's flustered.

Maureen is staring up at her and you can tell she's thinking,

Come on, you're a big woman. She says, 'Yes. But why didn't you stop him?'

'I couldn't. Poor thing was that bashed up.'

It was kiddo again. I'm shouting, 'Where is he now? Anyone seen him?'

I'm thinking, He must have done a runner.

Steve points the neck of his bass towards the back of the room and nods. 'No. He's still here.'

The next half hour, it's like a Tom and Jerry feature. The kid keeps popping up at different spots around the room and I'm too slow. I catch a glimpse of him, three separate times, but he just slips underneath the crowd and reappears somewhere else. And what he leaves behind, it's like a dust trail of confusion.

A guy catches him with a hand in his coat, another has left a leather jacket hanging on the back of his chair and the kid almost gets away with it. Then it's quiet for ten minutes and the band's started up again – 'Pub Crawl' by Brendan Shine – and I give up looking. Then another purse goes missing.

I'm getting no help.

Everyone is trying to point me in the right direction. But any one of them could have grabbed hold, given me a hand and held him until I'd lumbered over. The kid is charmed, it's unnatural. We've got some of the biggest nuts in Manchester in the room and none of them wants to hurt the kid because he looks so sweet and vulnerable. I can't believe what I'm seeing.

I'm standing in the middle of the room, trying to get my bearings. Actually, trying to cool down because I'm still wearing the puffa jacket and I left off my deodorant this evening. I never thought I'd be getting into heavy athletics. Barry's hammering the chords for the intro of Johnny Cash's 'Folsom

Prison Blues' and he goes and snaps a string. He stops the song right there, flagging it down like he's flagging down a taxi late at night in Rusholme.

The band's got no feeling for how to start or stop together. They kind of slither to a halt – like if they really were a taxi, it would be an unlicensed minicab, pulling a handbrake turn on a patch of black ice. It's the best they've sounded all night.

Barry's shouting, 'Hold up, I just got to change my guitar.'

Barry plays a Strat, a genuine one though it's bottom of the line. But he has a catalogue copy as back-up, for when he breaks a string. He once told me he's a professional. No one wants to wait for him to restring and tune up. I asked him, 'You serious? You ever tune up?'

Now he's shouting, 'Where's my fucking guitar?'

Half the pub turns, pointing to the exit. The beaten-up Irish boy is walking out the door, he's got Barry's catalogue Stratocaster under his arm.

Fortnight later, I'm in the Arndale Centre, I see Dicky Stocker outside JD Sports. We've not worked together I don't know how long. We did security at the Apollo for yonks but you got to be talking fifteen, twenty years ago now. That long at least.

I go over, tell him I didn't know he was working as a store dick.

Dicky says, 'Trainers, mate.' He nods his head back into the store, all these brand name trainers standing on little plinths like they been knocked out by Picasso. Signed, too. Except the betting is that this Michael Jordan didn't actually do the sculpting work, that was likely a Taiwanese teenager with a glue gun and a roll of Velcro.

I say, 'Nice.'

Dicky says, 'Trainers would run out on their own, they didn't put a fat cunt like me on the door.'

I'm thinking of asking, This nice work or what? Only I value my afternoons, gives me time to wander around and do my own thing. Like today, I got down the market, bought myself a piece of pecorino cheese and a pot plant. Dicky nods at the plant, says, 'Begonias?'

'Yeah.'

'Nice one.'

He has a walkie-talkie stuffed in the front of his puffa jacket. I only realize because it starts with the electronic burp noises. Dicky reaches through the collar of his jacket, his nose tucked down as he answers the call.

I know it's bad news. It's like he's bleeding swear words. The call over, he looks up, tells me, 'Sorry, mate.'

'What's up?'

'It was the Olympus shop on Market Street,' he says. 'They just seen Dyl McDonagh, and he's got a right pair of shiners again.'

I know he is talking about the beaten-up Irish boy and it isn't a case of intuition. I've purposefully gone out and learnt the kid's name. I also know, the only time anyone sees him he has his eyes blacked. It's like a charm. It renders him inviolable, as every bouncer and store dick in Manchester has now learnt to say.

I ask, 'What are we going to do?'

'We see him first. We twat him.'

'You reckon?' I wasn't so sure. 'You ever seen him up close?'

Dicky nods. 'You kidding?' He's got this story: 'I tell you, two months back, he comes in hooded up in an anorak, like a Tommy Hilfiger but with the colours all wrong, must be a DIY job. Two minutes later, I hear a shout and he comes running out with a pair of Filas still in the box. The assistant's seen him but done nowt. Now the kid's moving so fast I only just manage to grab the hood off his anorak as he screeches past. I tell you, I swung the bugger clean off his feet. I'm standing there, tightening my grip and waiting for him to stop swinging. He's choking, trying to get his breath and stretch his toes to the ground. Then I fix him with a stern look and he looks back with these miserable eyes and the rest of his face is beaten to a pulp. It's like, ''Did you have to kill my puppy dog, mister?'' I tell you, I'm almost in tears.'

Dicky looks right and left across the tiled mall floor, weighing up the passing customers. Then he leans in to me. 'I had to let him go. I couldn't help myself. The next thing I know, he's back in here. He must have got away with five, six pairs of trainers just that one day.'

I say, 'We'd be doing the whole of Manchester a favour.'

'Too right. We catch him, I'll hold his arms, you give him a right twomping.'

'Okay,' I say. 'Or else, we do it the other way around.'

There were different theories about our beaten-up Irish boy. One, that there was an evil Fagin-type character in the background who would black the lad's eyes in the same way that medieval beggars were supposed to break the legs of their own children, give them a trade as professional cripples. Another story, that the bruising was make-up applied with a trowel by an auntie who worked on a make-up counter in Kendal's. I gave this story some thought. I even took a turn round Kendal's ground floor, trying to penetrate the inch-thick foundation on the different make-up ladies, searching for a family resemblance to McDonagh. I didn't have any luck but,

I knew, it was wishful thinking. I was hoping he was wearing make-up. I wanted it to be a trick, not real.

The truth, I reckon, the kid is nothing but an inept chancer. He might go out of a night, get into trouble. Maybe he's on the sniff, the girl's boyfriend catches him and leathers him. Or someone catches him stealing their pint and decides to teach him a lesson. Or it might be a bouncer gives him a clout, say he's too lippy or he throws up over the wrong pair of shoes. Or it might happen down the shops, he'll be slipping the Danepak down his trousers, the store dick steps on him. Who knows? It could happen a million ways.

But once he's got his magic black eyes, he is transformed. The difference between the idiots you see any day you care to walk down Crown Square, the kids going into court, and the kind of master criminal who's got plans for a big job. The black eyes are his edge, his badge of genius, a Zorro mask, pummelled out of his flesh.

And it looks as if me and Dicky are going to be the ones to save the world from his reign of terror. We're ready for him, we're geed up. We see him appear around a free-standing pay-phone, we start running.

I scream to Dicky, 'Whatever you do, don't look at his eyes.'

The boy pauses, a tremor running through his body. There's a moment when he is not sure: we really coming for him? He's got a long, thick fringe that swings across his face. Only as he turns, I catch a glimpse of the bruising. It seems to me I feel fine. I will be able to do what I have to do, when the time comes.

He runs for the far side of the concourse, trying to keep as much street furniture and potted plants as possible between us and him. Dicky signals to me 'You go that way.' I nod. The idea, we'll try a pincer move, catch the bugger between us.

The boy makes his decision and puts on a turn of speed. He takes a corner so tight his body's at an angle to the floor, like a speedway champion. He slithers round a woman pushing a baby buggy and evades capture. Dicky, he's practically left standing.

I come pounding up, say, 'Pull it out, for cheese cake.'

Me and Dicky, we have to weigh thirty-five stone. Moving at speed, you can multiply that. We're like a juggernaut, our big white trainers pounding across the pale floor of the Arndale Centre. The beaten-up Irish boy is way ahead of us but he has to dart around the shoppers, he's so jockey-light. We steamroll right through, the path clears for us and we're gaining ground. By the time he reaches the escalator, I reckon I can hit him, I only need a lucky throw. I could bounce my pot plant off his head, I'm just scared I'll hit a civilian.

McDonagh leaps for the side of the escalator, riding the rubber strap on his backside. Dicky follows, trying to shoulder his way, but the escalator is rammed solid. He doesn't have room for manoeuvre. I keep to the upper concourse; ahead of me there is an open section with balcony views over the floor below. I have my plan. I've got my pot plant nestled under my chin like a shot putt. Pretty soon, I'm looking down and I see our boy. He's scrabbling to find his feet after over-shooting the end of the escalator. I lead with my left arm, getting the whole of my weight moving forward, whipping from a point in the centre of my back. My right arm comes thumping up and the begonias are out of my hand, flying through the coolly conditioned air of the Arndale Centre and tumbling, tumbling, tumbling . . .

It catches him such a clout, he goes sprawling. Like an ice skater in a comedy fall, he's spread-eagled on the floor, spinning clockwise across the smooth surface. Now he's face down but as the crowd begins to form, a woman kneels and turns him over to cradle his head in her lap. The racoon stripe of his black eyes seems to swell and throb, the whites of his eyes flicker at me. The crowd follows his gaze.

I am frozen. If you put industrial rivets through my feet, I couldn't be more firmly rooted to the spot. There is nothing I can do. Thirty pairs of eyes staring up at me, then forty, then fifty. And then a voice, shouting, 'That's him.' I recognize the voice but I still can't believe it's Dicky Stocker. The bastard's even pointing.

'It was him.'

Oh god, I swear I'm sorry. Tell me what I can do to make it better. When this moment is over, this crowd is going to kill me for sure.

Lucky
Jane Rogers

There were 7 tests. If the 8.20 to Victoria was on time. If there were no empty seats. If I saw the weird couple. If I could get across the station concourse without them making any change-of-platform announcements. If the beggar was in that doorway just round the corner from the post office. If a pigeon walked across the pavement in front of me without me dodging to get it there. And if I arrived at work before 9. Check check check check check check check! He loves me.

Each day I make it more difficult and each day it's proved – apart from Tuesday which was crap in every other way as well, what can you expect, it would be unbelievable if it did always work, there has to be an exception to prove the rule. Like spelling.

He brought the report back in to me at 3.07.

– Well done Janine, you've done a good job. He smiled. – Apart from the usual problem. Have you turned that spell-checker off, or simply converted it to your own personal language?

– It's on, I said. I was trying to stop giggling. – There wasn't a single underlining. Honest.

He laughed that deep brown glow in his eyes it warms you through to your guts.

– Creative spelling. I love it! OK, I've underlined in pencil here. Can you get it in tonight's post?

He was starting to go. Like the sun disappearing behind a huge dark cloud taking all his lovely warmth away.

– Dr Anderson . . .

– Yes?

– I – d'you want to see the corrected copy?

– No, Janine, I trust you.

Of course he does. He trusts me. He closed the door gently and you could hear my heart banging like a drum, sometimes it's dangerous, I'm afraid the others will notice – the bitching, the gossip, they'd have a field day. You only have to listen to the way they talk about Maggie. Lisa was on the phone though and Laura was taking her printer to bits, the paper feed was jammed again. They don't notice. Because they can't imagine. They can't imagine he'd like someone like me. They think they're so great with their Wonderbras and lipgloss and step-ladder shoes, they don't even ask me what I did on Saturday night.

Well fuck them. They know nothing.

Once he sent me a note. *Jan – articles from BMJ on post-abortion depression, May 95–97, by 10.30 if pos? You're wonderful*.

I keep it folded up in my pocket. I can feel it through my jeans, secret against my thigh.

You'll be wondering how it started. I'll tell you. It's good to tell someone at last, it's been like this secret balloon inside me, this lovely growing swelling thing that makes me so huge and light I sometimes think I'll burst – burst with happiness or just take off and float into the sky. The secret wants to burst out of me, I want everyone to know.

It was instant. First sight, on my second Monday there. He came into the office.

– What's this? Can't a man turn his back for an instant without everything changing? He smiled at me. He's got grey hair but he smiled right into my eyes and I had that feeling you get in a high-speed lift when it suddenly plummets 20 floors and you think Omygod.

– This is Janine, said Laura. She kicked Lisa under her desk then she said, She's filling in for Maggie.

– Welcome Janine filler-in-for-Maggie, he said. You let me know if they're not looking after you.

My hands were sweating, I couldn't hit a single key right. I had to get out a pen and fiddle about pretending to make a note of something. He went over to Lisa's desk asking about some letters, his voice is deep and soft and furry my ears can pick it out anywhere it's right close up to them, in a crowd I can sometimes hear it too, low and close murmuring beside me as if it'll keep me safe from everything. When he'd finished at Lisa's desk he came back past me and he slowed down he couldn't walk past me he couldn't help himself he had to stop.

– You girls get younger every week. How old are you Janine – or is that an offensive question?

– No. I was afraid I would giggle. It's horrible. It comes out sometimes and then they laugh at me they used to laugh at school. – 18.

– As old as that!

– I was giggling. I couldn't help it. He would hate me and think I was an idiot. He started to laugh.

– She's a giggler! he said to Laura and Lisa. Wonderful! A

dose of that all round every morning and you'd halve the NHS waiting lists!

He went then and I was giggling so hard I was gasping for breath, I could feel my face like a beetroot. But the other two didn't notice, they were whispering together, Maggie this and Maggie that, he can't wait till she gets back. He's been to see her twice in hospital. I wasn't interested in Maggie. I knew he liked me. You can tell.

You know it but you don't believe it. You have to keep checking, you don't dare to let yourself think it might be true. That someone like him could fall for me. But everything that's happened – every single thing – reinforces it.

The library. I go to the library for my lunch. Often I think I won't, I think I'll go to a wine bar where there are foreigners or businessmen doing deals but in the end I go to the library. The others send out for sandwiches but I don't like sitting listening to them, I like to go somewhere where I can watch people without them feeling sorry for me and trying to drag me into the conversation. In the library you go through the revolving door and past that expensive card shop then down the stairs to the café. I like the posters down the stairs, all the plays they have on there, one day I'm going to go to that theatre. One night, I should say. I bet it's different at night full of glamorous people holding drinks from the bar, chattering away, reading their programmes. Maybe I'll go with him!

At lunchtime you can sit by a pillar or the wall, usually you can get a table to yourself and there are invisible people there, old codgers with lots of coats and a cup of tea, sometimes studenty types, I suppose they use the library, or ordinary people, fat with a shopping bag. There's a man with glasses who always reads a book, everyone ignores each other and you just queue and pay for your sandwich, none of that embarrassing waiter business. You can buy theatre tickets there – I've seen where they do it. Also the toilets are good, very big with gigantic mirrors, there are four cubicles and when you come out it's like you're a film star reflecting back and forth and back and forth in the mirrors in front and behind.

He came into the library café. July 2nd. July, the 7th month. I still don't know . . . did he follow me? I can't believe he did but how else did he end up there when I was there, what are the chances of him going where I was going at lunchtime with the whole of Manchester and all the important people he has to meet for lunch and the girls asking if he wants a sandwich when they pop out – how did he end up there with me?

I was in the right-hand corner by the pillar near the stairs and he came down the opposite stairs. We saw each other straight away. Instant. He smiled then there was a little frown, I was afraid he wasn't pleased to see me. But he didn't have to look at me, it's easy enough for people to pretend they haven't seen you isn't it? They do it all the time. Or he could have just smiled and waved from a distance. But no, he came straight to my table like he was drawn there by a magnet.

– All on your own Janine? Not having lunch with the other girls?

I shook my head. I was afraid I might giggle.

– Is everything all right? You all getting on OK in the office?

He was so kind, he *is* so kind. He's the kindest person I ever met.

– Fine thank you. I just – I didn't want him to think I was stupid but I couldn't think what else to say. – I like it here.

It's a marvellous building isn't it? A jewel in the heart of the city!

He understands everything I think.

– I'm waiting for a book from the depths. May I join you?

He went to the counter and when he was there he turned back to me and made sign language pointing to the teacups then back to me. I mouthed back coffee and he smiled and I felt as if I was melting into a puddle. I *was* melting into a puddle it was awful my nose started to run and I had to swallow my mouth was full of saliva I was all warm and watery inside I was afraid I might have wet myself. I didn't dare to look at him until he was sitting down, he ate his sandwich in 7 bites. 7 is my lucky number.

– D'you use this library? he said. I shook my head and he leaned forward. Have you ever been upstairs?

Upstairs. I can't believe he asked me that.

– No. The giggles were rising in my throat nearly choking me.

– Well if you've finished come with me and have a look. You might want to use it one day.

He stood up and drank his coffee in three gulps. It was coffee. The same as mine – not tea. We went up the marble steps together there are 26 to the ground floor, I stepped on each one at the same time as him. We moved at the same speed.

– Wonderful institution, public libraries, he said. But we must use them. Use them or lose them, eh Janine!

He says my name so beautifully. I was giggling and he laughed too, he joins in my giggle. I thought I would never tell anyone because people would probably sneer, my mother would say something terrible and crude like he's a dirty old man or something because he's about 20 years older than me but she doesn't understand anything. Now I have to tell someone but you won't laugh because you can see he's not dirty he's kind, he's kind to a person like me when he doesn't have to be, he notices me he talks to me he looks at me he loves me.

We turned round the corner and went up the next lot of steps – 35 (definitely lucky – the sum of my birthday and month, the 27th of the 8th). There's a desk where you get books stamped then he turned in through an archway into the centre of the building and I followed him in between two tall bookcases into the middle where it opens up. He looked at me. He was looking at me to see if I liked it. It opens up under a vast round white dome smooth as an egg, with a glass circle at the top. Around the edges, gilt lettering: SHE SHALL BRING THEE TO HONOUR WHEN THOU DOST EMBRACE HER. SHE SHALL GIVE TO THINE HEAD AN ORNAMENT OF GRACE. Me. Me and him. It must be. He knows it. Brilliant sunlight pouring through the glass dome.

– It's beautiful I said and he patted my shoulder his fingers touched my blouse.

I can feel the shape of them still on my skin I could draw round it with a biro today if you wanted me to show you. It was only for an instant and he went ahead of me towards the round counter in the middle of the room he moved away pretending it was nothing. He had to, in a public place like that we had to be careful.

My legs were trembling I sat down at the end of a long table, there was a young black woman writing away at the other end with a pile of books around her. I can come here. This magic place he wanted me to know about. All the round walls are lined with books and mustard marble pillars and tall book-cases come inwards like rays of the sun and there are big metal cabinets with newspapers and maps in, and quiet voices and pages turning. Our special place.

He picked up a book from the counter then he went round to a photocopier, I watched him fish in his pocket for change. I wanted to run over and do it for him, I could have done that.

He copied 2 pages then he took the old book back to the counter. He handed it to a librarian and she smiled at him – I couldn't see his face, his back was to me but I saw the way she smiled at him and I thought Hah! You don't know. Forget your smiling like that you slut, it's me he loves.

He came back with his papers he was looking at his watch I counted his steps, 17 from the counter. 17.

– Shall we be getting back? It's nearly 1.30.

We didn't talk on the way back, we didn't need to, we each knew what the other was thinking. He stepped in front of me and held the lobby door open for me and the security man saw us come in together smiling and happy a couple.

He's married. You guessed that. I know everything about him. The others talk; he's got 2 kids at university. His wife's a doctor, his name is Paul. They talk about him and Maggie but they know nothing. Paul. In my dreams every night he's smiling – he's reaching out to touch my shoulder – he's leaning towards me and his voice is stroking, tickling, inside my ear.

Sometimes I don't see him for days. But I know he's here. Inside the building, talking, smiling, thinking of me. We can feel it – each other's force field. I know when he's in the building and when he's out, I don't have to see him to know that. Lisa had a phone call for him and I said He's not in – and she rang through to his office because she didn't believe me. But I was right.

They had a kind of party. It was to launch something – a booklet, "Maternity Care into the 21st Century". We were invited to stay for a drink after work. Lisa dared Laura to ask Paul if Maggie was invited and they laughed like a pair of hyenas but I ignored them. I didn't know what to wear. They dress up like secretaries, he knew I wasn't like them. He knew I was different. I was afraid his wife would be there and that

I might let something slip. If I met her I might start to giggle –
I wouldn't be able to help myself – she would stare at me and
she would begin to realize – she'd quickly understand that
this is why Paul has been so strange lately, so dreamy and
absent-minded, smiling to himself and humming a little song.
Because of me.

I worried about it all night, the fear of it kept me awake. I
didn't want to make things difficult for him. That was the last
thing I wanted. And I had nothing I could wear.

In the end I decided not to go, when the others finished at
5 and locked the office I put on my jacket and went down the
stairs. They got in the lift, they didn't bother to say goodbye.

As I was going across the lobby he came bursting in from
the street carrying a huge bouquet.

– Hello, he said. Coming up for a drink?

– I have to go home.

– Oh that's a shame. He wanted me there. He knew how
much I wanted to be there. – Well have a carnation. I'm sure
the chairlady of the AHA won't miss one!

He pulled out a long-stemmed bright red carnation. As red
as blood as red as my heart thumping Paul Paul Paul. It's a
promise. He knows why I'm going home. He knows we will be
together one day – soon. I keep the carnation pressed inside
Rebecca.

Maggie was coming back to work the week after that so my
job ended but on my last day I saw 2 magpies when I was
walking to the station – 2 for joy! And they gave me a card
signed by everyone in the office and he'd put *Thanks for all
your hard work. Good luck, giggler! Paul X*. With a kiss. He had
to be careful because everyone would see the card, but even
so, he put a kiss.

I'm working in the accounts department now at Debenhams.

It's 7 minutes to the library, I go there every lunchtime. I don't like it so much since they redecorated, the café is navy blue and yellow, a depressing combination. There are even blue lights, they seem to shed darkness. It's been a long time since I saw him, I think that's why I'm bursting to talk about it. Sometimes I go upstairs to the big white domed room and sit at a table and look at a book. That's where we'll meet again. He knows I'm here. I can sense it. Soon it will be July, our anniversary.

Robinson Street
Livi Michael

For my mother

Everything has changed; it is full of blank spaces where the houses used to be, where grass grows now, interrupted by dirt, cobbles, tarmac, metal canisters and council flats, built sideways on to the street. The old engineering works is Apple Plastics now, and further up the hill there is a modern, cheap terraced row. It is possible to stand in one of the open spaces that used to be Robinson Street, Bin Street, Cartwright's Buildings, and look straight through to the main road and the old school beyond, where the path used to wind up to the old Hall . . .

. . . I remember carrying big buckets of sheep dip to wash outside lavvies – tippler toilets that stank to high heaven – our mam used to send me and I couldn't have been more than nine or ten, and I had to carry them buckets all the way from down by side of library where there used to be a big tank and anyone could get it for free, back up Caroline Street, across bridge and up the hill, big metal buckets banging my legs all the way, scraping your shins if you weren't careful, till they bled. I remember my shoulders hurting, and having to keep putting them down, by Connie Cotterill's, that made the wonderful dandelion and burdock, it were lovely, she used to come up to us when we were playing and ask us to get dock leaves for her, then give us a cupful after, but her door were closed so no cupful there, then by Edie Batt's who lay in bed eighteen year sipping tea, and pouring tea leaves all over carpet to settle dust, until she changed doctors. Get up woman, new one roared, it's nothing but thyroid. So she did.

I remember Mr Birdsall coming by with his son Ernie, him that had eyes rolled right back in his head, but his dad always took him walking, linking arms. He were a big, proud man Mr Birdsall, with a big stiff moustache like a brush, and he looked at you as much as to say, who are you looking at? who are you? and his son only a poor, wizened thing, and Mabel Carnie went by as well, walking and stopping, walking and stopping, and every time she stopped there'd be a big puddle on pavement.

There were always the smell of baking bread on our street, or else tattie ash. It made me hungry, and the next time I stopped was outside the shop, where Florrie and Annie Evans always let our mam have tick, and if you had a ha'pence you could get a hap'orth of sherbert, only I didn't have one. But the door were open, I remember it well, and inside were Clara Bath, her that used to have clogfights with Elsie Coghill because, folk said, Elsie Coghill's youngest looked just like Ronnie Bath. Anyway, Clara Bath were telling Florrie Evans all about poor Mr Storr up at Hall. Stabbed fifteen times, she said, in the head and neck . . .

. . . What I remember is cleaning that pantry floor, scrubbing hard tiles with my knees that swollen with arthritis it was like kneeling on blades. Every day for twenty years I sank to that floor with a groan that came from the heart of all labouring souls since time began.

Man that is born of a woman is of few days and full of trouble.

He is chastened upon his bed and the multitude of his bones with strong pain.

See if there be any sorrow like unto mine which is done unto me, wherewith the Lord hath afflicted me, and sent fire into my bones.

So I got myself from one side of the floor to the other. When I look back I don't know how I did it, one day after another, year in, year out –

On this day, I remember well, there was no warning, I just looked up and he was there, muffler wrapped round his face, gun in hand.

I didn't think nothing, I thought, so you've come then, and strange to say I felt no fear at all, more a kind of lightness or relief as if to say what's done is done.

He said, Not a sound, I can hear him now, and I leaned forwards, almost as though to lean on him. Then the door bursts open and in comes Nellie Flitch, and he catches hold of her.

Not a sound, both on you, he says.

But Nellie Flitch ups and breaks away from him, screaming like a steam engine, which goes to show, as my Alf always said, that it'd take more than a loaded gun to shut Nellie Flitch up, and she ran down the landing and up the lobby stairs crying Murder, Murder, for all she was worth, and him following, you might almost say she took him straight to the master. Me, I got up slowly, as best I could, and hobbled slowly to the door. The

*Lord giveth and the Lord taketh away, I said to myself. Blessed
be the name of the Lord . . .*

. . . Nellie Flitch told Edie Batt and Edie Batt told Clara Bath
who told Florrie Evans in shop. So that's what I heard that
day, Clara Bath telling Florrie Evans, and she wouldn't lie,
clogfights or no, she used to go shuttling with our Alice. And
she said that Nellie Flitch said that master and mistress, and
young Miss Lindley, their niece that lived with them, all
come out of parlour door at once, and that brought villain
up short, and they all stood staring, one at another. Then
Mrs Storr drew herself up – she always were queen-like – and
said, Give me the gun young man, I can hear her now. And
believe it or not that's exactly what he did, just handed it over,
meek as a lamb. And muffler round his face had slipped by
that time, but still no one knew who he was. And he just
stood there, mazed-like, and it might all have been over
there and then, but all of a sudden he lunged himself at Mr
Storr with a cry like a wild animal – Clara Bath said Nellie
Flitch said she'd never forget it, not if she lived a hundred
years. So there they were, master and madman, locked
together just like mud wrestlers at Wakes. But then madman
drew a knife.

Well, after hearing all that I picked up my buckets and ran
all way home, never heeding my poor scraped legs, because
I couldn't wait to tell our mam. I ran past our Maggie, playing
with Eddie Clegg that died of diphtheria, and Amelia Brooke
that were run over by a tram, and our Billy with hardly any
clothes on his back.

Maggie Durkin, look at our Billy, I said. You'll catch it.

Catch it yourself, says she sharp as a knife. I haven't taken
all day with them buckets.

I won't then, says I over my shoulder. Not when our mam hears what I've got to tell her.

Tell us then, tell us, calls Maggie after me, but I were already running into house shouting, Mam, Mam. My mother was where she always was, in the kitchen by the dolly tub, up to her arms in suds. She did washing for all street as well as her own, and what a good washer she was, she rinsed every scrap three times by hand, people came from all over wanting Nora Durkin to wash.

Mam, Mam, I said. Mr Storr's murdered.

Now our mam never paused in a wash once she'd got going, thump thump with the dolly regular as a heart, but she stopped then.

Don't talk daft, she said.

It's true, said I, offended. I heard Clara Bath telling Florrie Evans.

My mam wiped the wet hair from her face with a worried look.

Are you making this up? she said.

Stabbed, said I. Fifteen times.

My mother's hand flew to her mouth, then she wiped both hands on her apron.

Go to shop Mam, I said urgently.

No, said she, sharpish. I dare say Florrie Evans'll be round here soon enough. That is, if you're not talking wild. Now get going with that sheep dip.

I picked buckets up and before I'd left room I could hear her again behind me, going on with washing, that regular, angry thump. I went through to the back house in a huff and nearly fell over our John, him that were always sat around all day while rest of us worked on account of his bad chest.

Watch it sheep dip, says he, and I said something back to

him that weren't quite nice for I were feeling a bit surly with our mam.

Want your mouth washing out with that, he said, kicking my bucket, but I ignored him, for our Rose, the babby, was holding her arms up. Whenever I went into a room her face lit up and her arms went out and I never could go past without picking her up. The others were all same to me, taking up room in bed and wetting it often as not, but Rose was like my own babby, lovely and laughing and just like her name, a big bonny brown rose.

Bylo baby bunting,
Pappy gone a hunting.

Are you doing them toilets or what, said John, him that never did owt, then one day upped and left to live with Mrs Prince and caused a right stir, her with one son in jail and the other one daft as a brush.

I went anyway, out back, where the sheds had no doors on and the bins no lids, and I sat there in a right mood till Walter Jackson came by and asked us what were up. That were before diphtheria, him and his sister Lilian both went, and everyone said they were beautiful children, too beautiful for this world, and when they died Emily Jackson their mam went just a little old woman though she couldn't have been much more than thirty, and when Ronnie Bath told her that war had broken out she only said, Nowt worse could happen to me.

Anyway, I told Walter and he were impressed, which cheered me up, so then I threw a bit of sheep dip down toilet hole and went to play murps* with Walter and Charlie Simms that were

* *murps* marbles

sucked up a pipe on Bin Street, and his mam never forgave Connie Cotterill. Then later Walter's mam called round on mine and so news got round. Nine days' wonder, Connie Cotterill said. A nice, comfortable woman, Connie Cotterill, one you could pour your troubles out to and know she'd never turn a hair but say something comforting like,

It'll all be the same in a hundred years' time, or,

Worse things happen at sea.

But it went on for a bit more than nine days. People talked about it as long as I lived in that street and after, when Annie Evans came to tell our mam that John Brooke, Amelia Brooke's father, had a house going on Cartwright's Buildings for 4s and 9d, and we moved in next door to Arthur Stelfox, him that were a bit funny and used to expose himself near playgrounds and we hadn't to go near. Then our Maggie were that feared of Daddy Ratcliffe that used to bang on desk with a big stick if you couldn't do your sums and she got in such a state about going that our mam sent her to Hob Hill, where the path at the side goes all the way up to Gorse Hall, only it isn't there now. And then of course they charged that young man . . .

. . . He cometh forth like a flower and is cut down. It weren't him of course. I sat back and waited while they worked that one out. And there was such a rumpus when they said Not Guilty, stamping and cheering, folk are fools by and large. Innocent, guilty, I've thought about them words, where one leaves off and the other begins, it doesn't seem that clear to me.

But that was the end of me cleaning at Gorse Hall, because Mrs Storr couldn't stand being there after, so she moved and eventually they pulled the old place down. And no one talks about it any more. Me, I'm just an old, old woman now. My days are faster than a weaver's shuttle and are spent without hope, as the

Good Book says. But sometimes I wonder about him getting clean away, how he managed it, when people saw his face, when I went hobbling one way as if to look for help, and Miss Lindley ran screaming to the Liberal Club, yet still no one caught him. Truth will out, they say, but that one never. God works in mysterious ways. There are times when my memories hurt just like my knees, but then I think about him getting clean away that night, no justice, and it doesn't seem that bad a thing to me . . .

. . . The wind whistles down from the top of the hill where the old Hall used to be, through the space that was Ducie Street and the gaps on Robinson Street where all those people used to live. It's cold, and though I walk up and down I can't quite place in my mind where the shop was, or the archway through to Cartwright's Buildings. Only if I stop looking and walk on the street as though I live here do the people come, out of the cobbles behind me, Mr Birdsall with Ernie, Mabel Carnie, Edie Batt. There is Connie Cotterill on her doorstep asking Charlie Simms for dock leaves, and Amelia Brooke skipping rope with Maggie Durkin. Behind them, further up the hill, May Durkin my grandmother pushes Rose out in her pram, past Eddie Clegg and Billy playing murps. Nora Dodd is hanging out her washing and Clara Bath is talking to Mrs Prince, while Arthur Stelfox goes by hands in pockets, looking at no one. And I know this is an unreliable part of my imagination, for all along the street the sun is shining, the atmosphere benign. And look, Emily Jackson is coming out of Annie and Florrie's shop, with Lilian and Walter by her side.

They have a hap'orth of sherbet each for carrying her bags and they are looking up at her, she down at them, their faces are full of light.

Timing
Jackie Kay

I have to get the timing right. Sometimes I do and they don't, which leaves me feeling flat and unfortunate. I have grown to depend on the order of things. On a weekday I leave my flat at eight-thirty on foot. I almost always see the first pair – the grandmother and granddaughter. My heart leaps when I see them – the grandmother with her grey straight hair stopping at her neck line, her three-quarter length navy blue padded raincoat; the granddaughter in her lilac anorak and her blonde spindly hair and her seven-year-old giggle. I often catch it. I never speak to them and they never speak to me. It is enough that I see them at the beginning of the day. Once or twice they've not appeared and I've heard a siren sound screaming right through me. They walk toward Didsbury and I walk towards Chorlton along the Barlow Moor Road. We pass right outside the southern cemetery.

I walk down Maitland Avenue and head for Chorlton Water Park. I pass the same little red houses every day with the same vulnerable, tender front gardens. On the corner of Maitland Avenue and Darley Avenue is a cherry blossom tree. In spring its pink is uplifting. I walk down the short steep hill at the entrance to the water park. Coming up the hill as I'm walking down is the man with his black mongrel. I catch this pair at the end of their walk. The man always tries to whistle his dog, but his whistle has obviously gone – maybe emphysema or something. He makes this breathless whoooo noise at the top of the hill to get the dog to come. Blowing air, a silent whistle. How the dog hears it, I don't know. Do dogs grow tolerant of their owners ageing? Perhaps the dog understands. This man – cap over his bald head, old tweed jacket, slack, loose trousers, slightly stooping back – always nods at me and makes a noise for me too; not hello, but 'ha' as if long ago he came from a place in a strange forest where the wood people said 'ha' to each other, as if all people made the same single sound.

I walk down the hill and round the west side of the man-made lake past the avaricious Canadian geese and then I see him, the third person. He has his bag of broken bread; I usually catch him at the beginning of the feeding of the geese. These are the geese that would happily bite the fingers of small, round-faced girls. He holds the bread in his hand and they come and snatch it off him. He is a hero. I am frightened of beaks. I dislike the snatch and fury of them. They stretch their too flexible necks, hiss, open their long thin mouths. The violent red inside the beak is horrifying. The cream, criminal stripe at the side of the face. I dislike the way they all land at his feet flapping their huge dark wings as if they were clapping. Their tails swish as they make their terrible noise, the honking of the horns. The geese make their dramatic desperate landing just as I am passing. I rush past the goose man thrilled and tense. Then I increase my speed. I walk around the west side of the lake until I come to the stile and then I head for Jackson's Boat Inn, alongside the river Mersey. There are golfers out already in their jumpers and shoes. They take a swing at the hard and clever white ball as if they were a new species altogether, old fit men, just landed on the earth somewhere between the first hole and the eighteenth.

It was at the river that I first saw them and ever since I've tried to see them again. I've tried coming at the same hour and I've tried coming at different hours. The different hours unsettled me because I missed my grandmother and granddaughter, my no-whistle man, my goose man. I walked past their empty spots with my eyes shut. No amount of tiny white terriers running optimistically along the riverbank or friendly old women and men joined arm in arm, almost surgically joined, who said 'Hello' and 'Lovely day' and nodded, no amount of any of these chance unknown people could compensate for my familiars. So I stopped coming at random hours, early afternoon, late afternoon, early evening, when the pink flush of the sky convinced me again and again that tonight would be the night because the very clouds were wearing highlights in their hair.

I went back to my regular time, leaving my flat at eight-thirty with my flask of orange juice and my soft bread roll with butter and thick-cut Old English marmalade to have on the wooden tables outside Jackson's Boat. I never eat breakfast in my flat. It makes me feel too lonely. Other meals I can manage, but not breakfast. I have slept on my own all night. I need to get out and see my familiars.

One of them had bright-red copper hair and the other had dark, dark curly hair; one of them was wearing a light-cream coat, the other was wearing a black fleece; one of them had black skin and the other had white skin; they were both walking along hand in hand when I first saw them in the distance walking towards me. They were just passing the old green bridge that takes you over to the inn where the Stuart sympathizers used to meet secretly at the time of the Jacobite risings. They would all drink from a bowl of water placed in the centre of the table.

Maybe it was the copper hair that first drew me – she looked Pre-Raphaelite. Then they stopped quite suddenly just in front of the green bridge where the fencing narrows the footpath. The copper one threw her arms around the dark one and they kissed at the side of the river Mersey. I have never seen a kiss on one of my walks, not a long desperate kiss like that. I had to slow down so that I wouldn't have to pass right by it. It just went on and on and on. The river moaned and rushed and the sun spilled right along the riverbank and this kiss continued. It looked to me, as I walked towards it, like the kiss of the century. It was stunning, compelling. I knew I should look at golfers, but couldn't. I had to pass close to them and hold in my breath in a sort of movement of sympathy. I had to pass them. I couldn't turn back. Who could turn their back on such a kiss? I have not myself had one. A long wet kiss like that. I started to lick my lips quite unconsciously until I noticed myself doing it. Strolling by the river licking my lips. I was about a yard away from them and my footsteps could have been heard, my presence could have been sensed. I walked past them and nobody looked up. I climbed up the stone steps to the old iron bridge. In days gone by I would have had to pay a halfpenny toll to cross this bridge, I thought to myself, clutching at facts to try and remove the impact of the kiss. When was this bridge built? 1816. I turned and looked to my side and the kiss was still going strong. Who was Jackson? Don't know. I was hot, sweating. My heart was beating like a bird's. I felt light-headed as if I had gulped a whole gale.

It puzzled me for ages afterwards, the kiss. What was it that thrilled me? Its length, its public place, the fact that it was two women standing by the river Mersey completely engrossed in each other, the fact that I myself had never had more than a dry peck? It came to me, standing by my kettle waiting for it to boil in my very small kitchen, that witnessing that kiss changed my life. I felt involved, that was it. They involved me. They might not have meant to, but they did. Now they are in my head when I go to bed at night, the dark, dark curly-haired one and the copper-haired one. I kiss them both, gently on the cheek. If I could see them again I would know for sure.

I noticed myself changing in small ways. I am usually a fairly tidy person. But after the kiss I left my bed unmade in the morning. I still covered my leftover foods with cling film and cleaned my surfaces with Flash with boosted bleach and hoovered twice a day. Pine Forest had to be used in the toilet every visit, no matter how small or meaningless. I could not dump hygiene. Crumbs, I still could not abide. But general tidiness started to slip after the kiss. I came home and my small pine wardrobe disappointed me, with my white shirts hanging together and my coloured shirts hanging together. After the kiss I mixed up the colour coding in my wardrobe. Then I went out to buy my supper. I suddenly decided to buy a kebab in that Greek place Panico's where I've often seen people queuing. I bought a half-bottle of a nice Rioja in Carrington's then I came home and played Strauss's Metamorphosen, crying and sipping my wine. That night, the night of the kiss, I took my clothes off and left them higgledy piggledy in a heap on my bedroom floor. I went to bed completely naked.

This morning I leave my house at the usual time, eight-thirty. It is raining. Lucky for me the rain never puts off my regulars. The grandmother and granddaughter are on the Barlow Moor Road, a little further up this morning. I have to hang around a little outside the cemetery until they appear, then I continue to walk. The grandmother in her blue padded coat stares at me and looks unsettled. She has given me this look ever since she realized our paths cross every day. Perhaps she dislikes fate. I don't know. How do I know what's inside the old lady's head? She takes her granddaughter's hand and holds it a little too firmly until we've passed each other, silently, meaningfully. One hand on her brolly and the other holding her granddaughter's on their way to school. I wonder which school. There is a school with a strange name just across Princess Parkway. One of those schools hiding itself in its own strangeness, that nobody seems to know about. A school that crouches behind its own trees where children – which children nobody knows – seem to arrive and depart with nobody witnessing. Perhaps she goes there. I have been tempted to follow them but I know the old lady would be on to me like a shot and would be alarmed. She might even start doing one of those terrible old lady runs where the leg does a semi-circle before it hits the pavement.

I never use an umbrella. If it is raining, I am meant to get wet. Why should I try and avoid the weather's will? Luckily the rain doesn't bother my no-whistle man. He and his mongrel seem to enjoy it. He nods at me and says a louder 'ha!' – one he uses for the rain. Of course in Manchester it rains all the time and the people here have a split personality to accommodate it. The bleak, rainy personality and the surprised, sunny one. My no-whistle man is more at home in the rain, evidently. He likes to be able to say to himself, Bloody terrible weather today. He enjoys the feeling that something bad is happening to all Mancunians at once and it makes him complicit with strangers. 'Dreadful, eh?' his emphatic 'ha' says.

The goose man is evidently of the opinion that the geese should not suffer because of the weather. This man, with stick and a stooped back, feels obliged to come out come rain or come shine. His bread is already broken up in the plastic bag. He must break it before he comes out. I noticed after a while that he seems to be able to differentiate one goose from another and that they seem to have some pecking order.

Today I hurry past the goose man, scared as usual. I worry that one of his geese might go after me and peck at the backs of my legs, even though this is quite irrational and they are more interested in bread than leg. I worry just the same and I take a sharp intake of breath as I pass and only let it out when I am round the corner. I know where the fear of beaks is from. My mother had two budgies, one named Yuri Gagarin and the other Martin Luther King. I might have admired the men, but I loathed the budgies. They would be allowed out of their cage to watch *Star Trek* and *Dr Who*, their favourite programmes. My mother would insist that Martin Luther King sat on my head whilst Yuri Gagarin sat on hers. They're just birds, she'd say. Don't be silly. I hated the soft shifting of light bird feet on top of my fly-away hair. I hated them joining in to the theme tune of *Dr Who*. I was terrified of bird-do in my hair. The morning Yuri Gagarin was not sitting on his wooden perch inside his cage but lying flat on the floor feet up was a glad morning for me. Martin Luther followed soon after, a heart-broken bird. For three months, he carried on bravely, but his budgie chest got less and less puffed and single feathers flew around our brick house in a flurry of grief. One day, the kitchen back door was open and Martin Luther King flew out and never returned. The back door had been open before but the bird had never wanted to go. 'He's gone in search of Yuri,' my mother said, full of understanding. She understood birds but not girls. How could this be? My mother would have been happier with a whole aviary and no daughter.

I can't say any of our budgies ever pecked my legs or neck, but I lived in fear of them doing so. Each flap, flutter, each sudden bird movement had me breathing soft, fast audible breaths. The goose man is not a great talker, thank god. He never says more than good morning. If he were a garrulous goose man I would be forced to walk in the other direction. Today, in the relentless pouring rain, the geese come untroubled by the weather and take the bread from his hand.

I am convinced I will see them again today, the copper and the dark, because I imagine that the kiss would be even better in the pounding rain, in the biting wind. Exhilarating? I venture to imagine, yes. Love in the rain. Love in the wild, windy north-west rain. I can hear the birds in the rain, the blackbirds and the song thrushes and the robins and the wrens. I spy a robin redbreast in a small hedge and I take it as a sign that today is indeed the day. The trees look the way they look in spring, like actors waiting for their moment of glory, their drama. Their bareness is exciting. On the tiny islands a clump of them wait. I imagine bare boys hide behind the tall thin trees like something out of *Lord of the Flies*.

I walk round the edge of the lake and on to the river. The Mersey is moody and morose in the rain; it has lost its ability to swell, to be menacing, to threaten farms or houses. The rain no longer allows the river its excesses. Flood control measures have taken away the natural form of the river. Near Jackson's Boat, the sluice gates open when the level of the river is high and the surplus water runs on to Sale Water Park. At night when I kiss the two of them, the river is in the background. I say to it, 'You too. You've seen the kiss as well.' What has this river not witnessed? What rich mud does this river not know about? My mother used to say to me, when we walked by the river, 'A river knows, dear. A river knows your secrets.' That terrified me then because I was having bad thoughts about those budgies. I was wishing them dead in their cage. My mother would see the alarm on my face and continue. 'Nothing can be kept secret in a river dear. Secrets rise to the surface and are discovered.'

It might have been the fact that the rain hid her from me or the fact that I was looking into the sulky brown river. But when I look up, I nearly pass out. The rain pours down my face. My hair is soaking wet. I can barely see now. I take my glasses off to wipe the big drops of rain with my handkerchief.

It is her. It is. My heart lurches. I am still holding my glasses in my hand. There in front of me is the dark, dark curly haired one. Alone. Am I imagining it or is she looking sad? She walks towards me along the muddy river path. Her hands in her pockets. She is as tall as I remember and as dark. Her head is looking downwards. She is wearing her black fleece. I want to rush up to her and say, 'Where is she? What have you done with her?' I want to say, 'I saw you kissing. I've missed you.' She walks by me, but this time she notices me. She notices the colour of my eyes. I know she does. My eyes are my only attribute, the only thing I've got going for me. I keep my glasses in my hand, too vain to put them back on. My hair is too wispy, my nose too sharp, my cheeks lack real definition, but my eyes, kind people have always told me my green eyes are beautiful. I have to do something. I cannot let her pass without speaking. How many people in my life do I let pass without speaking. How often do I go home wishing I had not crushed my own passion? How many times have I sadly opened my fridge and peered inside at the neat contents, the low-fat yoghurts, the bags of red and green lettuce leaves, and felt a crushing despair? When will I let it happen? Why have I kept my lips shut tight? If I let her pass me and do not speak my whole life will be one long regret.

In the past, as a girl, when I was about to say something difficult, I would count down from ten. When I got to zero, I would bottle out and start again at ten. Finally, I'd say the difficult thing I had to say to my mother. My petty admissions of guilt and she'd say, to my absolute horror, 'Are you completely lacking in sensitivity? You have to get the timing right!' I used to repeat this phrase, 'Get the timing right!' but counting down from ten didn't seem to help. Today I don't count. I just take the plunge. I say, 'Hello. No friend today?' And she stares at me as if I am stark raving mad.

The Joy of
Sexism
David Bowker

In 1977, we really imagined that a new revolutionary spirit was sweeping the world. It was the age of unschooled energy and insolent thrashing guitars.

Andy Wallace, Pete Dinsdale and me formed a punk band called the Three Zeros. The word 'zero' held a chilling significance for us. We were the only male sixth-formers we knew, apart from the swotty Christians and the sweaty scientists, that were still virgins. That is to say, virgins without deserving to be.

So we formed a band, in the hope of amassing hordes of sexually rapacious fans. We rehearsed at Dinsdale's house. We never played gigs. We only rehearsed. I sang, played guitar and wrote the songs. Wallace was the blushing bassist. He always wore tight jeans that showcased his big fat enormous arse. In theory, it was okay for a punk to be overweight. But Wallace's arse was the wrong kind of fat.

Dinsdale looked like a badly dressed George Harrison. He always wore khaki, and the reflected light made his moustache look green. He was friendly, easy-going and shockingly tight with money. But he was a wonderful drummer.

Every Sunday night, we piled into my mini and drove all the way to a condemned shithole in the poorest part of Manchester. While I worried myself sick about what might be happening to my car, we watched the Clash, the Buzzcocks and the Adverts and spat at them to show our appreciation. Sometimes they spat back. We also danced the pogo, which was a great dance for people like Wallace who couldn't really dance, as all it involved was jumping up and down. We were young and rebellious but unfortunately not rebellious enough to challenge the banal notion that having sex turned boys into men.

Caroline, or Caro as she liked to be known, had newly arrived at our school from Kent. She was small and bitchy, with Icelandic hair that was not so much fair as devoid of colour. Her face was fashionably pale and when she applied dark lipstick to her insolent mouth she resembled a vamp from a 1930s' melodrama.

She wore black, listened to records by Nico and Siouxsie Sioux and used a red ball-point to underline the words 'death', 'bald' and 'moon' in her copy of *The Colossus* by Sylvia Plath. Within weeks of her arrival, Caro had distinguished herself with her academic prowess and her willingness to have sex with any boy she found remotely interesting.

I wasn't one of those boys. She liked the bastards, the bastard bikers and the revolutionary communists, all of whom were fairly thick on the ground in our sixth-form common room. Whereas I, nice Guy, seemed altogether too friendly, a hippie ten years behind the times, too fond of Keats and the Beatles to be considered dangerous. And despite my utter lack of religious convictions, I was adored by the girls in brown tights who comprised the school's Young Christian Fellowship Society.

But one night, at one of those interminable schoolkid parties that were not so much celebrations as conventions for people intent on making their forefingers smell, Caroline found a use for me. I tripped over her on the stairs, where she was pathetically crouched, sobbing into a stylish black lace handkerchief. She was pissed out of her skull. Over the raging stereo ('Do Anything You Wanna Do' by Eddie and the Hotrods) I asked her why she was so upset.

She shook her head, unwilling to communicate. I persisted, until she raised her face to glare at me.

'You all want to fuck me!' she snarled. 'But none of you want to love me.'

'I don't want to fuck you,' I assured her calmly.

This was almost true. She was pretty, but I'd never really fancied her. Yet my ingenious denial transfigured the poor weeping minx. Her face began to radiate light. Too late, I realized my mistake. She had inferred that if I didn't want to fuck her, then I wanted to love her.

'Do you really mean that, Giles?' she said.

'Guy. My name is Guy.'

'Guy,' she repeated, smiling through her tears. 'That's a nice name. Are your parents rich?'

'No,' I replied. 'But my mother's pretentious.'

A red-faced oaf in a rugby shirt heaved past us, singing: ''twas on the good ship Venus, by God you should have seen us . . .'

Caro touched my face gently. She tilted her head back and studied me through narrow glittering eyes. My pulse quickened in fear. It was the way I'd seen women look at men in *Emmanuelle* films. Then she leaned forward to kiss me and threw up down the front of my jacket.

Reeking like a toilet, I drove her home. She lived in a village called Disley, not far from beautiful Lyme Park. As children, my brother Ben and I spent many happy hours in Lyme Park. On my eighth birthday, he had tied me to a tree there, pulled down my trousers and charged a group of posh children two pence to come and laugh at me.

Caro's house had three storeys and six bedrooms. I had never been near a house like it. There were seven tall cedars in the front garden. The white front door was framed by bogus Ionic columns. Two cars gleamed in the driveway: a Jaguar and a little Honda with golf clubs in the back. The house was in darkness.

Caro took a spare key from under a brick near the front door and let us in. There was no one at home. Caro's parents were spending the weekend in the Lake District. I felt a bit sick myself on learning that we were alone. Was this it, then? The night I 'saw the sun go down as a boy, but saw the sun rise as a man'?

My fears were groundless. I spent most of the next six hours holding Caro over the lavatory. Her vomit was purple and brownish-black; a nightmarish soup of Guinness and rum and blackcurrant, with the inevitable sprinkling of carrot and tomato. In between bouts of retching, Caro apologized. 'I am so sorry . . . bleuchhh . . . what must you think of me?'

I thought she was just fine. I helped her out of her clothes, the jettisoned my own. As she dozed uneasily, awaiting the next attack of nausea, I lay beside her, marvelling at my good fortune. She may have been as sick as a dog, nay sicker, but she was a real girl and I was in bed with her.

Caro's stomach settled down by dawn and we slept until noon. Wearing only my jeans, which were thankfully vomit-free, I went down to the spotless fitted kitchen, made some toast and listened to the radio. The DJ was Jimmy Saville

('I'll give you one point if you can tell me the name of this tune and two points for the name of the group . . .'). It was that long ago.

When Caro had risen, showered and dressed she lent me a T-shirt and her father's sheepskin jacket and we went for a walk in Lyme Park. It was a warm, clear afternoon in October; the kind of day that you spend the rest of your life searching for. We found a quiet glade, far removed from the deer, the hikers and the happy families.

After her night of heaving, Caro's face was as pale as an ivory shield. We sat on the grass and she impressed me by unzipping her bag and extracting a small chunk of dope wrapped in tin foil. Then, with nonchalant ease, she rolled a joint. I omitted to mention that I had never smoked dope before, but she noticed that I wasn't holding the perfumed smoke in my lungs for the customary time-span and encouraged me to copy her technique.

I tried and coughed and coughed and failed, but presently I experienced a pleasant floating sensation. We lay on our backs, staring at the beckoning sky, and discussing our brief and not very eventful lives as if we were the most interesting people on earth.

Caro told me that she was an only child and that she'd been seeing a therapist after suffering from something she described as a 'semi-breakdown'. Her parents had been considering divorce for more than a decade. Caro felt that her unstable home environment was to blame for her tendency to have sex with anything in school trousers.

In the late afternoon, we returned to her house to smoke more dope and listen to a Captain Beefheart album called *Unconditionally Guaranteed*. There was a song called 'This Is the Day' on that album that summed up my mood perfectly.

'This is the day that love came to play. The day love came to stay.' When we were really stoned, we threw off our clothes and played about on the living-room carpet. Then we had sex, but I was too stoned to feel anything. Jesus, I remember thinking, this is worse than wanking.

Caro wanted to join the band. Because she was a girl, and unlike me could more or less sing in tune, Wallace and Dinsdale agreed. They were impressed by the fact that she'd shagged me. Although neither of them said anything, they were certainly aware of her loose reputation. I think they were secretly hoping that if Caro joined, it would only be a matter of time before they also saw the dawn rise as men.

One Sunday afternoon, Caro and I drove to Dinsdale's house. His dad let us in, grinning sheepishly and pointing up the stairs. 'May the revels commence,' he joked awkwardly. We didn't laugh. We didn't even know what he was talking about.

Caro sat on Dinsdale's bed with her arms folded while we played her the six shitty songs we'd been rehearsing since the summer. She listened thoughtfully, without obvious enthusiasm, then stopped us.

'Right. Yeah. A bit bland, don't you think?'

Wallace and I exchanged puzzled glances. Dinsdale, ever on the defensive, said: 'I'm a jazz-funk man, myself.'

Caro frowned. 'I just think you need a bit more fire, you know? A bit of bollocks.' She unfolded a sheet of paper with words scrawled across it, the lines sloping wildly. 'I mean, have you got anything that might go with these lyrics?'

Still smarting from the 'bland' remark, I said, 'How do we know? We haven't fucking heard 'em yet.'

She consulted the piece of paper. 'This is called "Blue Period",' she said quietly. ' "Bleed, bleed and smell real foul. Eat your dinner off my sanitary towel." '

Wallace blushed deeply. Dinsdale turned as green as his moustache. And even I was taken aback. This was the rudest thing we'd ever heard a girl say.

Every evening, after school, Caro and I treated the top floor of her house as our personal apartment. Her *Daily Mail*-reading parents, Dot and Gordon, seldom bothered us. Unless they were arguing, they seldom bothered each other. Gordon, an ex-RAF pilot, spent each night in his study, drinking whisky and swotting up on the history of aviation. Dot stayed in the living-room, watching TV into the early hours.

Caro's shrink had advised that she be allowed plenty of space and freedom. So Caro virtually lived away from home on the top floor of the house, only meeting her parents for the occasional meal, or when she wanted money or a lift to a party.

She insulted her mum and dad constantly. They accepted her abuse with sad, anaemic smiles, longing for the day when she would be well again. One night Caro's mother, bearing a tea tray, entered the bedroom to find her daughter sitting on my face. With chilling composure, the brazen Caro warned her mother to 'fucking well knock, next time'.

It was quiet at the top of the house. We smoked and drank and Caro played me records I'd never heard by people like the Doors, Patti Smith and the Velvet Underground. Often we'd fuck or write a bad song together, spellbound by our own dazzling creativity.

Caro's private bathroom contained a bidet that was piled high with books, enabling us to read while sitting on the lavatory. It was this bidet that introduced me to Simone de Beauvoir, whom Caro considered to be her intellectual equal. There was a fat book called *Sexual Politics* by that lesbian with white hair whose name I can never remember, and a thin book called *A Woman's Life* by someone called Ellen Quirke.

There was poetry, too; slim, poisonous volumes by Plath, Anne Sexton and Marianne Moore; female alchemists who had converted their inability to cope with life into art. Caro advised me to examine these books with care. 'These women are the future,' she predicted.

Caro proved to be a capable organizer, when she took the trouble to get out of bed. On her advice, we changed our name from the Three Zeros to the Thinking Reeds. She also secured us our first ever gig – an all-women's disco at Manchester University. Dinsdale was wildly optimistic: 'All those birds in one room, there's bound to be one for me.'

We had to pool our meagre savings to hire a van and a PA, but Caro assured us that it would be worth the sacrifice. We arrived early and as we were setting up, the event's organizer, a gigantic woman called Frank, demanded to know what was going on.

'What are you talking about?' said Caro.

'When we spoke on the phone, you promised me this was a feminist band.'

'It is.' Caro turned to me and the band. 'You're feminists, aren't you, boys?'

Wallace and I nodded.

'What's a feminist?' said Dinsdale.

Frank would not be moved. 'But this is an event for *women*.'

'Look,' said Caro. 'I'm a woman and these three are gay.'

This was certainly news to Wallace. 'Good God,' he hissed in my ear. 'We're not, are we?'

After a cold lesbian silence, Frank gave in. 'All right. If they're gay, I suppose they're not going to hassle anyone.'

It was a lively evening. Many of the women on the dance-floor ignored us altogether and played *tick* all night. The rest of the sisters were rather too interested in Caro's body for my liking. A big posse of women clustered around the front of the stage, swilling beer from plastic pint pots and shouting out non-sexist pleasantries like 'Show us your tits!' and 'Get 'em off!' Some of them actually had moustaches. Not that I have anything against women with moustaches. I mean, it depends on the woman. It also depends on the moustache.

We didn't have enough up-tempo numbers for an event like this, so we supplemented our repertoire with a few cover versions like 'Roadhouse Blues' and 'Brown Sugar'. No one complained but at the end of the night, when the empty dance floor was awash with lager and sick, Frank stormed over to make an announcement.

'You're not getting paid.'

'We fucking are,' snapped Caro.

Frank shook her head. 'You were crap. You played sexist music. You don't deserve to get paid.'

Caro was seething. 'What fucking sexist music? We never played anything of the fucking kind.'

Frank walked off and Caro followed her, shouting and swearing. When they were out of sight, Dinsdale, who didn't expect much from life, shrugged and sighed, 'A fitting end to a typically crap night.'

But as we were lethargically loading the gear into the van, Caro returned, smiling and triumphant. She was clutching five twenty-pound notes.

'How the fuck did you manage that?' I marvelled.

She gave me a tired smile. I could see that she'd been crying. 'There are some secrets a woman never reveals.'

Two weeks passed. Then, one Monday morning, Caro failed to turn up for school. I phoned at lunchtime and received no answer. That night, I went round to her house. Her dad said that she was out with a friend. 'What friend?' I said. 'She hasn't got any friends, apart from me.'

He smiled unpleasantly. 'It would appear that your theory is contradicted by the facts.'

The pomposity of the statement robbed me of the power of speech.

Tuesday arrived. Still no Caro. I waited until eleven, when I had a free period, and drove to Disley. I met Dot on the drive. She was busy piling golf clubs into the back of her Old-Bag-Mobile. She refused to admit me into the house, explaining that 'poor Caroline' was still asleep and really it 'wasn't as if she were married to me'.

'What the fuck are you talking about?' I said. 'Do you have to be married to someone to call round at their house?'

'And language isn't going to help!' hissed Dot, slamming the boot of her car for emphasis. I waited in my car until the old cow had driven away. Then I slipped the spare key from under the brick by the front door and entered the house. Stacking a breakfast tray with fruit juice, tea and toast, I climbed the stairs to the top of the house.

My curiosity was stirred when I saw that the short hall leading to the bedroom was strewn with articles of clothing. I had no memory, for instance, of seeing Caro in the oversized Donald Duck boxer shorts that were now draped over the handle of her bedroom door. Gingerly, I dislodged the shorts and sidled into my lady's chamber.

I surveyed the king-size mattress that dominated the floor, and wondered why two pairs of feet protruded from the Laura Ashley duvet. And when Caro raised her head from the pillow to peer at me through the gloom, I couldn't help noticing that she'd grown a moustache.

A strident female voice said: 'Breakfast is served.'

Unsteadily, I inched forward, nausea wrenching my gut. It was Frank, the organizer of the Women-Only disco. Frank had clearly organized another Women-Only event in Caro's bed. Caro groaned and buried her face in a pillow while Frank smiled at me reassuringly.

Feeling sick, I staggered round to Caro's side of the bed and slowly placed the breakfast tray on the floor. Caro emerged from hiding and stared at me. Her expression held a great deal of resentment and very little warmth.

'Caroline,' I said, my voice shaking. 'What in God's name have you done?'

'You're supposed to be the clever one. Work it out.'

'Oh, you fucking cow!' I whined.

'Don't start,' she warned.

Still smiling, Frank got out of bed. Not surprisingly, she was naked. She had enormous breasts and more hair than seemed humanly possible. Under different circumstances, I might have taken a photograph.

'Frank, don't go,' Caro implored.

Frank slipped into her Donald Duck boxer shorts. Then she gathered up the rest of her belongings. 'This is between you and him. Sort it out. It's nothing to do with me.'

Frank left in a hurry. I argued with Caro for the rest of the day. Needless to say, I was shattered by her infidelity. But what astounded me was her apparent incapacity for shame and remorse. 'You cold-hearted bitch. Can't you see what this is doing to me?'

We were seated at the kitchen table, me with my head in my hands, she stirring her coffee and smelling like an alley cat. 'You're doing this to yourself, Guy. I can tell you haven't read that Kate Millett book I lent you.'

'Oh, fuck off. No one in the world has read it.'

She chose to ignore this perfectly valid point. 'Women are not property. You do not own my mind and you certainly have no claims to my body.'

My schoolwork went to hell.

Everyone in the sixth form knew what Caro had done, and found my plight hilarious. I'd been dumped for a fat woman with a moustache. Whenever I entered the crowded common room, everything went silent. It was like walking into the saloon in a Western. People that I'd considered to be friends nudged each other and exchanged knowing smirks.

I spoke to Wallace about it, hoping he'd offer me a few words of comfort. 'Tell me they're not laughing at me, Andy.'

'They're not laughing at you.'

'Really? They're really not laughing at me?'

'No. They're laughing at you.'

Throughout the following weeks, I hounded Caro obsessively, in the feverish and irrational belief that she would not dare to err as long as I was standing beside her. Every day, I visited her at home without an invitation until the Saturday afternoon that her father refused to admit me.

'Look here, old chum,' he said in his best 'bandits-at-four-o'clock' voice. 'Don't you think this has gone far enough? Caroline doesn't want to see you. Comprendez? Be a good chap. Plenty more fish in the sea. She's not strong, y'know, and you're making her ill. So I can't let you in. Sorry and all that.'

'Gordon, please. I just want to talk to her.'

'No. You're upsetting her.' He waved a bony forefinger. 'I won't have it. She's my daughter. I won't have it.'

'I fucking love her.'

At this, the leather buttons on Gordon's cardigan began to quiver. He adopted a fighting stance worthy of a sad old man. 'What? What did you say?'

I couldn't believe it. There was I, suffering the worst pain of my entire life, and this silly old sod wanted to punch me for using a rude word. Gordon pursued me round the garden, stumbling over the flower beds, his face empurpled by rage. Then Caro appeared. She was wearing jeans and a white T-shirt artfully torn. She hugged her dad, who stopped being angry and started to blubber. 'Go inside, Daddy,' she urged softly, 'I can handle this.'

Exit Gordon, wiping his eyes on his sleeve. Then Caro took my hand and led me down the path to my car. We got inside and she instructed me to drive. While we journeyed through the melancholy hills, she calmly attempted to reason with me.

'You're losing control, Guy. And if you carry on like this, you'll lose me. I'd like to see you again. Of course I would. When we're together, it's nice. But I can't stop seeing Frank and frankly I don't see why I should.'

'Frank-ly,' I echoed bitterly.

'Look at it this way,' mused Caro. 'Until Frank came along, you thought that you owned me. But in reality, you didn't own me then and you don't own me now. Nor does Frank, for that matter. I mean, I'll probably only get to see her twice a week.'

'Caro, don't lie. You know what's going to happen as well as I do. First of all, you'll see me for three nights a week and Frank for two. Then you'll feel the need to see her three nights a week, then four, until finally you'll realize you might as well live together to cut down on all that fucking travelling.'

I hoped that Caro might make a token effort to allay my fears. Instead, she shrugged and sighed hopelessly.

We were in the Peaks. I stopped the car by a small roadside shrine where lonely pilgrims stopped to pray and give thanks, until the wind made their ears ache and blew away their flowers.

I switched off the engine and turned to her. 'Please, please,' I said tearfully. 'I love you. I really love you. It kills me when you sleep with other people. Why can't you just be faithful to me?'

'Guy, listen,' she said. 'It's 1977. The world is changing. Like all women, I have a responsibility to myself. Try to understand.'

She saw the tears coming and hugged me as they fell. Her heart was not completely dead.

I realized that this was the last time; that whatever I hoped, whatever she claimed, Caro had outgrown me.

Thinking to console me, she unzipped my jeans and took me into her mouth. A battered old Volkswagen pulled up behind us. A door slammed. In the dusk, I saw an old man in a flat cap shuffle over to the shrine, bearing a bunch of lavender. He laid this offering before the virgin in her weathered cage. Then, removing his cap, he crossed himself and lowered his head.

The wind ruffled his thin hair and flapped the legs of his voluminous trousers. I felt a sharp pang of grief, knowing that this was a moment I would always remember; the darkening windy hills, the golden head in my lap, and the flapping of the old man's trousers.

Trainers
Cath Staincliffe

It all starts off as a bit of a laugh, right. Get our hands on some cash, have a good time. Bit of a giggle not a friggin' horror show. I can't believe it. Keeps going round in my mind like some advert off the telly, the sort that makes you mental 'cos it's on twice in every break. Doin' my head in, I tell you.

Kelly comes round earlier, acting all natural.

'What you doin' here?' I says.

'You comin' round Becca's?'

Daft cow. 'No.' I shut the door.

'Linda,' she starts whining at me through the door. I whip it open quick.

'No.' I say it again so it'll filter through.

Girl of little brain, our Kelly. She blinks about a million times then says, 'You're not going to grass us up, are yer?'

Oh, yeah. And find a knife in my back. Yeah, love to, shop the both of yer. I don't actually say this, right, 'cos Kelly can't cope with sarcasm. She'll take it for gospel and go running to Becca.

'No,' I says. 'I'm not. And I'm no fuckin' grass. Right?

Doesn't mean I have to hang round with youse lot any more.'

She looks at me a moment. Opens her mouth. Starts to blabber, a rush of words, trying to say it all before I twig. ''Cos it weren't us, really, it were Becca. We were just there, innit?'

Just like school, I'm thinking, it was always Becca, we were always just there. Like the time Ryan Curtis calls her a slapper and she leans close to him, arm round his back, asks him to say it again, burning her fag through his Nike top and into his back till he howls with pain and surprise. Or smacking Nicole Smith up in the toilets, banging her head against the sink. Becca. We were always just there, thinking how the fuck did this happen?

'Can't blame us, innit? Wasn't as if . . .'

'Shut up, Kelly' – I make my voice very small and tight and pointed – 'we don't talk about it. Not now, not never . . .'

'But . . .'

'Never.'

She swallows.

I shut the door.

I feel like shit. I want to cry. I want to tell Mam, like some big kid with a knot in her belly. Let her soothe it away with gentle words and cuddles. Make it all all right. But I can't. Not this. Not ever.

Some things she can take. Like our Angie falling pregnant at fourteen and then the baby dying and Angie getting all fucked up and sleeping around, trying to get caught again, starving herself, cutting at herself with little scissors. Mam went to hell and back with Angie – and what for? Oh, granted she's married now, to smarmy Trevor and he's got her all set up in a canal-side apartment off Oxford Street, right in the heart of the city. She can't work. Barely makes it out of bed most days. He takes her out, round those new places by the canal. Bars and restaurants, dresses her up and drags her round, showing her off. Good looks our Angie has. Like a model when she's all tarted up. They took me once. Bar in one of them old railway arches. Freezin'. Loads of glass and crumbly old bricks, with the pipes all showing and wavy doors in the toilets. Everyone's drinking little, fat bottles of Spanish beer. I order a double gin and tonic, then a Pimm's – let him flash the cash.

But she's not there, Angie. You talk to her and it's like she's gone out. Back in five minutes. Nothing touches her any more. She never even asks about Mam or me. There's Mam killing herself, up at six every morning, walking to work, serving dinners at the hospital for a poxy few quid and going to the moneylender when the video packs up and all the time our Angie's got money to burn. He's got a four-wheel drive. They even went skiing last year. Skiing. Mam thinks three nights in Dublin is the break of a lifetime. And it never occurs to Angie to slip us a few bob. I hate her.

He smiles. He thinks we're joking. A wind-up. He doesn't clock Becca – most people can tell, that look in her eyes, fearless, so they don't push it. But he starts to argue. Reasonable, not nasty, like he can talk us out of it. Becca's already wound up 'cos the whole enterprise isn't going exactly as planned. Friggin' nightmare, truth be told.

We all think it's a brilliant idea first off. Round at Becca's, well sorted. Her brother's dealing so we can always get hold of something tasty. Spend half my life round here. Her dad has the front room, sleeps all day, lives on strong cider and pills; jellies to calm him down. He looks like he died sometime last year, smells that way too. Hasn't left the house in months. Becca's Mam ran off with a guy had a burger bar in Marbella, years back. People ask, Becca says she's dead.

Becca's going on about wanting a good time, about crap jobs and signing on and no money and living in the dead-end of North Manchester and wanting to get a few bob, have a night out, a real good one. New clothes, some good stuff off of Becca's brother, have a make-over, hit the clubs. A night to remember. Planning what we'd buy with fifty quid, a hundred, a grand, a million. Fly to Ibiza, get a trunk full of designer gear, a different pair of trainers for every day of the week. Kelly wants a boob job. I tell her she'd be better off with a brain job. She nearly asks, mouth open walking into it, stops herself just in time, snaps her gob shut. I nudge Becca and we both get the giggles, rolling about, I can hardly breathe. Mad.

Becca says she'd get a band together, with shit-hot PR, someone to push them to number one like they did with the Spice Girls. Sings like an angel, Becca does. I want all the usual things, lots of money in the bank so Mam never has to go short, no more queuing up at the Post Office for telly stamps and phone stamps and all that. I'll get her a bungalow, somewhere dead nice, all new stuff. And a stables for me, full of horses, out in the country. People working for me.

Becca rolls another, good and strong. Kelly says her uncle used to do students 'cos they always had a bit of cash or you could take them to the hole in the wall and most of them are soft as shit.

'Oh, yes,' says I, 'there's a lot of students round here aren't there? Millions of them. Not.' And Kelly looks miffed.

Becca says, 'We don't do it here, we do it over the other side of town.'

'Didsbury,' says Kelly, 'Richard and Judy live round there.'

'Where they filmed *Cracker*,' says me. 'Mansions.'

'We're not doing a house,' says Becca.

'There's a lot of rich bastards there though,' says Kelly.

'They're not out walking around though, are they? Yer stupid cow. They've all got cars,' says Becca and then she's going on about which areas students live in and how we'll do it.

I can feel the stuff rushing its way right round to my fingertips, blood singing.

'We might be famous,' I says, 'Girl Gang Terror.'

'Yeah,' Becca laughs, 'get a name for ourselves like the Gooch Close Gang.'

'If we did cashpoints,' trying to keep my face straight, 'we could be the hole-in-the-wall gang.' I crease up. Hysterical. Becca's pissing herself. Kelly doesn't get it. Sad.

We talk some more about what to say and pretty soon we're acting it all out like bleedin' highway robbers and putting on student voices and cracking up.

He has a nice voice. Not posh at all. Geordie, like Byker Grove, and his trainers are fuckin' shocking.

I think about confessing to Father Ambrose. He's not bad for a priest, better than old MacIver who looked at you like you were a piece of shit. But he'd make me tell, I just know. I don't go to church now, anyway, not for the last couple of years. I liked Midnight Mass but they had to stop it, too much bother. Lads all tanked up, people puking up in the aisles.

'Course there was Angie's wedding. Mam bawling her head off. All the relations over from Killarney. Angie looking like a doll and Trev all puffed up. Grinning like a dog. Itching to get her away from the mad Irish crowd and lock her up safe where he can play with her all by himself.

We get the bus in. Down the Oldham Road, through Miles Platting. They've ripped off the top of the maisonettes to make them into houses but they're still crap. Some of it looks like Bosnia round here, places trashed, abandoned buildings with weeds growing in the windows, glass glittering bright in the sun. Mam gets mad when I say stuff like that, goes on about community and respect and people doing their best. But it's always the same ones I tell her. Sian's mam and the Nolans, Betty Clarke, the Conroys. Running the play scheme, doing a petition, bothering to vote, blockading the road when Anthony Sherwood got run over. The rest don't give a fuck.

It's not true, Mam says, of course people care, they're human beings, Linda, just like me and you. Sometimes people feel there's nothing they can do but there's always something, some small thing.

Union talk. Shop steward for years my mam, still banging on about it. Goes off to her local history evening class and comes home all excited about things that happened centuries ago. Peterloo, suffragettes, the Chartists. Half the time it's about people standing up for themselves and getting killed. Brilliant.

I keep trying to tell her – it's over, right. There ain't any unity any more. All right, Nelson Mandela, but he's in bleedin' Africa isn't he? Why can't she see it's all dead now, all that. History.

We change buses at Piccadilly Gardens. Claim we're half-fare. Driver doesn't give a toss. But it's the wrong bus. We get off somewhere in Whalley Range, big houses, trees like a forest but the mansions are all split up into flats and there's weeds in the garden and the shops are just like ours – half of them closed down. There's a couple of girls working the corner. Loads of black people.

'Where's the students?' Becca says. 'This is no fuckin' good.'

Kelly's getting nervous, talking too much. Becca's gone quiet. I notice straight away. I always do. She's wild and hard and she can make you feel like the only person who matters in the whole friggin' universe and she can make you feel like a pile of shit. You never know what's coming. One time I tell her to fuck off 'cos she's winding me up. She walks straight into the middle of the road, stands there, cars swerving round her, horns blaring, brakes shrieking, she never moves. I run out and drag her back, I'm screaming at her, shaking her and her eyes are shining. She's flying, high as they go and it ain't the drugs.

Now she's not talking and I feel sick.

So we're waiting bleedin' ages for a bus. I'm the only one with any fags left and they're all tapping off me and I'm dying for a drink but we haven't even got enough for a can of Coke. I'll have to lend off Kelly for the bus fare back anyway, unless we get lucky. The bus says West Didsbury. Kelly says it's okay, next to Didsbury and she's sure there's loads of students there. I think maybe it'll change. Next half hour. All come right. One or two hits and we'll be sorted. Money in us pockets, grinning wide, ready to roll. Into town for a long cold drink and a Big Mac and on to some serious shopping. Made up.

We get off the bus and we're going down this side-street, quiet, lots of trees again. Massive they are, dead old. Hiding the houses. Makes the sun look softer. How come there's no trees like this round our way? Just a couple near the church. The rest are all weedy little ones that the kids bend over, snap off. Mam would know with all her history talk.

No one about. I don't know where the fuck we are any more. It's that hot. This is no fun. This is not my idea of easy money. I just want to go home and get a bleedin' drink.

I tell Becca, 'Let's go home. This is stupid.'

He comes out of one of the driveways. Smallish guy, black hair, white T-shirt, black jeans, crap trainers.

' 'Scuse me,' Becca says and it sounds like a threat.

'Yes, how can I help you girls?' Perky like. Not posh. Ferrety face. Gold cross in one ear. Gay? Catholic? Both?

'Empty your pockets,' Becca says. He shakes his head grinning.
'Aw, come on now . . .'

'Just do it, fuckin' do it.' Becca is totally still.

Do it, I'm thinking, do what she says, please.

'C'mon, look.' He lifts his hands up like it's a Western and he's surrendering. He has spatula fingers, flat and wide at the end. They look babyish on him. 'I've no more money than you, ya know –' Becca doesn't even enter the argument . . .

I keep filling up. I've got to pack it in. If Mam cottons on, if she ever finds out why, she'll end up in Prestwich. First Angie, now this . . . so I'll not tell, see. Even if I wanted to. I swear on my mam's grave.

They couldn't tie it to us, anyway, could they? No one saw us. He was just a stranger. Don't even know his name. If he'd only waited a few minutes before he went out. If he hadn't bleedin' argued. It'll be all over the paper tomorrow, on the telly. He probably wasn't even a friggin' student.

'I've no more money than you, ya know –' Becca doesn't even give him chance to reconsider. She pulls a blade from her pocket,

flicks it open and slices it across his throat. That quick. Smooth as silk.

His hands flutter and a crease of red splits across his neck. He's still smiling and he looks at me. Straight at me. Soft, puzzled. Like Mam did when the baby died. Why doesn't he close his eyes? Stop staring at me. I didn't friggin' cut him. He falls to his knees. I move to catch him and Becca pulls me back.

'Frigginell,' says Kelly.

'Oh, Becca, jesusmaryan – what have you done? Shit. Aw shit.'

Becca snaps the knife shut and pockets it. I turn to her. One of us is shaking. She pulls me close, pushes her mouth against mine. I can feel her teeth through the skin of her lips. I push her away. Wipe my mouth. Kelly's gawping.

He falls on to the pavement now, bum in the air like a baby. Like Angie's baby. Still. A shadow spreading below him.

'Home,' says Becca.

'The money,' says Kelly.

'Fuck you,' I say, tears stinging my eyes, my throat hurts.

'Leave it,' snaps Becca.

Getting home takes ages. We don't talk. Becca is spacey and Kelly is doing something weird with her fingers, probably saying the bleedin' rosary. The bus takes us up through Ancoats. It all looks sharper, like I've had my eyes cleaned. Everything is shabby, seedy. Even the pavements look worn out. This is it, I think, this is all there is. I want to weep.

I get off at the corner.

'See yer after,' says Becca.

Mam comes in from work. I tell her I've got the runs. I can't eat.

'Are you all right?' Her face goes all concerned. 'I do worry about you, you know. Come here.' She holds out those strong skinny arms and I can't go near. I cover my mouth to hide the lie. 'Feel sick.' Rush out.

Kelly calls while Mam is out, round at her friend Carmen's. Carmen's dying, right. She keeps having chemo and Father Ambrose goes once a week but Mam says she can only get worse and isn't it an awful shame that the good ones have to suffer. When Mam comes back she puts the news on. I can't watch it. I go to bed. She lets me rest. Later she calls up. 'Night night, darlin'.' She breaks my heart. I can't ever be her darling again.

I won't look in the mirror. He may be there, over my shoulder or in my place. Looking at me. With Mam's eyes, with his cheery lad's voice, his pale spoon fingers. Looking at me. Why? What can he see?

STOP FUCKIN' LOOKING AT ME.

I just wish it was yesterday.

For ever.

Morietti's Super-Swirl
Andrea Ashworth

'Chocolate *chee*manay?'

Sunshine snatches at the girl's coins, a glint of copper faces.

'Erm . . .' She squints at them, then, 'Nope', lifts her freckled arms as high as they'll reach and lets the pennies cascade. 'Haven't got enough.'

'How much you got?' Mister Morietti palms the change.

Pish-clink, pish-clink, pish-clink. He swipes the coppers across the metal counter and they plink into his box.

The ice-cream van grumbles. Alex looks up, emerald eyes wide in spite of the fierce summer light, which makes a fiery halo of her ginger hair.

'Nine pence, eh?' Mister Morietti frowns. ''Aff to see what we can do.'

Turning to his Super-Swirl pump, he breathes deep and swells into song. Something passionate spirals up from his chest while the whipped vanilla oozes out, white and wonderful.

In the lull of his aria, he throws over his shoulder the usual pantomiming: '*Rass*-purr-ray?'

Alex grins; she knows he knows.

'So ... *Bwonno!*' His moustache is lively silver. 'Ow-eezat?'

A voluptuous, melt-in-the-mouth mountain, sweetly bleeding. Her tongue lunges to catch the syrupy scarlet before it dribbles down the cornet, over her fingers to the cracked pavestones. Nosing out of the ice-cream: a stick of flaky chocolate.

'Mister Morietti!' the girl gasps, her eyes smiling thanks, between licks. Raspberry slithers and the vanilla slides into its melt and Alex's bright-green eyes grin.

'Mister Morietti.' She levitates back along the terraced row of low, slate-hatted houses, her face plunged in a creamy kiss.

'Why's Mister Morietti's wife got a wooden head?'

Alex's mother sighs, 'Why are little girls nosy?'

One of the questions you're not to ask: why does Mrs Morietti keep a head made of wood smack in the middle of her dusty front window? Its shiny baldness nestles among the aspidistras, tickled by wilting, spindly leaves. And, while Mister Morietti trundles his whipped ice-cream and his hearty songs from street to narrow street, Mrs Morietti is nowhere to be seen.

Alex has heard of people, especially ladies, disappearing – *poof!* just like that – only to turn up later, under the floorboards of the house of the nice quiet man down the road. Or stashed inside the walls of their own front room, freshly decorated with leafy or bird-patterned paper. Houses that look and sound like all the others (though the smell gives them away in the end). You might think someone has gone off on holiday for a bit of a while, then discover them right there in the back yard, drowned under a porridgy avalanche of concrete. Or chopped into freezer-sized bits, wrapped in tin foil, tucked under the frozen peas and fish fingers.

Alex gets an attack of the creepy-crawlies whenever she glimpses that wooden head – faceless, unsmiling amid the aspidistras – in the Moriettis' smudged front window.

'On holiday,' grown-ups mutter, looking over her, past her or right through her, when Alex plucks up the spark to ask. 'On holiday, Mrs Morietti is. Now shush up.'

Red-white-and-blue billows, slaps, sopping wet, in the wind that comes gusting out of nowhere.

'Aw, Christ, me Union Jack!' Thrusting his shaved head out of the window, the rough lad over the road hauls his beloved flag in out of the sudden rain. 'Me bleeding Union Jack!' The red dye is running, streaking across the white.

Alex spies through the front window nets. Cross-legged, she sits on the sideboard, her feet trapped in fluffy orange slippers, her freckly face pressed against the lacy bars of the nets. Eyes on the drenched outside, her ears are tuned to her mother's murmurs within.

'One minute it's sunny as you like . . .' Cradling sugary coffee in the mug with the wonky, glued-back handle, Alex's mother tries chit-chatting like everything's hunky-dory. 'And the next blooming minute . . .'

'Aye. That's Manchester for you.' The lady called Maggie shakes her head at the sky as if it were a naughty child letting rip an almighty, tears-and-all tantrum.

'But' – her lips go all holy – 'it's only the weather.'

Only the weather. Alex unwraps the lady's phrase and rolls it around under her tongue. Rain jails the seven-year-old indoors, where she has to sit good and still. Ladies in the street tighten their crinkly, see-through plastic hoods over their curlers and grit their teeth, grimacing against the devil of a downpour as they cart their spuds and tins home. When it's like this Alex's mother grows quieter than ever; she lets the sky do the sobbing.

'But it's only the weather.'

Maggie's mouth crimps into a smile that lets you know she can see beyond the rain and the clouds, the stars and planets and everything. The lady has her eyes on a higher element, and her smile is set so you don't forget. 'You were saying, Julia, about your baby . . .'

Her mother's murmurs resuming, Alex's ears heat up, sting a bit.

'My baby, he . . .' Her sighs give the girl shivers; dreadful pleasure churns around her tummy; the hairs at the nape of her neck spike up.

'My poor baby . . . all that time I was carrying . . . when I think . . .'

It's not the one-by-one meaning of the words – higgledy-piggledy, spilled, or painfully cranked up from deep down – that Alex laps up, but the music of them cascading out. After so much silence. It makes her giddy, the scent of pent-up thoughts, hot from her mother's mind.

Coming home from the yard where he smooth-talks people into cranky, used motors, Alex's father can't help saying: 'Had that psycho Samaritan round again?'

His oily patter burns out on him as soon as he leaves the yard of shabby, stubbornly still-going cars. He drags off his blue anorak and hangs it in the old coal cupboard under the stairs, where its rubber tyre scent can't go rolling around the house. Washes his face like a dish in the kitchen sink, runs wet hands through his dirty blond curls and tries to make light of things.

'All right, Ally love?' Bending down to tickle his daughter, he feels the spirit fall out of him – klunk, a leaky pen dives out of his breast pocket. He stops tickling his daughter, gropes for the pen, then straightens up stiff before winning giggles.

'All right?' he says to his wife.

'Aye,' she sighs, and tries for a smile.

It comes out upside-down, her lips sagging glum at the corners.

Another sigh heaves. A slow, sucked-in sigh, it slides back down to her chest, rolling into a pebble that adds to the ache. She finishes dishing out beans while the eggs hiss and quack in a pond of hot lard, spitting gobs of wet gold out of the frying pan.

Her father pecks her mother's hollowed cheek and they both pull away – slightly, quickly – as if it burned.

'Bread and butter?' Her mother scrapes the bread plate across the table to her father. He picks a slice from it, sniffles: 'Ketchup?'

Nobody touches the tomato sauce.

Under her nose, the yolk of Alex's fried egg gleams, trembling liquid held by a milky film. She wants to roll up a slice of bread and dunk it right in the Cyclops' eye, to watch it weep.

A week of wondering, since that day they came back with no baby: her mother ushered home from the hospital, auburn hair straggled, unshining; the brand new silver-and-blue carriage looking burgled, gaping bare like her ransacked face. Her father's face terrible too: traced by the slug-trails of tears – real, grown-man tears – that nobody had taken a hankie to. Alex watches her mother's face empty and empty, her father's growing cold and congealing.

Although her tongue is not crying for it, the girl makes a grab for the salt; she feels like grasping the glass pot and giving it a good shake. She makes a shy start on her baked beans, noiselessly pronging them, one by one, with her fork.

Laying down the knife and fork poised over her own unpunctured egg, her mother makes a little noise, *hucka-huck*, in the back of her throat. The sound of a car whose engine is not sure to start. More dry sputters, and she announces to her husband: 'Maggie is *not* just some Samaritan; Maggie happens to be my friend.' She speaks with a wobbly voice, like someone straining to ice-skate: 'Maggie listens to me.'

Lashes lowered over her oyster-grey eyes, she rubs her stomach with slow palms, and her daughter, swallowing a single, stinging, salty baked bean, watches the veins throbbing bright blue in the back of her hands.

If only the Jehovah's Witnesses didn't have to go on about God, Wednesday afternoons would be heavenly. Maggie turns up with Rosie and that other lady, Lil, or sometimes she comes by herself, and she always fetches with her a packet of custard creams. The biscuits come out of the green string-bag that holds the pamphlets that tell you how to be holy in the Jehovah's Witness way. So the first one always tastes odd, as if you're nibbling a bit of the Eternal Beyond.

'Alex!' her mother chides, 'stop pulling a face. The wind'll change and you'll stay that way – squished.'

'Right, Mum.' Chewing, she concentrates on taming the muscles that make up her face, always scrunching and stretching and giving her feelings away. Turning her insides out.

'That's much nicer, now, in't it?' Maggie chips in. 'See, you can be right pretty, like, when you want to.'

Alex has the look of someone sitting on the pointy end of an umbrella.

She turns her face to the window, to give it a rest, and devotes herself to the biscuits. The second one has much less holiness about it. The third, the last one, is good old custard cream, no spirit business to get in the way.

Her mother and the other women talk in low, silky voices that slink off the settee and swish around the living-room while the girl sits cross-legged at the front window, munching. Pretending not to listen. Watching the world in the street.

'Indians moving in over the road,' Rosie, looming behind Alex, reports to the other women in the living-room. Over the rim of her mug she narrows her eyes; sups up the goings-on with her milkless coffee. 'Come away from the window, luvvie.'

Why? Alex's mouth is crammed full of custard cream rubble; the question stays caught in the creases of her forehead.

'Come away now.' Rosie puts down her mug and lifts the girl off the sideboard. 'There's a love.'

Through the lacy blur of the nets, Alex steals sight of the new lady, swathed in a sari. A glimmer of seaweedy green, veined with gold. And, holding her hand, a small, brown and bony boy wearing a pink turban. A cornet of strawberry ice-cream.

Ray. The new boy has been stuck into the register at school, and although his name sounds like Red Ginger, Miss Chapman says everyone is to call him Ray. At dinner-time, he doesn't have to plough through the same potatoey goo as most of the others. He and some of the Indian and Pakistani kids spoon their own: nosh that looks strange – muddy, steaming gobs of orange and green this-and-that. In class, the new boy sits right in front of the blackboard, as if that will help him absorb its chalky mysteries.

Nobody talks to him. Alex would like to, but does not dare.

'He speaks funny,' Big Tommy Tanner has declared, 'gin-gan-gooly-gooly-gooly-gooly-wotsit.'

Nit nurse. Nit nurse.

The school is a hive of hysterical whispers.

Nora the nit nurse is here.

A jolt of fear, that the nurse will discover a party of lice in Alex's red curls, mingles with desire: divine tingles crown the girl's head when the nurse runs cool fingertips, strand by strand, through her flamboyant mop. Closing her eyes, she slides into a daydream. For a few goosebumpy moments, the nurse is her mother. Alex can be touched, stroked like this, whenever she likes.

'Okey-dokey?' The nurse smiles as she opens her eyes.

'All clear,' she scribbles on a bit of blue paper, which she slips into Alex's fingers, before turning her back and bending over the sink to soap up her lovely long hands. 'Next.'

Big Tommy Tanner is next, and he comes out beetroot, a yellow slip in his hand.

'Got the mange!' Jacqui wastes no time in taunting the one who is usually quick to taunt everyone else. She holds up her head in disdain, tossing her regal mass of lice-free plaits.

Ray lurks at the end of the shuffling, giggling line. His hands are a pair of snails: fingers fisted around tucked thumbs, nails razoring into his palms.

'What 'aff we here?' Mister Morietti's eyebrows scrunch when Alex lifts up her hand.

'. . . I've got enough for a chocolate chimney,' she blushes. 'From my mum.'

A fifty-pence piece blooms in her palm. Fresh-minted, blinkingly shiny under the sun.

'Nottattoll!' Mister Morietti shakes his head and folds the girl's fingers back over the silver. 'Thees one on me, eh? – and the Meesiss Morietti. She's come home tomorrow, you know that?'

Where from? Alex is dying to ask.

But her thoughts are jumbled and lost, along with Mister Morietti's aria, under the jangly blast of *Twinkle, Twinkle*.

Alex goes home eager to show off the fifty-pence coin, still handsome and heavy silver, unchanged into the slighter silvers and paltry coppers that usually pass through her palm. Fifty whole pence. It is warm from the oven of her fist when she hands it back to her mother.

Who snaps: 'What's this?'

'Mister Morietti wouldn't take it.'

'You're always mithering me for extra pennies for your precious ice-cream' – the woman's jaws lock and unlock – 'then I go and give you more than enough, and what d'you do?'

The child hovers in front of the settee, where her mother is slumped, shoulders demolished, in her salmon-pink satin housecoat.

The woman tuts and mutters on in a low, moaning-to-herself voice, '. . . trying to make me feel guilty.'

A sulk of clouds swings overhead, and the room crashes into gloom under a wave of dark seawatery light. In the murk, Alex's mother looks like a fish that has given up swishing and flopped on to the settee.

Then the sun cracks through the clouds for a few wheeling seconds, and her mother looks up. Entranced by shifting light. Light that reminds them both of the rainbows you Catch, trembling, in the skin of a soap bubble on the brink of its burst.

The woman's silver-grey eyes stay hazy, but her mouth slices into a rare, sharp smile.

It knocks Alex dizzy, the smile. Her mother's young, still-girlish beauty flashes. A hint of her dimples. The child imagines hugging her, nestling her face in the warm auburn curls that smell of baked flowers; the swoony blend of pie and perfume she knows from before. When a cuddle was something soft you could just go on and do, not something prickly you fretted about doing.

Over the road, a letter is being cooked up at the rickety kitchen table. On the stove, rice and vegetables gurgle, steam writhing upwards in genie clouds, undulating, unleashing spicy promises into the air.

D. E. A. R. S. I. R. S.

The boy grips a ballpoint pen. Under his nails, the pink flesh is pressed pale with effort. His tongue is alive, worrying circles inside his cheek while, over his head, his father and mother bow. Holding their breath. As if that will help the words to emerge.

W. E. R. E. G. R. E. T.

Ray's father knows the bare bones of business English. His mother knows that something sacred is at stake, though the English to express this eludes her. She steps back from the words now and then and bends over the purr of her pots, adding piquant pinches, the odd yellow or red powdery dash, to punctuate her sauce.

Some unlaughing game: the family jigsaw their message

together, using toy pieces of learned and borrowed English –
our religion, *kindly*, *forbidden*, *please*, *thank you*, *sincerely* –
gathered scraps of street-speak and letter-speak.

'The Meesiss Morietti is back, eh?' Mister Morietti is too fired
up to sing. Taken over by a vast grin, his mouth will not pucker
into an O.

'Ees *bwonno*, eh?' His glance jumps over his shoulder from
the Super-Swirl pump to Alex, then zips back to his missus,
a shadow hovering inside the van. Her face is obscured by the
glint of the sun-bouncing window, spotted with stickers of
cartoon ice-creams and lollies.

'So!' Mister Morietti presents the girl with her Super-Swirl:
'Ow-eezat?' His hand is quivery, as if electricity is crackling
all through him.

Instead of the usual marvellous marble sculpture, the cornet
is crowned with a lop-sided splat of white. Crazy speck-
splurts of raspberry, where a scarlet crochet of syrup
would normally have been squirted with exquisite, extravagant
care.

Alex is all eyes and no tongue. So keen to get a glimpse of
Mrs Morietti that she lets unslurped syrup snake down the
cornet until it clings, a raspberry bracelet, around her wrist.

'Ow've yer bin, duckie?'

Mrs Morietti was Agnes Angela Davies until Mister Morietti
came along all those years ago; she pours out her sweet mushy
Manchester voice, but stays out of sight.

'Okay,' Alex squints up, straining for X-ray vision. She can't
keep her voice from squeaking, tight with trying not to sound
nosy: 'Did you have a nice holiday?'

Mrs Morietti chuckles. She shifts off her seat and leans over
the counter to talk to Alex.

Wow. Alex's eyes shout. *Wow*.

'Wh-where did you go, Mrs Morietti?'

Alex stares at the lady's hair, which used to be silvery-grey and wiry, like a Brillo pad whose pink powder has been scrubbed away. She laps up the new vision. Great, swirly blonde curls curving in and kicking out around Mrs Morietti's heavy, purple-framed glasses.

'Nowherz special,' the lady smiles, 'just over to Liverpool, like, to see me old mate Betsy.'

'And maybe' – petting her curls – 'to find meself . . . *Rejoov'nate*.' She winks at Mister Morietti. 'Get back me old spark, eh?'

Alex watches as Mister and Mrs Morietti kiss. They actually kiss. Nothing squishy, but still: the lip-to-lip kind of kiss.

Her head feels too small for all the stuff in it: busybody rumours swapped under this and that neighbour's breath – so She's leaving Him, is she? No, no, He's leaving Her – mixed up, jostling, with the gaggle of confused but colourful flyaway fates the girl has been imagining for Mrs Morietti during her days away.

'You look like somebody,' Alex can't help saying.

'*Marry* Lean.' Mister Morietti, sliding his arm around his wife's skinny waist, is podgy with pride. 'Ees *Marry* Lean, no?'

'Marilyn Monroe today' – Mrs Morietti's dark eyes blink, suddenly bashful, behind her glasses – 'who knows who tomorrow?'

Next morning, Alex spots Marilyn Monroe in Mrs Morietti's front window.

Afternoon, and Alex is buckled into her sandals, her feet hot and shifting, shuffling and hopping on the front step, more than half an hour before the ice-cream van is due to come jangling.

Twinkle, Twinkle, and Mister Morietti finally chugs up. His van is a boat, floating up the street, bearing a short-sighted Cleopatra: satiny black curtains of hair parted around purple glasses.

The magic. Alex can feel it. Can taste it in her ice-cream as she flitters home, licking, skipping to conquer the cracks in the pavement. The magic of being able to become somebody else, somebody new – part of a world bigger, shinier than their street – just by changing your hair.

Whispering. Hot and snaky in your ears. Whispering. About Ray, the new boy. He definitely must have the mange. Definitely. Else why wouldn't he let the nit nurse look at his hair, then, eh?

Fascination had fizzed through the school when the new boy was sent home with a sealed brown envelope, addressed to Mr and Mrs Singh, and tears quavering – frightened and proud – refusing to plunge from the fleshy tightrope rim of his lower lashes. He wouldn't let anyone, not the nit nurse, not Miss Chapman, not even the headmaster, who unlocked the stippled-glass door of his office and came clicking his shiny black shoes down the corridor, lay a finger on his pink turban.

'Wot about all them nits?' someone had started it off, 'crawling around under there. That's why he won't take it off, innit?'

On the way home from school, just past Manchester City Football Ground, she sees it, bobbing along: Ray's pink turban on the other side of the street.

Should she cross?

She eyes the cars and the trucks.

Zooming, zooming.

Belching petrol fumes in sinister, ground-skimming plumes.

The lights change.

The road clears and falls quiet.

Blood is speeding under Alex's skin – fear of fast cars and trucks, poisonous clouds and what else? – as she legs it across Claremont Road.

The other side of the street.

The way home looks odd, feels funny, on this side. As if she's not going home at all. Strange graffiti on the red brick walls, spattered with dirty words; curious initials carved into lampposts; yellowed nets with patterns she doesn't know by heart, hanging in windows she's not in the habit of peering through.

At number seventy-three the girl's glance snags on a ghost.

A woman with accidental, old-lady-lilac hair and a lost, loose mouth is glaring out into the street. Below her grim and toothless face: a hymnful of fingers and thumbs marching this way and that, unstoppable soldier crabs, along the yellowed-white and cracked black keys of an ancient electric organ. There is something horrible, funny and horrible, about the silence that shines out of the glass while the old lady stands there, framed in her front window, playing her heart out.

Loneliness. And vinegary anger. Alex knows what they look like. She drops her stare and studies her sandals. Hop-skip to escape the curse of the cracks. The pavestones aren't smashed in the right places. The weeds and dandelions are all wriggling the wrong way.

And there is Ray, bobbing along in front.

In a minute they'll be side by side.

What should she say?

The girl falls back, begins to take sludgy steps. His pink turban blurs in the sun as a slow distance swells. The blood calms and cools under her skin, then, as the pink promises – threatens – to shrink out of sight, it starts hammering again. Her sandals pick up, chase the cracks. The pink grows pinker, and so do her cheeks.

Candy floss. The hair wisping out of the turban around the boy's neck is finespun as candy floss. Alex is so close she could touch it.

Hullo.

'You're home late.' Alex's mother has taken to following the second hand on its steady-go-round and around and around. A kind of countdown, her heart is caught up in watching the clock. Sometimes a tic starts up in the pearly blue shadows below her left eye, pulsing in time with electric seconds. When Alex sees it, her chest corkscrews.

'I walked home with Ray,' she speaks in a small voice, 'that new boy, you know, from over the road.'

'That little Indian boy?'

Alex nods and says, 'Ray.'

Ice-cream gets whipped up in the girl's dreams.

She is not to eat any more Super-Swirl, Maggie and Rosie have told her. The reason being that Mrs Morietti has upped and moonlighted to Liverpool without her hubby, and has, to cap it all, come back a Loose Woman.

'Shameless as you like!'

Alex listens to the Jehovah's Witnesses describing Cleopatra and Marilyn Monroe as Women of Due-Bus-Morrels.

'As for Mrs Morietti' – they seem not sorry, but gleeful – 'the trouble her soul is in!'

The soul stuff is a big fat yawn to Alex, who has had its 'jeppaddee' drummed into her, hellfire and all that, since her mother fell sad and stopped shutting the door on the Jehovah's Witnesses.

But curiosity tickles the girl's tongue. *Re-Joov'nate*. She remembers Mrs Morietti smiling, winking at Mister Morietti. She blurts out:

'What's it mean, Re-Joov'nate?'

The grown-ups look flustered. They glide over her big-eyed, asking face.

'Never you mind!'

'Oi!'

It's Jim Todd, the lad with the spoiled Union Jack.

'Oi, you!' He's shouting to them, to Alex and Ray, as they make their way home from school.

Meandering along Claremont Road in the glorious sunshine of home-time, they don't even know he exists.

Zillions of things they've discovered to giggle about, since that day they found themselves on the same side of the street. The girl's shyness has evaporated. The boy's English is sprouting. It's not just the words. Even his eyes have come out of hiding. Now they play-skate between earnest and silly. Shiny, not frosted by fear that people will laugh or sneer, even flick stuff at his face. Alex has knocked a great wall of dominos tumbling, just by saying hello: Alex talks to him, so Jacqui talks to him, so Brian talks to him, so even Paul and all that lot talk to him. So Big Tommy Tanner decides to leave off. Nobody fires chewed paper bullets to smack the boy's temples, nobody pings paperclips to scratch and shame the high-boned cheeks beneath his blushing turban.

'Oi!' Jim Todd is crossing the road in some kind of huff.

They hear him and see him at once.

'Oi, Paki lover,' he barges up to the pair, sweating: 'You!'

Squares his chest in front of Alex: 'Wot you doin'?'

Squinting up at him, she sees the sun – kingly, high – behind his shoulders and shaved head.

Thinking, *anyway, the sun is bigger than he is*, she says: 'Going home.'

'Not with 'im, yer not.' The lad grabs her, wrenching, by the wrist.

'Why not?' She tugs to free her arm, but stumbles over the older lad's feet. A gasp of hurt escapes her proudly sealed lips as her knees smash and grate against the pavement, come up bloodied like the palm of her free hand, smacked down to break her fall. She swings in the big lad's grip, then falls again, hard, as he lets her loose with a jerk.

'Bastard!' He stands open-mouthed, questioning his hand, freshly tattooed with tooth marks. Ray has chomped a gorgeous rose shape into the fleshy heel of his palm.

For a moment they share the same look, the little lad and the big: smiling, sort of, stunned, at the stopped hand that hangs in the air between them.

Then the hand flexes to life. Swoops, fists and yanks at the boy's head.

'Not!' Ray's voice spurts up towards screaming as the pink cloth flies out of its knots and whorls and reels into a billowing, blushing banner. 'Not!' he cries and pulls away, but the pink cocoon is already pierced and spilling bright, sun-glinting black hair.

He dashes into the road.

Ray. Alex's head is full of his name, Ray, as she watches sunshine spill from the boy's head.

A burst of sunshine is what Mister and Mrs Morietti see: sunshine exploding across the windscreen as they jangle down Claremont Road. A burst of sunshine so bright it blanks out all other sights and sounds; kills the twanging, twinkling tune of the ice-cream van.

So bright they see nothing else.

Cleopatra is among the aspidistras, whose leaves are so thirsty they look fried at the edges. Behind her, Marilyn rests, a tad oily and rumpled, on a gold-tasselled lampshade whose bulb is no longer switched on and off.

When people pass by the Moriettis' front window, they shake their heads, turn down their voices and start up a storm of whispering wonder. Down the street, the nets have not stopped dancing. So many lacy spies. Rumours rustled over the hedge. Opinions pegged up and blown about on the washing lines.

Tripping in the road after Ray, Alex saw cornets scattered, crushed, like so many bones. An oasis of spilled, pooling vanilla. And Mrs Morietti's blonde kick-curl wig lying, trampled by tyres, a world away from her grey-haired and still, still head.

A spirit uncaged from the overturned van. Lurched off its wheels, thrown sideways and right over – smash – in its sharp, screeching swerve to avoid the boy and the girl dashing into the road. It kept jangling, feebly, jolting, to the end of the tune, before cutting out on its final twinkle.

Alex's mother is shocked out of the treacly nightmare she has been sunk in since the stillbirth of her baby boy. Now her eyes, her arms – her pores, even – have opened back up to her daughter: she can feel her, smell the scent of talcum powder and Palmolive soap and sweet, sweaty play when she holds her. The woman imagines inhaling the very freckles off her child's skin.

When Alex's father comes home, he doesn't have to smuggle love into the cave of her mother's cheek. Her mother cracks eggs on the edge of the gabbling, hissing, exuberant pan. Flicks her wrist to swirl oil over splashes of now-clear, now-milky jelly buoying up rich yolk hearts. Then turns her lips on his lips while they do their sizzle.

A new jingle has been rigged up in Mister Morietti's bashed van. 'Que Sera, Sera' – a plinky-dink version that hobbles and clangs and does its best to be a tune.

When it stops, there are no kids clamouring. No whipped vanilla on the swirl. Just the restless growl of the sore engine, wondering, Where to?

Mister and Mrs Morietti are off.

'Second honeymoon.' Smiling mysterious goodbyes in the face of the neighbours, leaving them to stew in curiosity.

They have a noisily unfolding chaos of maps, veined with roads unravelling through fields, dawdling, trickling along the seashore. Far from the city of drizzle and dancing nets.

No more custard creams, which is a bit of a pity. But no more holy pamphlets flapping around, either. And no TV Times:

Alex's father has forgotten to buy it. Nobody can be mithered about God or TV.

On the sideboard is a white cardboard box, and Alex teases it open from time to time.

'Just to look,' she assures her mother.

A glistening sticky rainbow lurks under the lid: honeyed pink, yellow, green, orange confections too pretty to eat. From the almond-eyed and velvety-voiced Mrs Singh.

'They're to be saved,' Alex's mother has decided, 'for Wednesday afternoons.'

She has a new idea of what's sacred, and the sweets are part of it. Mrs Singh comes over on Wednesdays and they talk talk talk. At first they said it was for English lessons. Alex's mother and Ray's both had fidgety bird fingers, didn't know what to do with their faces, when they were introduced in the wake of The Accident.

Twin statues of politeness.

The solace of small, stilted talk.

They sat at opposite ends of the settee and spoke about the state of the sky.

Simple plastic words they clicked together between them, like yellow and red Lego bricks.

Laughing over mistakes.

The delight of misunderstandings.

Then surprise understandings.

An orchestra of muscles warmed up, started playing, around the eyes and mouth of each woman.

They took to the air of each other.

Now they skip the weather. Alex's mother has discovered the wizardry, the winding, tucking secrets, of wearing a sari. Ray's mother has been to a Tupperware party, made friends with the Avon lady, and mooned with Alex's mother over the glossy tease of the shopping catalogue, Great Universal.

Alex is perched, cross-legged, at the window with Ray. The pair of them nibbling on a rainbow of sticky lumps as they take peeks at the street, which stands for the world, through their greedy kaleidoscope minds.

The drizzle of the street passes right over them, sparkles silver, as they sit there, sharing the weather of one another. The colour of the street is changing – slowly, fantastically, its colour is changing – as the pair sit there, swallowing honeyed pink, green, orange, yellow.

The Rialto
Richard Francis

The bloke, little round bristling fellow, really did used to come into the barracks of a morning and shout rise and shine. Nincompoop David referred to him as, lifetime ago now.

Now, all that there was to sing him reveille, at six twenty-seven or six twenty-eight of a dim Manchester morning, was his bum.

Out of bed, hands on lower belly to stop his bowels knocking too hard on the door, tippy toes to avoid jarring, what do they say in ballet, *sur les point* or to that effect, delicately trotting *sur les point* to the loo, carrying his burden of turd.

Nothing like getting that done to give you wings.

Some have a nice loose flap, some a tight one which you have to roll the paper up into a tight little tube for, like as if you're making a telescope, and probably on the other side it would slowly unroll again like a crisp bag does, but not all the way, so whoever wants to read it reads it bent. Like: I'm the ghost of a newspaper, rising from the grave. Like Gavin wrapped in a sheet for Hallowe'en with his arms out and the sheet flapping down from each one like wings, and the way his hands curved round at the end, going woo-oo.

One box had a sort of tooth on the flap, which tore right along the top page no matter how hard you scrunched it. Jacko kept waiting for them to complain to Mr Denby. What he was going to say was, you try it, Mr Denby, see if you can get it in without. Only way it can be done if they take a smaller paper, like the *Sun* or *Sport*, plus you get tits.

But they never dobbed him in. Perhaps they thought your paper was *supposed* to tear down the middle.

Some of the customers came to the door. One big guy in Norman Road used to lie in wait. He was like a child-abuser sort of a guy who didn't have the bottle to abuse in real life, or didn't know how you did it, needed a teacher to draw a bum on the blackboard with an arrow pointing. The light was never on in his hallway, and he had those bubbly windows in his door that look as if they've got measles or something. His box was a biggy, but you never got the chance because just as your arm was going up, bingo, light flashed on, door opened, and there he was in his big fat pies with one of those white holey type cords tied in a bow round the middle. I'll take that, thank you very much, he said, like as if you were trying to nick it in the first place. He needed to shave so much his face looked scribbled.

One girl at another house who came to the door sometimes, one time mashed her teeth all together then fell on the floor in a dead faint. Her mum came out from somewhere and put a ruler in her mouth. Don't worry, she said, it's just a fit. Thanks a lot, Jacko wanted to say. Like: you drop down dead, and she says, don't worry, duck, it's just dy-ying. Right as rain for two pins, she said.

But this was the worst one of the door-comers, who lived in

Stanley Road. The streets round Heaton Moor all had names like as if they were people, and they'd christened them or something. The O'Donnells were all right, who you went to first off. There were lots of them, all sizes. Some of the kids had kids. The mum one had big boobs, even though she was about fifty. But she was quite nice, if she saw you.

They had a front door that was white with sort of black metal studs in it, a bit like a castle kind of one, even though they had a blue van in the driveway without all its wheels. Black letterbox too, like a castle one as well, all doodled round the edges.

It wasn't them, it was the bloke next door to them who was the arsehole, but this morning their door had gone really wild. It had little cuts all over it, with pink wood showing through, just like somebody who'd got slashed by a mugger. The curtains were still closed.

Jacko shoved the paper in the box. While the flap was open he thought he heard somebody meeping inside, but it probably just needed an oil or something.

But it was the next bloke along who was the arsehole.

Paperboys in wintertime, what a topic, David thought as he made his way to the door, each one nosing through his round in the dark like a mole. If you had to pick an animal to be, moles were worst of the lot. Always alone in the pitch-black. Storing earthworms in their little pantries. Biting each one in half first, stop them scurrying away.

And for the rest of the time, just breast-stroking your way through soil like a bird through the air, except no view whatsoever.

David made a point of taking his paper from the lad in person. The human voice, as it's been called.

Each morning when he opened the door the boy jumped as if he'd been caught doing something he shouldn't, brought back the days when he'd catch them abusing themselves on the back row of desks; they'd jump then OK.

'What news on the Rialto?' David said, giving the lad a moment to get himself together. He took the paper and snapped it open with that sharp movement you do to open a fan. Some politician on the dodge, same as usual.

'Can't keep their fingers out of the till,' he said, nodding at the headline.

The boy cocked his head on one side, like a dog does waiting for the word biscuit.

'Bit brisk,' David went on.

The boy still gormless.

'Brr brr,' he said, acting out a shiver, just to get the point across.

'Somebody's tried to bash their door in, next door,' the boy said, uncocking his head and pointing it the other way, towards the O'Donnells.

'Have they just,' David replied, looking over the spiky bump of the boy's head. Hedgehog more the case than mole. Waste of time in any event looking at a bashed door side-on.

Suddenly David's flesh crept, as a memory came back. It caught him on the hop so sharply he said out loud, 'Watches of the night.' What he remembered was a sweaty moment, early hours of the morning, lying half awake as the bed throbbed, imagining he was suffering palpitations of the heart; when all along it was some hooligan whacking the house next door with an axe.

'Probably one of them locked himself out,' he explained. 'Or herself. They come and go all hours of the night. I used to put it down to hot-bunking. What they don't have, is any −'

he put his fingertips to his mouth and nearly kissed them, then tossed the nearly-kiss into the black January air – 'finesse.'

But the boy was already through the gate.

A squirt in each of the upper corners of the bar. It felt like doing your armpits with deodorant, only on a larger scale. Cynth always chose the same air-freshener, pine, with a picture of a river on the can. What you don't want, at eleven o'clock in the morning, is the pong of yesterday's beer. Her words.

Hand on heart, Rob quite liked it, at least in the wintertime. You come down of a morning and there's a warmth in the air from yesterday evening's customers, and the smell of their drinks and cigarettes, something cosy about it.

He'd had a conversation on the subject once with Davy, who agreed with him, or at least didn't like the smell of the freshener.

'If I wanted to smell pine, I'd go to Canada,' Davy'd said. 'Or Scandinavia, some godforsaken place like that. You don't go to all the trouble to live in Heaton Moor if what you want to smell is a forest.'

'I like the way the customers have long gone, and the smell stays put,' Rob said.

'Footprints in the snow.'

'You what?'

'Smell-prints.'

'Ah.'

'In the pub.'

Sharp enough to cut, Davy was.

But Cynth had a point. What she said was, the George had phases. Eleven in the morning it was the coffee crowd, even a lot of women. At twelve, boozers. At one, lunchtime, office people, reps, that type. Two to four, just a few boozers, maybe a courting couple. Four to five, tea-time crowd, though not so much a crowd, more a sprinkling, though sometimes they got the university of the third age in after one of their classes. Five to seven, home-from-workers. Then as the evening wore on, it got younger and younger. It was a young people's pub at night, they'd had popstars, the lot. Before they became popstars. Before they popped, Davy said.

At eleven a.m. on the dot, it was always Davy, like a bloke clocking in at work, carrying his newspaper for the crossword. He was a boozer by nature, but from eleven to twelve he was a coffee-drinker. Then he went over to the Queen's Head to be a boozer. Man of habit.

Sat down at the table by the window, shook his paper open, took out his propelling pencil, and began on the crossword.

Timmy came in, more decrepit than ever. He seemed to limp with both legs, hardly possible, like squinting with both eyes. Surely you've got to have a normal leg, to set the standard. Like in those medical researches: a pilot study. You need a pilot leg, before you can be said to limp. Or a pilot eye.

Though on the other hand, plenty of room in nature for both of somebody's legs to be buggered.

But in this particular case probably neither was, except for a little stiffness in the hip-joints, tempus fugit. The thing was, Timmy *wanted* to go into a decline. Couldn't wait for a wheelchair. To be followed by retiring to bed, wearing an enormous nappy. As he sat across the table now, opening and closing his mouth like a fish: pure affectation. He was auditioning for dementia.

'What news on the Rialto?' Davy asked, stirring the coffee.

Gob gob. No more effect than on the paperboy.

Rob came over, with Timmy's half a pint. Gob gob again. That probably meant, thank you very much. Half Timmy's arm disappeared down an enormous trouser pocket, and came up with some loose change. He held it out on his red swollen paw, and Rob took what was owed.

Timmy shook his head, not that he was disagreeing. What it was, he wanted his head to wobble as part of the ageing process, and so he shook it on purpose at just the wrong moment, so that it would look inappropriate and involuntary.

Sure enough, Rob clapped him on the back. 'No danger,' he said, and went off back behind the bar.

'Can't keep their blooming fingers out of the till,' Davy said, nodding himself, but in his case down at the paper.

Timmy hissed, getting a head of steam up. Then at last he said something. His eyes nearly popped out of his head, and the emphasis round his mouth made you expect a shout, but what came out was a voice so tiny that you could almost imagine there was an intervening wind blowing the sound away.

'My girl was bawling her head off.'

Timmy'd never had a girl till this stage in his life, so far as Davy knew. All she had to do was tidy round a bit. Tide him over till he was eligible to book into a hospice. Prepared him a sandwich lunch, according to the grapevine, to eat at his convenience.

'Probably got women's problems,' Davy said grumpily, keeping his voice down. The George was awash with women this time in the morning.

'What she's got, she's got men's problems,' Timmy said. Beneath all the trembling and dottle he gave out a cunning look, having topped Davy's remark.

'Good for her.'

'Silly apeth gave her a car for her birthday. Two days later, a constable came along, asked her some questions. She asked the lad about it, turned out he'd pinched the bugger. The police come to take it away, she spends best part of the day in hiding under her bed.' His little croak came to a halt, then picked up again. He had a way of looking all over the shop as he spoke. Just as well really, he had dirty eyes: not pornographic, just looked as if they could do with a scrub. 'The day in question being yesterday,' he went on, perhaps imagining he was the policeman himself. 'She says she feels as if she's been publicly humiliated.' The last word, albeit intricate, came out as a sort of squawk, like goodbye from a dying chicken. Timmy sat panting from the effort.

Davy pictured it, young man without a bean, wanting to do something quixotic, gets hold of an iffy vehicle. Stealing probably a bit of an exaggeration. Trying to explain to his enraged girlfriend, hoping she would see that dishonest acquisition was more of a gesture than merely spending money, especially in view of the lack of it. But sadly he'd not picked a romantic opposite number, and all he got was an earful instead.

To his surprise, Timmy renewed the subject. His mind ought by now to be on childhood memories or the cost of lard, if he was to properly surrender to the discipline of aphasia.

'He took it the wrong way in his turn,' Timmy said, 'made a terrible to-do.'

Dried-out eyeballs, Timmy's problem, which let grit and fuzz get bedded down on them.

'What he studies,' Peter said, 'is very minute bugs. Well, I don't know whether they're bugs. I think they belong there. Not like catching a cold or something.'

'Belong where?' Jeff asked. He looked like a monkey, always had. His nose was upturned and he had one of those heart-shaped hairlines like chimpanzees do. More a gorilla type these days, big beer-bellied so-and-so that sits and scratches itself.

'Wherever they are, I suppose.'

'What you talking about, Peter?'

'Louis. He has a job at the university. I was –'

'About the bugs, I mean?'

'I don't know, do I? The little bastards are a closed book far as I'm concerned.'

'Is it like, this is a round one, that's a measle. Here's a square one, the common cold. Or what?'

'That's what I'm saying. I don't even know if they're medical ones in the first place. They might just be normal bugs, for all I know.'

'What the fuck is a normal bug, when it's at home?'

'What I'm saying. Hello, Dave.'

Dave was stood at the bar all of a sudden. He had his usual expression, that you'd caught him halfway through crapping a piano. At least it was a change of subject, even though the way Dave behaved, as if he owned the shop, could get you down.

'Thank you, Peter.'

Peter poured him a pint.

'The usual,' Peter said, passing it over.

Dave had it down him in two goes.

'Cheers, Dave,' Jeff said.

'Oh. Santé,' Dave said, putting his empty glass down. Jeff wandered off. He didn't like Dave, said he was too sarky. True enough.

'What news?' Dave asked. 'On the Rialto.'

'I haven't had it switched on,' Peter said. 'I'll have a look at Ceefax a bit later, before the start of the horse racing.'

Louis came into the Queen's Head, bought an orange juice, and stepped over to Dave's table. He took his paper without a by-your-leave, and sat down peering at the crossword. 'Carbuncular,' he said.

'You beauty,' Dave told him. He liked to think of him, big and rangy as he was, bigly and rangily peering through his microscope at things the size of those swarms of angels that used to fit on the head of a pin in medieval times.

'I've been called a lot of things,' Louis said. He passed the paper back over, and leaned back and began to talk about DNA. Dave just listened. He loved to be on the edge of a subject, getting glimpses of the shape of it looming through mist, without being bothered by any actual knowledge. The alternatives, as far as he was concerned, were utter immersion or pig-ignorance. Beware the middle way, where you know exactly enough to not see the outline any more, or not to see it yet, according to which end you're measuring from.

Then who should come over but young Liam, blob of oil on his nose and sad sad eyes like a couple of broken eggs.

'Hello Lou,' he said. He sat down. 'Dave –'

'You look like a wet week in August,' Louis said.

'I am. Dave –'

'I was young once,' Louis said, DNA gone for a Burton.

'Yes,' said Liam, 'Dave –'

'Tell us all about it,' Louis told him.

'Oh, nothing to tell. Chuh,' Liam added, that funny noise between a sob and a disclaimer.

Louis's eyes narrowed. 'Oh well,' he said. He swigged down his orange. 'I better trot.'

Thank you, Liam, Dave thought.

'Dave,' Liam said, 'I've gone and done something daft.'

'Oh yes.'

'I made a goof-up. She took it the wrong way. So I had some in here, drowning my sorrows. Then I went back and lost it when I got to her place. I went bonkers.'

'What do you mean? You didn't –?'

'No, no, I just. You know. I lost my head for a bit. I had this tyre lever. I must have got it out of my car.'

'Jesus.'

'No, no, I didn't even see her. I just did a bit of.'

'What?'

'You know. Damage.'

'To her?'

'No, I didn't *see* her. I said.'

'To who, then?'

'Not who. What.'

'You did damage to what?'

'Yes, that's all it was.'

'That's all right then.' Liam throws a tantrum, and that's the end of intelligent conversation the following day. Not only stupid himself, but the cause of stupidity in others. Also the sheer self-importance of it, the way he thinks his little concerns with some girl somewhere should be brought to the attention of all and sundry. And sending Louis on his way so he could confide. Needn't have been so coy, my lad: Louis is an expert on micro-organisms.

Dave extricated himself when he could. 'Time to bugger off for lunch,' he said. You can ask what news until you're blue in the face, he thought as he went, but nobody ever seems to tell you any.

Sad Cunt
P-P Hartnett

'Michael won't be going swimming today.' That's what she said.

Michael's mum had been in a mood, not a strop, but it was clear to Lenos that something was up. The woman was exercising a control over her face, her voice, perhaps even the beating of her heart.

Lenos had been tempted to give the door a little kick after it had swung closed. He didn't. Just stood there, cotton wool quiet. Lenos: a nice boy, the potent combination of a Lancashire lass and a long-departed Greek Cypriot actually named Stavros.

Lenos evaluated the situation: Michael's mum was pissed off with her son and him, so it had to be the IT lunchtime club incident the day before, right? Ms Prakash had done her nut with Michael, singling him out in the usual way. She said she'd pop round with a print-out. Must've.

The two of them had been hard at it, a bit of Info Titnology.

```
┌─────────────────────────┐
│         (.)(.)          │
│         NORMAL          │
│                         │
│        ( . )( . )       │
│         LARGE           │
│                         │
│       ( . )( . )        │
│         MELONS          │
│         ( ; )( ; )      │
│         PIERCED         │
│                         │
│       ( * )( * )        │
│        IMPLANTS         │
└─────────────────────────┘
```

Within a minute of clanging the front gate behind him, Lenos had begun ambling back in the direction of Sandheys Grove thinking he'd just stay in and watch telly, but the bells of Brookfield Church were ringing like fuck and to him they were roaring a big Radio 1 *Come on!*

That Saturday, the last day of October, was the first time he'd ever gone swimming alone. His mum would have killed him had she known. Ever since that Gorton boy had gone missing only to be found in a shallow grave, she'd been an ol' worrier: that's why the mobile was a prominent bulge in his pocket – she loved him that much.

The warm wind blowing down Hyde Road decided it for him. At last, a nice day after a month of brittle rain, so he'd turned, knowing he could still get the 10.01 if he legged it.

Cutting through Sunnybrow Park, racing past Old Hall Drive Primary (only stopping to spit at that A PLACE TO GROW bit of the Perspex sign for the nth time), Lenos made it to Ryder

Brow with a minute to spare. From that station the two of them had ridden on trains to Marple, New Mills Central, Strines and Sheffield. Best was the other way – into town: Piccadilly.

'All right Lenos?' two girls with pushchairs sing-songed his way.

Slags, Lenos thought, S-L-A-G-S. All that baked-bean foundation on their faces, all that teased hair whooshed up like pineapples. He gave them a smile and a hiya and walked to the exact point where blackberries had stopped growing.

KEEP BACK FROM THE PLATFORM EDGE
PASSING TRAINS CAUSE AIR TURBULENCE

Though neither of the boys had ever shared the idea, the drop to the lines had always seemed like a plunge into the longest, narrowest pool. The idea of swimming into town was lovely. Sweet. Staring at without seeing the blue sky, it'd be backstroke all the way, their thin bodies gliding through the water so gracefully that the surface would hardly displace.

There was a really big bird's nest up a tree that had shed all its leaves in the night. Way off, beyond the branches, there was a bang. Before the bang, a quick staining of bright red, white and blue. Some fool was letting off rockets at that time of the morning.

'In daylight, too!' Lenos tutted at the waste.

Lenos and Michael had always had better things to do with their pocket money: swimming. Each week a different pool. They had a list. One week it'd be slides, high-board diving the next. Michael had taken such a pride in being the school swimming champion since Year 7. The occasional BDCA certificates and those thumb-sized medals hanging from thin ribbons which decorated a corner of his bedroom were such minuscule rewards for the innumerable hours. Time when his mind drifted during dozens and dozens of hypnotic pool lengths.

Michael was a born swimmer: he had been in the water as an infant and swam without water wings by the time he was three. At five he was swimming underwater with ease and began diving aged six.

Together they'd seen the sights of Oldham, Tameside, Stockport, Macclesfield, Trafford, Salford, Bolton and Bury. Faves were the Abraham Moss Leisure Centre (Crumpsall), Broadway Swimming Pool (New Moston), Chorlton Leisure Centre (Chorlton Cum Hardy), The Forum (Wythenshawe), The Y Club (Castlefield) . . . and Pendle Wavelengths (Nelson) – off the beaten track – well over an hour away on the X43, but fab slide.

Sure, there was the occasional Saturday when the lure of HMV or Afleck's Palace was too much. The odd day when Michael would punch in the four numbers of his Abbey National pin code, withdrawing surprising amounts to spend spend spend. The odd day when Michael would turn heads down Market Street with his T-shirt off, discussing the finer points of Umbro, Kappa and Ellesse as jaws dropped in the most satisfactory way.

Odd days that had odd moments, like when Michael would insist on a quick walk around St Ann's Church, and – weirder – the John Rylands Library, Deansgate way. Moments when Michael went silent, into another mode. (It wasn't his sparkly yo-yo on the go that made unseen controllers of CCTV gulp, it was that semi-baked erection fer-loppin'.) The walks would invariably lead them to Canal Street. They'd sit on the cobble-stones by Manto and Metz, pinching pint glasses and taking the piss.

Both were good swimmers, but both were far better divers.

That had something to do with standing around next to naked in the open air high above the glazed water. Luscious and gleaming, the boys weren't the only ones who knew they looked good on the various collected levels of diving platforms, posing as they chatted together in the hilarious ozone just above the plane of regular mortals. Both were very conscious of their bodies because that's what they were judged on, form. Foul-mouthed and sadistic, both appeared elegant and lovely when up on a five-metre platform, awaiting their allotted time for a dive.

The yellow head of the train approached like the most deter-mined caterpillar.

For the last year, Michael and Lenos had a chant they used to perform for the benefit of the train driver – Ryder Brow, Belle Vue, Ashburys, Wicked Willy! They'd do it with appropri-ate hand movements. That's what they'd hear in their heads to the chh-chh-chh as they rocked on the velour of a paired seat: Ryder Brow, Belle Vue, Ashburys, Wicked Willy!

Two old women bitched about some old man's aftershave all the way. Normally Lenos wouldn't have noticed, wouldn't have heard a word. Michael's bubble-gum breath would have been against his face telling sad cunt jokes. Like what kind of file makes a small hole bigger? A paedo-file.

At Piccadilly there was the same Crimestoppers poster up as last week. Same bloke from Blackley missing. Since May.

'May, June, July, August, September, October,' Michael had whispered to the face of the missing man seven days back. 'That's six months. You're dead meat mate.'

Michael always insisted they pinch one of those posters – he had a collection of them back home, neatly stacked under his bubble jet. Michael's mum didn't approve. She wasn't too keen on his interest in such addresses as 23 Cranley Gardens, 25 Cromwell Street or 10 Rillington Place either. She'd have preferred him reading Dickens to true crime.

'You too can be a MISSING BOY,' Michael used to enthuse. 'You too can be a MOTHER'S GRIEF, an UNSOLVED MYSTERY,' he'd say with a wink each and every time they arrived at Piccadilly.

Lenos did all the things he'd have done if Michael were with him; went for a slash upon arrival, preferring to use one of the nine lock-ups rather than one of the nine urinals, then washed his hands really quickly at one of the six sinks avoiding eye contact because – as Michael put it – 'There's always some sad cunt loitering with intent.' Michael knew a lot about paedophiles, like how they seal a friendship – then sexualize it. They'd done it in PSRE.

Bladder emptied, Lenos sat quite alone in the Photo Me to have four flashes go off in his face. Normally Michael would have been crushed up beside him, trying to look cool/insane/ buzzin'. He didn't go into Menzies for a stand-read, didn't pick up fries at Burger King. Without Michael, the usual routine was all a bit flat.

Same route as always, Michael's route. Right at the blood donor centre into Ducie Street, a left into Dale, then 1–2–3– 4–5–6–7–8–9–10–11–12 goose-steps across to the great gaping mouth of the Rochdale Canal entrance. The towpath walk was smellier than usual – sopping wet after so much rain.

Not yet eleven and already a few pacing beyond the green bars.

'Sad cunts,' Lenos muttered in exactly Michael's tone of

voice, quite an achievement considering the age difference of three years.

Had Michael been there he'd have teased the fuckers in the usual way, like he was acting in some movie. This always started with the reversing of his Nike baseball cap so that the silvery polycotton stitching of JUST DO IT struck out. Michael – down there – taking his T-shirt off, flashing a bit of teenage flesh. Lenos didn't do that, only Michael. He said it was fun, funny. To Lenos it felt dangerous.

Every inch of Michael was sixteen-year-old perfection. Years of swimming had done something magical to the colour of his skin. It was pale with pink smudged in. The tightest pores. Pubescent essence smeared up into the air around him as he rotated gum in his mouth really slowly.

Michael knew how to look and the look was not to look. Looking down at his trainers, both laces undone – that was sexy. Changing angle of the eyes slowly. Mmm. Gliding the eyes over the stinking wet until they made contact – an erotic ten on ten. The sneer, the clearing of the throat in a cartoony spit, scratching the back of his neck – star stuff. Hands plunged so deep into those shiny white polyester shorts he wore all weathers . . . waistline sinking to pubes . . . that brought them both close to laughing because they knew the effect it was having on those sad cunts down there.

The close proximity of such a boy (and his little pal) felt like a highly punishable offence (or trap). The policeman in many a head moved some along – fast. The driver's door of car after car could be heard slamming within a minute of the duo's arrival. Jailbait, and not worth it.

Leaning against one of those filthy walls, with his head tilted back as if being eaten alive from below, it was a full frontal come on, come and get me. Young pelvis thrust forward, crotch contours clearly visible and excitingly impressive.

His body language whispered to all within a radius of fifty mutual masturbators' steps: I've a calling. I'm every sad cunt's cute kid brother, the one you all wish you'd had to abuse. Body language can be interpreted so many ways, perhaps someone somewhere was interpreting his stance as, Nail me to your living-room floor, mount me like a butterfly.

Some followed. Up on street level, around Richmond Street or Minshull, around the Crown Court car-park, some offered money – usually more interested in 'the littleun'.

One of these followers once opened up a thirty-second exchange with, 'The dark line above a young lad's lip is a lovely, very special texture to tongue, so long as 'e 'asn't 'ad 'is first shave.'

Michael had taken a look at the man, deduced that he was a pretty typical, absolutely average variety of sad cunt in search of a fresh face, a new body – some magical quality to feel complete. In hopeful anticipation, greasy lips got a licking as the SC craned his neck slightly forward to hear what that young looker was about to say. Maybe he was hoping to inhale a little of the boy's exhalation as he spoke, too.

Michael had turned to Lenos, like he'd just smelled shit . . . then . . . showing the single, steel, horizontal line across his upper teeth, he'd taken a delight in sneering, slow and low, in a really crap attempt at a Birkenhead accent, 'Haven't you got anything better to do?' Lenos had added, 'Sad (pause for dramatic effect) cunt,' and they'd both gone into a fit of giggles and handclaps at that.

'Bloom Street, Chorlton Street . . .' Michael used to announce as they headed towards the bus station toilets, '. . . stand A1 is full of 'em. Better off dead.'

Neither used to use one of the three lock-ups or nine Armitage Shanks urinals. They'd go in to wash their hands, comb their hair, teasing and torturing the willy wavers from the side.

'Wish I had a gun,' Michael used to say. His cue to gob and run.

From TV, films, extensive secret reading, pool changing-room chats that toured the world and the occasional 0989 phone line (hard on pocket money in payphones) Lenos knew lots about the wonderful world of sex. Michael knew more, Lenos had seen it in Michael's eyes. Three times it had happened over the summer holidays, Michael had shown Lenos how his penis worked. Lenos had seen it flaccid often enough, seen the short 'n' curlies amass over the years, the sturdy development . . . but holding it . . . all hot and stiff and rubbery – like a dog's toy bone: something else.

Three times Michael had instructed Lenos to wank him off, give him a few fast up and downs so that his arm hurt the next day. Three times he'd made that thing wet and white and slippy. Michael had said it was important for Lenos to know how to mass-dur-bayt, someone had to show him. Best a friend, not some slag or – worse – some sad cunt.

'No fear of shit at the end of your dick when you fuck pussy,' the young ejaculator who'd never so much as Frenched a girl used to say afterwards.

'It's not a queer thing what we've just done,' Michael would half-explain, 'it's . . .' and his words would peter out – making Lenos feel guilty, as if he were supposed to finish the sentence like some dumb English exercise.

As they waited for a bus to – wherever – Michael always pointed out how easy it'd be to make a bit of money and run away. There, all around the station, were the names of places nudging and winking and breathily whispering, Hey you, this way!

Of all the planets spinning that day through the planetary system, only one had the vast collections of liquid water known as public swimming pools. As Lenos walked towards the golden lights of Bury's Castle Leisure Centre, pound-coin admission charge warming in his pocket, he inhaled the rising scent of chlorine and – and something that's not sweat exactly but something that swimmers give off – a mix of excitement and fear.

'And curry,' Michael had once piped up. 'Pretty soon the water's gonna taste of the stuff.'

Michael had a strong racist streak in him. He was bent on eliminating all non-white swimmers to keep the waters pure and their white women unogled.

Lenos hyperventilated to expand his lungs, flattened his soles against the roughened surface of the block. He looked at the water until the glints and shatters of sun stabbed through his eyes. His toes gripped the very edge.

'Judges and timers read-yy. Swimmers take your mark,' Lenos announced internally. He stood motionless for a long moment, gearing himself up to show them, then the especial slenderness of youth leaped out – hanging suspended for a freeze-frame moment before he entered to do six splash-out-and-die lengths of crawl.

That dive was a moment. Every lifeguard bears witness to a special moment every day. That dive was the dive which made colour shatter into a million wavy panes as the water prismed from surface to pool bottom. People who'd missed the dive heard it, only to see the fine net of ripples giving off fluorescent light in infinite repetition.

It was 1 – flip – 2 – flip – 3 – the astonishing whites of the soles of his feet turning on that slippery tiled wall no problem. Back and forth, one end to the other like the neon tetras he kept in a tank back home. 4 – 5 – flips, converts, and gone all in one yet again, breathing to the right every four strokes. Added to this, somewhere well in the back of his mind – was the one-two one-two of a flutter kick. His little heart was ticking fast as scoop after scoop of water was thrown back, cunningly moving him forward.

He wasn't in the mood. That day the water wasn't water, it was honey. No, giant spaghetti hoops that encircled his arms. He had to pull pull pull. Usually being in the water was like being with an old friend but his old friend wasn't with him today so the water was just H_2O and that was b-o-r-i-n-g.

He sat on the side for a while. Took a rest he didn't need. What, he wondered, had happened to stop Michael from going swimming?

The same old faces were there – the regulars. That was the funny thing about the boys' routine. They always ended up wherever they were going at more or less the same time. There they'd be, kids fresh from bouncy castle, badminton, circuit training, five-a-side, skating, squash and trampolining. Shiny-faced and ready for Mum to take 'em home for tea. Michael and Lenos never actually made friends, but got talking to a few. Got into a few races and the occasional scrap. Michael could always spot a sad cunt at thirty-three and a third metres. He'd invariably seduce with glittering aquatic displays, then let them know what he thought of them in the gentlest whispers.

Lenos half-recognized one of the faces, the one Michael had nicknamed The Swimmer – someone Michael seemed to have a muted respect for. The man had the kind of body that'd be expert in judo, kendo, karate or aikido. The kind of body that had cooled sun-tanned limbs in the irregular cold currents of many a warm sea.

Just for a microslice of a second, Lenos thought the man was watching him as his head emerged from the aquamarine blur of breast-stroke. A millisecond. Long enough to greedily, guiltily, sneak a peek.

Out of the water, adjusting the little gold crucifix the man wore around his neck, Lenos saw that the man had gained a bit of weight, yet still retained a gymnast's trim, a supple grace. The jet black curls had been carefully cut away, sheared down to a military #4. Suited him.

Amidst the commotion of Saturday swimmers, Lenos and his friend Michael had long been the focus. The boys arriving, making that first entry, every sexy exit from the water – trunks clinging and unplucked. Always laughing. Occasionally sliding into the water like knives – hands palm-down to hips, or, more nostalgic, one hand crossing heart, the other clothes-pegging nostrils.

To the man, the boy had become a shivering fascination. The direction in which the boy wore his hair varied each and every time he saw him. The first time he'd worn it parted dead centre, swept off the forehead in two perfect wings. Then it went kind of, oh, Oasis. Moppy. Then cropped. It was nice cropped. A #1, with a few zig-zag lines. Now he'd returned to his former glory, how it had been a couple of years ago: parted dead centre – perfect wings.

A tiny vial was dissolving in each of the man's eyes: the contents first freshened then widened his pupils, making them hungry for more glimpses to save and replay. It was a struggle to keep them off the boy, but he had to. Didn't want to get caught staring at the kid about to take a dive.

Lenos entered the water like a bird: he was going to swim a length under the choppy surface. It was a beautiful minute, a minute that'd be caressed in the man's memory. That boy body, flying out into the air the way kids dream of doing.

Smoothly, evenly, again and again in lovely slow motion, the man did a stretching exercise. With arms raised as if about to dive, armpits on show as if for an examination, he was up on tiptoes. Over to the left he went. He held the position. Back. Up, keeping his trunk straight, no leaning forward. Tiptoes. Arms down. Relaxed. Same again to the right. Then he shook his arms out, rolled his neck, all the time watching the approaching mini-missile streak of Lenos coming nearer and nearer, blade-like feet fluttering.

Breath fizzled in a champagne of its own making as Lenos came up fast and flushed and eating air – a great grin on his face, his teeth a white flash as he gasped, 'Did it!' The vision of him down below, between the man's legs, emerging so high – so unexpectedly – was snapped, captured. Saved.

Lenos tossed his hair out of his eyes like something amphibious, full of bubbling thrill, then a wave slapped water down the back of his throat making the boy splutter hot nosefuls of chlorine. Had Michael been there then it would have been different – he'd have entered with a somersault, coming up to shoot water out of his mouth, trailing arcs of spray behind him.

There was a catch in the man's throat as he watched the boy walk the perimeter of the pool, leaving delicate footprints on the tiles. Once he'd been a boy like that – a dripping teenager – and he'd enjoyed the eyes upon him.

Lenos felt he'd been lazy, hadn't pushed himself. The feeling had now turned into a mood: he was pissed off. Swimming wasn't so much fun without Michael.

That boy had always enjoyed showering. Long showers. With Michael. Together. Sometimes he thought he did all this just to have the joy of the showers, firmly fixed nozzle-heads spraying their fierce jets down. He was not alone. Standing beside him was The Swimmer.

Tiny bubbles gathered in the boy's hair, making it seem like glass. The boy was like a sampler, a taster. Like those use-once-only tiny pots of jam and marmalade you get in hotels. Miniature and perfect he was, a tiny bird-boy – fragile bones displayed in a neat tracery under thin skin. Eyebrows to lick for hours.

Soap me all over with your big bare hands, that skin seemed to scream. Turn me, wipe me. Around me, under me. Slide and skid all over with this warm, soapy water. Move your fingertips there and there and through my hair. Now. Lather me up then rinse off my shoulders, this thin chest. Now.

Would those hands ever have enough of the boy? Would each finger ever want to stop stroking in a way that was so gentle, seeming to go on and on, breaking the trust of all that warm water?

The intimacy of the gaze was long and detailed. He knew the exact shape of the teenaged child; the swell of his lower lip, the little bones running down the length of his spine like neatly stacked ornaments.

The kid was in the final days of boyhood. That particular shade of skin in the perfect space under his arms, behind his knees, in the delicate bend of the inside of his elbow, would soon be darkened with hair. Soon that pretty head would be weighed down with facts, figures and . . . Lord knows. That head, which had stretched his mother's vagina and split her vulva before he gasped his first breath in her world, that head . . .

The baby mouse of his penis stirred. Lenos had the desire to piss or bleed through that cock of his as he thought of Michael, mass-dur-bay-ting Michael. Michael down by the canal, the Michael he knew and didn't know down by the canal. That other Michael . . . with his trainers . . . both laces undone. That mystery boy Michael, changing the angle of his eyes slowly – gliding the eyes over the stinking wet until they made contact with his. Michael, sexy Michael. The sneer, the clearing of his throat, the rapid scratching of his neck. Michael's hands plunged so deep into those shiny white polyester shorts he wore all weathers.

A vertical stripe of his Speedo trunks was pulsating, getting the best stretch of its life. There was an unhappy realization on the thirteen-year-old's face.

LENOS = SAD CUNT, Lenos thought.

A thirteen-year-old boy checked that no one was looking, then squeezed his dick – bending it, bruising it. Bursting tiny blood vessels. His eyes were fixed upon Michael – standing on a pedestal at the end of an Olympic pool, shaking his muscles loose among a line of other older boys doing the same. Then he was there beside Michael, not at poolside but bedside, Michael's eyes seeing whatever it was he saw just as a thirteen-year-old's hand made a sixteen-year-old's dick go splashsplashsplash.

LENOS = SAD CUNT, Lenos thought. Better off dead.

It kind of hurt, kind of got on his nerves. He liked it, and it made him sad. He wondered when his penis would do what Michael's could do. It'd have to get hairy first, he knew. A bit. Then he'd be able to do what he had helped Michael do three times, that difficult word: e-Jack-you-late.

The way that full grown man was showering there in the corner was still, like he was listening.

'Friend not with you today?' that full grown man asked.

Lenos kind of stood up straight for a moment, looked over his shoulder and scanned the body beside him, sort of like browsing, before making eye contact.

'No.'

Not a single soul had ever seen the prints on the walls of that man's home, painters from the late-nineteenth century 'aesthetic school'. Subjects were young working-class men by water, ready for action. Rowdy crews of cheeky lads, stripped for the plunge. Some naked, some sunbathing, some swimming and relaxing. Casual. Boys being boys in the hot summer months, full of fun. Some with mouths parted voicelessly – lips with whimsical curls, dimples in cheeks and buttocks. Pretty dimpled boys, like smiling Cupids. Golden-skinned, slender and vigorous. Idyllic, innocent of self-conscious aerobics, liposuction and implants. With arms around shoulders and waists, drying off in the sun, they were mates grinning spontaneously, looking into each other's eyes, inviting admiration unaware, happy in their warm congregations, not a designer label on them.

A child ran into the showers, chased by an older boy and a man.

'But *Daaad* . . .' the little one screamed, 'I *wanna*!'

'Come on, Vinnie,' the older boy encouraged, 'not *yet*.'

Before escorting both boys back to the pool, that father of two turned to the man with the kind of body that'd be expert in judo, kendo, karate or aikido and said, 'Why do we 'ave 'em, eh?'

Time to go, Lenos thought, I'm completely waterlogged.

'See ya,' he said in the rough direction of The Swimmer's

neck as he slipped away towards a misted mirror for a look at himself.

Lenos rubbed a porthole of vision on to that mirror. It looked as if he were waving a giant bye-bye. He looked at himself – smiling like a lover in a song – then his eyes adjusted, gulped a rear view of The Swimmer. Turning, the man knew how to look and the look was not to look. Looking down at his feet – that was sexy. Changing angle of the eyes slowly, that clearing of the throat in a cartoony spit – porn star stuff.

By the time Lenos would be almost towelled dry, The Swimmer would be close enough to smell the fabric conditioner of the boy's underpants as they rose up past his knees, over those thighs. Close enough to shiver a delicious coating of pale green goosebumps at the sound of a tracksuit-top zipper rise in one. *Zzzzzp.*

Thinking about that boy and only that boy, that full-grown man's thoughts became more enclosed, dense. Breathing deeply, going more into himself, in deeper, thinking only about the boy, and the feeling of him, he let out a little sigh.

Any minute now, the man thought, he'll be wrapped in a towel, like a parcel for me.

It was then that a man known to a couple of kids as The Swimmer did what he could not find it in himself to do during those long hours in his office, his car, his home. He turned, leaned against the cold tiled wall and, to his own amazement, allowed himself to cry.

Blackley,
Crumpsall,
Harpurhey
Michael Bracewell

The clouds of a late November storm have been blown to white remnants, high in a pale blue sky. Winter is here; the day is held in freezing stillness. Sunday lays sorrow on the heart; all the cobbled back alleys are empty. Tall grey bins have been left upturned at crazy angles, and some stacked waste timber, swollen with damp, is catching the pink light of the afternoon sun. A mongrel dog, its coat the colour of cigarette ash and its wet, square-bearded muzzle lowered to sniff the length of a wall, is trotting towards the main road – where shattered glass glints around the edges of a telephone box, and the low sweep of vivid turf makes a child's drawing of the new estate. This is north Manchester, cut from Collyhurst to Crumpsall by a tapering valley in miniature, which is obscured by scrub and brown saplings.

The male exhalation of a bus's brakes gives way to the rising drone of its engine, then a pause for the gears to change and the hiss of heavy wheels advances into silence. It is as though the people have locked themselves away from their neighbours; as though these mean houses were hiding their poor like a lie. Here are quiet streets of descending terraces: they fall away to the floor of the shallow valley from a kind of civic campus, where a formation of dust-coloured tower blocks has been set down on the cleared land. The sky looks vast above them. But ruddy Victoriana remains: the church of Mount Carmel, its mullioned west window like the stern of a dry-docked galleon; the old steam laundry, buttressed with engineering brick; three pubs; the damp husk of the Conservative Club. At dusk, the near future appears to intrude on this northern Gothic, in the calm, violet forecourt light of the big new petrol station on the Rochdale Road.

Lank and dark-eyed children play in thin clothes on the cold streets. Some bouquets of rusted flowers, their paper wrappings sodden, are wired to the low railings beside the pedestrian crossing. Straggle-haired little girls stand on the kerb to stare at nothing, inert but ready to run; their teenage brothers are walking away from them: a loose-knit squad of stragglers, six abreast, whose excited conversation, made up of shouted challenges and sudden exclamations, fades in the twilight with their passing. Heedful to their own supremacy along these empty streets, these boys each have the awkward physique of early adolescence, but the gruff, deep voices of men. Heads down, their red fists pushed hard into the seams of their shallow pockets, they make their way up the damp incline of Russet Road and disappear from view.

This is their way most evenings: a watched pack, indifferent to surveillance, led by the teasing drift of habit to group on the steps of the corner shop; and then, gaining the swings and derelict parkland of Boggart Hole Clough, to fan out like advancing bandits across the open grass, before plunging down the sudden slope of what can only be called a dark ravine. Their destination, a burned-out car, crouches in the depths of this ravine. Down there, the light is the colour of mud on the brightest of summer days; today, as the afternoon gives way to dusk, the pale, enfeebled rays of the low winter sun will do nothing to penetrate the darkness which has settled like sediment on the bed of this chasm. The lads will light a fire inside the blackened car, the heady smell of liquid butane hanging in the freezing air; soon, the spears of yellow flame from the damp, hissing wood will be reflected in the oily trickle of the stream which passes close by. By midnight, helicopters – the urgent shudder of their engines sounding directly overhead; the inverted funnel of a searchlight snapped on, its elliptical disc the colour of moonlight, sweeping the rooftops, park and streets, in search of five youths and a stolen car. The four lumpen syllables of the park's name, Boggart Hole Clough, find an accurate translation in 'the crack in the earth where the devil descended'.

But not all of the local boys have been ready, as though by instinct, to join the roving pack of lads. Mark, for instance, would sit on the wall outside his father's house, alone, thinking of how the houses on one side of the street had tiny front gardens and low garden walls, and how the houses on the other were a single terrace, with scuffed and battered front doors which opened directly on to the street. And the more that he sat and looked at that terrace, in all weathers, the more it looked to him like a heavy curtain of bricks and mortar, which had come down with a thump on the stage of outside – show over, the final curtain.

In summer, Mark used to play in the street with John and Paul, at any game which involved a ball; during the humid, still evenings, when the heat seemed to thicken the air, they would just sit on the wall and talk. All around, they could hear the sound of televisions – broadcast voices and laughter booming through the open windows; then they would hear the man down the street who sat on his back step, singing 'Lawdy Miss Clawdy' or 'Love Me Tender' to his own accompaniment on a steel-string guitar. This is big Elvis country, for the parents, at any rate, and some of the children are born into the cult – baptized, as it were, not only into the rituals of the Holy Catholic Church, but also to the worship of the King of Kings, born in Tupelo, Mississippi, one frosty morning many years ago. Mark couldn't say that he liked the King, but he had a respect for him, and for other people's beliefs, which set him apart from the bulk of the lads. As for John and Paul, they thought that Mark was okay, but too quiet for the gathering pace of adolescence. By now, Mark was fifteen.

That year, there was a brief autumn – a few high, roaring days of deep blue sky and golden leaves – which gave way within weeks to a cold wet winter. When they drove down the street, people would see Mark sitting on his father's garden wall, a thin figure dressed in a thin black track suit; more often than not, he would be drenched, having sat there for hours in the monotonous, vertical rain. 'You're fucking cracked,' his older brother, Tom, would say, as Mark crept into the house towards ten o'clock in the evening, hoping to get upstairs before he was noticed. 'Either stay in or go out,' his father would add, looking up from the television, 'or do some bloody homework.'

But Mark, reaching his own small room at the back of the house, would kneel beside the window with his chin resting on his hands, and stare out over the dark, narrow gardens which dropped away, street by street, to the odd little valley below. Continents of light and shade would drift across this valley during the day, as big clouds passed beneath the watery sun. Blackley, Crumpsall, Harpurhey: the districts of his home, those flat, familiar names, could often seem like regions of himself. Now, at night, the gleam of orange street lights marked the length of a road, invisible from Mark's window, but running along the bed of the valley. At one end, on the opposing ridge, the stark silhouette of an old Jewish cemetery; at the other, brooding like some alien pyramid in a science fiction story, the hundred black and hive-like windows on the east facing side of Hexagon House – UK headquarters of a petro-chemicals company, the hinterland of which, behind its high wire fence, was bathed in a moat of security lights.

This view from Mark's window was a mosaic of shadows, mottled with luminescence; and as he looked down upon it, the same words would form in Mark's mind, flashing out a signal to the wholly indifferent darkness: 'Change, strange, range' – but there were no other words that seemed to fit into the pattern. They repeated themselves in his mind like an incantation: a statement of difference, muttered with neither comprehension nor remorse, to the immensity of the night sky.

There was little in Mark's bedroom to suggest that he was any different from any other boy of his age, living in that part of the world. There were the two posters of Manchester City Football Club, and one of a big-breasted Californian blonde, her pale pink lips pressed into a teasing pout and her parted thighs dusted with a light coating of fine sand. On a narrow table, three model cars, clumsily painted, and a few cassettes which had long since lost their cases, were scattered beside a pile of paperback schoolbooks. The wallpaper was left over from Mark's infancy, from the buried time before his mother died, and had once been bright with the print of teddy bears flying space-ships; now the pattern appeared washed-out and subdued, as though it, too, had died.

On one particular night, just as the rain had blown itself out, and the first frost was bleaching the pavements, Mark was sitting in his room when he heard the group of lads going by. It was a sound that he knew well; the far-off clamour of raised voices growing nearer, the impression as they passed that the lads had actually stopped outside the house, to have a fight or twist the wing-mirrors off a car; and then the sense of relief that the voices had in fact moved on, and were growing more and more faint as the lads went on their way.

Running to the window in the front bedroom, Mark looked down into the street. He didn't know what he had been hoping to see, but he was surprised to see his friend Paul, loitering at the rear of the procession, with another boy he didn't recognize. The night ahead seemed long and empty; sleep distant. Mark went back to his room and looked at the rumpled sheets on his bed; then, on an impulse, he rushed to pull on his clothes and anorak, and headed downstairs for the front door. His brother was out; his father couldn't hear him above the noise of the television. As soon as he got outside, he felt the sharp cold air hit his cheeks with a burning intensity; he was aware of the clear night sky, filled with a brilliant scattering of stars. The street was empty, save for the bobbing heads of the straggling gang who were making their way towards the main road. It was late, after eleven, and there was a sense of purpose in the way that the lads were striding ahead, which was seldom apparent in their usual ambling procession. Taking a breath which seemed to hurt his lungs, Mark ran off to catch them up, his footfalls sounding loud on the cold road.

The first person he saw was Paul; the familiar arched eyebrows and slightly mocking smile were a comfort to him in the darkness. Paul showed no surprise at Mark's unexpected appearance, he simply grinned. Behind Paul, Mark saw a few faces that he recognized from the school.

'He's all right – I know him,' said Paul; but the rest of the boys had already turned away from the encounter and were walking on ahead.

'Where're you going?' Mark tried to sound uninterested.

'Over the Boggart; down by the park – you just fuck off!'

These last words were spoken by the boy directly ahead, who had stuck his elbow into Paul's stomach for no particular reason. The two of them grappled for a moment, before the other boy hit out with his right arm and caught Paul just beneath the throat. 'Fuckin' get you for that later. Fuckin' Giggsy.' Mark had caught the mood of the battle, and made no effort to intervene or even comment. He was looking at the two boys at the front of the gang, who were passing a large plastic bottle between themselves. One of them had turned around to see the fight, and as he did so, Mark saw what he could only describe as a weirdness in the boy's eyes – a flattening of response in his gaze, as though he was no longer capable of reasoning vision, but merely a mute audience to events. It was a look which chilled; and, if Mark could have found the words, he would have said that this chill came not because of the intensity or intentions of the boy's expression, but because of its seeming incapacity to make a moral judgement; it was the look of a person who has seen everything, but who feels nothing. Mark didn't know the boy's name; he was taller than the others, and his white face looked as though it had been chiselled out of a marble that was sickening from some pollution in its veins. He wore a black, low-peaked baseball cap, and his trousers were too short for him, flapping above his ankles.

By now, they had crossed the Rochdale Road and were

heading into the park; in the distance, the tops of the trees looked like a low black wave, sweeping towards them, its crest a silhouette against sodium orange. The grass was thick and heavy to walk through; there were hidden puddles and swathes of softened mud where the ground was waterlogged, and the earth seemed to tug at each footfall as though it was trying to suck you down. A bizarre game of tag had been started, in which the prize seemed to be the plastic bottle that one of the boys was carrying; here and there in the darkness, as Mark tried to keep up with this crazy pursuit, he could see the orange dots of cigarettes and smell the pungent warmth of their smoke. Someone buffeted into him, and he nearly fell, but seeing a glimpse of a grin he buffeted the stranger back. 'You cunt!' came a voice, suddenly cold and hard – and then he went sprawling full length in the mud. 'C'mon,' said Paul, 'you going to fucking stay there or what?'

Was this, after all, living? Later, Mark would time the remainder of that night from this memory: of looking up into the sky above the park and seeing the three-quarter moon, the edges of its ivory sphere softened by mist, the yellowing amber of sulphur. Staring up at the veiled, portentous moon, he felt the magnetic pull of circumstances drawing him into the throng of boys; he felt as though he had become a mist himself, swirling around the legs and shoulders, the passed bottle and the swift tread of feet through the heavy grass. And when he blinked, he found himself returned to his own body, overly-sensitive to the jolting heaviness of his own footsteps, and of the serial forcefulness of the swaggering expedition.

Soon, the lads were approaching a set of dark and muddied steps which seemed to ascend from a gap in the trees; above them, a single lamppost, elegantly curled about its bulb, with a mirrored cowling, shed pink light. One of the boys threw a stone at the light, and hit it with a sudden crack; he let out a cheer, but the pink light remained – a feminine gauze of soft illumination, which appeared to expose the very texture of the freezing air. Panting and silent, the lads made their way up the steps; some were holding wet sticks which dirtied their palms, and smacking the rotten wood against the cast-iron railings. The taller boy whom Mark had noticed earlier was already at the top; he looked as though he was surveying a new territory, and determining its greatest exploitation for the boys in his command. But as Mark climbed the last few steps, aware that he was on the far side of the park, which he had seldom visited – even during daylight – it suddenly occurred to him that only a few of the original gang were still around him; the others, bored or tired, or enthused by other schemes, must have peeled away: at the top of the steps, in the sudden arena of pink light, there were only five boys from the fifteen or so who had started out.

At first, Mark didn't recognize the old boating lake. He had been there in the summer, when the path around its edge, bordered on one side by a low iron fence, and passing beneath the dusty shade of ancient trees at its farthest end, had seemed like a snapshot from a bygone age of innocence and gentility. At school, a teacher had shown the class some old photo-graphs of the park, as it had been – when? It had looked like hundreds of years ago, to Mark, but the teacher had said that the photographs were taken just eighty years ago. To see that ancient sunshine, and those stern faces, grouped in obedience to the camera – two little girls in heavy stockings and strange-looking dresses – to think of that summer afternoon as having really happened, had seemed almost unbelievable to Mark. He had found the pictures mesmerizing, too potent, as though they were casting a spell on him. Now, he guessed, he was standing somewhere near their location, with Paul and four strangers – two of whom were thrashing the path with sticks.

The water in the old boating lake looked black and stagnant, and the leafless branches of the trees were like thin, bent fingers, clawing at the sky; an icy wind was getting up, and on the overgrown island in the centre of the lake, the tree-tops were creaking like dried out floorboards beneath a stealthy tread. Mark could hardly articulate, in his own mind, just how defeated he felt by the pointlessness of the night's escapade; it was merely cold, and boring, but a somehow shameful experience. Nor did he relish the walk home, alone. He was just turning to look for Paul, when he suddenly saw, ahead in the darkness, what looked like a white plastic bag – caught and half-ripped on the edge of the lake. The light made distance hard to judge, and the white form appeared to be jumping in his vision to illogical angles. It was only as he drew nearer that he recognized a swan.

Mark's first reaction was one of child-like wonder. How could this swan – a bird which he associated with summer postcards from Stratford and the pictures on jigsaw puzzles – have found its way on a winter's night to the fetid waters of the old boating lake? And why was it staying in one place, as though to the warmth of a summer sun? But close to, the swan's white feathers were blackened with mud, and the graceful curve of its long neck appeared to be trembling with fatigue. Only the black band around the swan's eyes retained the bird's imperial serenity, and made it appear aloof, from the ceaseless tugging to escape from the invisible snare of some submerged wire or debris, which was slowly killing the creature by wearing it down with exhaustion. Seen in the farthest edge of the pink lamp's radiance, rearing, splashing the freezing water, and then falling back again, the trapped white swan, to Mark, looked like a mythological beast. He made his way towards it, ready to call the others to help.

The tall boy, the one with the vacant eyes, had reached the creature first; he was kneeling close to it, with something like a smile twitching across his pallid features; and as he paused to strike a match, he turned, and with the same smile, looked directly into Mark's eyes. At first, Mark nodded, and smiled back, unable to form the words to tell the smiling boy that he wanted to help; then, he couldn't work out what the older boy was doing: there was a new urgency in the stranger's gestures, a terrible intent on working out the precise geometry of evil. From a small yellow can in the boy's other hand, an arc of liquid flame spewed out across the edge of the dark water and on towards the flailing swan – to lassoo the trapped creature with molten fire; then there was a hideous beating of wings and churning of water, and over all of this, triumphant, a bray of laughter – 'Fuckin' magic!' The graceful white neck, buckled – then the massive side-swipe of a pure white wing, scything the air . . .

Mark had felt himself turning away, in slow motion; he was touching his forehead with two fingers, and aware of a sudden expanse of darkness between himself and the other boys. The swan was nowhere to be seen; only the cold black water, its surface shivering and rippled, showed any signs of movement. Then the still parkland, seeming lighter, but held in a flat monochrome of orange-tinted darkness, appeared to flow by on either side of Mark's vision as he made his way home – sometimes walking, then breaking into a sullen run, as though pursued by not only the echoes of a braying laugh, but also an opposing urgency, to settle this confrontation of wills on a higher level – to engage the psychic processes for which this moment, and this defeat, had been a mere preparation.

Reaching his little room once more, Mark sat down on the edge of his bed. For a long time, it seemed, he didn't move or even think; he felt as though he was still running; he could feel a warmth which centred his racing thoughts, and stilled his recollection of the mocking smile on the face of the boy with the empty eyes. And as he sat there, gathering strength, Mark felt an ecstatic tension in the freezing night: the streets of north Manchester, the Clough, the valley and Hexagon House, the deserted market and the old Jewish cemetery – every shard of red brick, neat front room and boarded-up window, were taut with some new meaning which he had never felt before, but which he knew would offer itself, colluding and eager, to his deft control. His incantation of repeated words, formerly meaningless, shifted in sense – lengthened, as it were, to the shadows of the park and the sulphurous moon. He reached for his old exercise book, and picked up a pen from the top of the bedside cabinet.

Blackley, Crumpsall, Harpurhey, Saturn (Cobralingus Remix)
Jeff Noon

START

INLET   Michael Bracewell

The clouds of a late November storm have been blown to white remnants, high in a pale blue sky. Winter is here; the day is held in freezing stillness. Sunday lays sorrow on the heart; the cobbled back alleys are empty. Tall grey bins have been left upturned at crazy angles, and some stacked timber, swollen with damp, is catching the pink light of the afternoon sun. A mongrel dog, its coat the colour of cigarette ash and its wet, square-bearded muzzle lowered to sniff the length of a wall, is trotting towards the main road – where shattered glass glints around the sides of a telephone box, and the low sweep of vivid turf makes a child's drawing of the new estate. This is north Manchester, cut from Collyhurst to Crumpsall by a tapering valley in miniature, which is obscured by scrub and brown saplings.

The male exhalation of a bus's brakes gives way to the rising drone of its engine, then a pause for the gears to change and the hiss of heavy wheels advances into silence. It is as though the people have locked themselves away from their neighbours; as though these mean houses are hiding their poor like a lie. Quiet streets of descending terraces, falling away to the floor of the shallow valley, where a formation of dust-coloured tower blocks has been set down on the cleared land. The sky looks vast above them. But ruddy Victoriana remains: the church of Mount Carmel, its mullioned west window like the stern of a dry-docked galleon; the old steam laundry, buttressed with engineering brick; three pubs; the damp husk of the Conservative Club. At dusk, the near future appears to intrude on this northern Gothic, in the calm, violet forecourt light of the big new petrol station on the Rochdale Road.

Lank and dark-eyed children play in thin clothes on the cold streets. Some bouquets of rusted flowers, their paper wrappings sodden, are wired to the low railings beside the pedestrian crossing.

Clouds
white remnants held in a stillness
where Sunday lays sorrow on the heart,
swollen with a damp pink light.
A mongrel dog.
Cigarette ash
descending.

A child's drawing of Manchester,
cut from shattered glass.
A rising drone and hiss of heavy silence.
The estate has locked itself away.
Thin cold streets, hiding their colour
behind blown dust.

Male exhalation,
a dry galleon of steam,
engineering a church of sky.
The crazy angled husk of the Gothic Club.
Dusk, the near future.
Northern Violet.

Lank and petrol-eyed children play
in bouquets of rust formation.
Sodden flowers,
wired to the cross.

Dusk, the near future. Saturday night at the Rust Club, where Mongrel Gothic perform songs from their latest release, *Bouquets of Drone*. Female singer with the band, Violet Sky, hisses like a dog, remnants of notes held in a dry stillness.

> *Shakespeare Walk   Brontë Avenue*
> *Wilde Street   Wordsworth Road*

In the audience, white cigarette smoke caught in pink damp light, and a rising sound of husky male breath. Their hearts, locked tightly inside, engineering hidden colours in formations of dust, shaping their pain. A northern day's pain, the estate of love. Cut from heavy silence, descending, a glass shatters. Sunday morning lays sorrow on the heart.

> *Keats Crescent   Austen Walk*
> *Coleridge Avenue   Ruskin Road*

Outside the club, lank children play, dreams of petrol in their eyes. While, in the nearby churchyard, a lonely kid makes a drawing of Manchester, all crazy angels

and swollen clouds. Sodden flowers, wired to a cross.
His sister's grave.

Tennyson Gardens   Waverley Crescent
Milton Grove   Chaucer Avenue

In the boy's mind, a dark galleon drifts by, steam-
driven through these thin cold streets, into the sky.
He sets fire to the drawing; flakes of carbon, mailed
to the stars. Sunday morning lays sorrow on the
heart.

$\boxed{\text{DECAY}}$

$\boxed{\text{CONTROL}}$

Dusk, the near future, Satur n. G a the r here rel ic
songs from the s ea. Bouquets of drone l inger
with the violet k isses. A dog man s of t in a
stillness,

       shakes a re al   b on e venue
        wild tree   word swor d.

In the d ence t igar smoke, ink a rising sound of
sky. Le t the Eart h 's engine ring our n ation of
dust, shaping the r ain. Or d ain the state of love, cut
from heav en, descending. A glass sun d orning lays
sorrow on the

         k at scent   st alk
        r aven   skin road.

The b lank child of petrol in the s hi n y church
makes a wing man, a crazy angel cloud flow,
wired to a rave

        son ar   wave crescent
        ton g   h aven.

In the boy's mind, a dark gall dr eam rive r gh o st.
To the sky he sets the wing. Lakes of ar o ma. Le t
the stars' g lays row the heart.

the compass

the lyre

the balance

the sails

the twins

the serpent

the dove

the net

the bird of paradise

the clock

the virgin

the telescope

MIX

INCREASE SENSE

At dusk, on the lakes of aroma, the people of Saturn gather relic songs from the mist. Along the parched shoreline, all the wild drone flowers linger with their violet kisses of scent. A dogman soft in a stillness, shakes a gentle word-sword in the circle of bone, conjuring out of dense tiger-smoke a rising sound of prayer. Together now, the people offer their songs to the engine of balance that shapes the virginal sky. Ordain the state of love, they sing, that heaven may descend in rain upon this, our paradise of dust.

At dawn, the dry glass sun lays sorrow on the planet. In the church of petrol a silent child watches a cat stalk a raven bird along the road of skin. In the boy's skull, a serpent girl sails a river of dreams, the ghost of his twin. The raven's dark shine of ink escapes into a tree of clocks. Seeing this, the boy constructs a wingman, cut from the strings of a lyre, a handful of drone petals, a net of wire; the plumage of a dove. Using telescope and compass, he sets a course through the ring of clouds, toward the distant Earth. Flow, my crazy angel, whispers the child, along the crescent of my tongue, along the sonar waves to your haven in the sky. Allow the glaze of stars to welcome your heart.

PURIFY

gather songs
                soft in a stillness of
      parched skin—
                      in raven tongue sky
   violet drone   let rain descend—
a circle of bone   heaven dust
                    is conjuring ghosts—

allow dark sky words
           ordain the state of love
      in sun sorrow—
                      the silent child
of skull twin shine
          uses ink wing and compass lyre
          to set a course
                 in cloud flow—
                along the crescent
         of the tongue
      allow stars
         your heart

$$\boxed{\text{CONTROL}}$$

$$\boxed{\text{OUTLET}}$$

Along the crescent of the tongue allow
These words; allow the skull's incessant drone;
Allow that thought be conjured in the flow;
Allow that heaven twin the rounded bone.
Within the violet parched-out mouth a rain
Allow to fall, that voices dark and hoarse,
In fluid tones the state of love ordain;
Allow the heart's encompass set a course.
To silent lips give song as from the lyre;
In raven's ink, the shine of stars outrun;
Allow the ghost, the skin, the sky inspire;
And soft in sorrow's cloud, allow the sun.
Allow that wings be fixed to every brow;
And every child of dust, a tongue endow.

$$\boxed{\text{SAVE}}$$

Letters to
Andy Cole
Karline Smith

12th May 1998

Dear Andy,

For as long as I can remember you have been my favourite Man United player. I'd watch you alone if you were on the pitch. I think Andy, you're the most baddest, beautiful person in the world. Your eyes are always smiling. I remember when the critics were hounding you. They had no faith in you. I kinda know how that feels. That's why I'm writing to you 'cos I feel we have a shared interest. I know what it's like to be hounded, I guess. My name is Shona Alicia Anderson. I'm 13, 14 next week. I've included a picture of me for you to see. I have jade green eyes. I wear my hair low and manageable. I'm tall but a little overweight I think.

Right now I'm in my bedroom, writing to you listening to Mary J. Blige and Brownstone. My bedroom walls are covered with posters of you, Jodeci, Keith Sweat and other R&B artists. I just love R&B. What sort of music do you like?

I live with my mother Jackie, who is black and divorced

from my father Anthony who is white. I have a little brother called Delany. My mother and father got back together briefly and Delany was born. He married Stella ten years ago and they have two white daughters, who are my half-sisters. Stella don't like me and I don't like Stella. If it wasn't for her Anthony would be with Jackie and Jackie wouldn't be crying each night. And I wouldn't wake up every morning worrying about what's going to happen today.

I live in a three bedroom council house in Longsight, Manchester. I bet it's nothing like where you live. I bet your house is like heaven. I'd like to go there one day and see how you live. I go to a school which is all right. But I have to tell you about that tomorrow 'cos Delany's crying. See you Andy. I love you.

Yours truly,
Shona Alicia Anderson

Shona drops Delany off at the nursery and crosses over manic-busy Stockport Road in Longsight. It's market day. The area is full of beautiful Asian fabric shops, mini-markets and is quickly filling with busy rainbow-coloured people. People from Vietnam, Bosnia, Africa, the West Indies and even Mexico. A diversifying Mancunian utopia. Shona's young but she knows the junkies are up and about too, burgling, pick-pocketing and mugging right there on the streets in broad daylight.

Today, the rain is falling like bricks. Shona's late for school. Her bag feels like she's carrying a baby elephant, and the 53 bus is nowhere in sight. Jackie hadn't bothered getting up to dress Delany. As usual it's Shona's responsibility. Jackie's hangovered from drinking wine last night, which means she won't get up to cash her book at the post office. It's Wednesday, half-day closing. There's no food in the house. Last night

Shona had put Jackie to bed, did the housework, cooked tea for her and Delany before doing her homework. She was never going to make it to hand her English assignment in, first period. English is Shona's favourite subject. Shakespeare, poems, stories. Shona wants to be a teacher when she grows up. Shona starts to hum to herself. Shona's got the sweetest voice you ever heard.

Two 53 buses arrive together like long-lost twins. Holding her breath, Shona flicks the driver her outdated bus pass and heads upstairs quickly. The noise can be heard before she hits the top deck. Candice and her crew are controlling the area. The atmosphere is thick with the smell of cigarette smoke although there are signs saying No Smoking. Silently Shona curses under her breath. She had hoped they would have been on the second bus. Candice is wearing red Kickers and a blue, white and red Tommy Hilfiger jacket. She's brought her boom box on the bus and it's pumping out the latest bashment beats from Jamaica, a new reggae dancehall style.

There's a roar of mock approval as Shona sits down as far away from them as possible. But if Shona gets up and moves now she knows it's a bad move. Candice shrieks out Shona's name. Shona tries to ignore her. Candice runs over laughing pulling her hat off. Opening the window she tosses Shona's hat on to the road. The cool breeze clears the smoke briefly. Shona watches her Nike hat hit the wet road. It had been a Christmas present from Anthony. Two cars drive over it to the delight of Candice. They then start on Shona's hair which is quite coarse in texture.

'Dry head.'

'How come you head so picky-picky, girl, and yu daddy white?'

'Yeah, Brillo pad head.'

'Want some relaxer cream, Shona, or will wallpaper paste do?'

Shona says nothing. She gives them no emotion. She just looks through the window until school draws near. The crew won't be visiting school today. The music changes. All Saints in the house. They all start singing and rapping. They back off, talking about fucking and Candice telling them the latest moves she has performed on her boyfriend Raymon, alias The Watchman. Shona gets up to go when it's her stop, ringing the bell as the bus tears precariously towards the school stop. Candice shouts after her.

'I'm calling you and you better answer this time gyal.'

'Yes?'

'We like yu style. How you show us respect an' all when we dissin' ya. If you want to be in the crew meet us this time tomorrow, same time same place.'

Shona heads downstairs.

'If you don't show up we'll know you're disrepectin' us and the penalty for that is . . .' Candice giggles. 'You'll see.'

Dear Andy Cole,

I feel so happy. They want me. I'm going to be a part of their posse. Candice is beautiful. She's tall, light-skinned. She has long straight hair and she could be a model. Candice has loads of friends. She's bubbly, her clothes always the latest fashion. Well dark. She's got money and is always talking about London. She's brilliant at sports. Her figure is gorgeous. All the boys in school want to check her but she's only interested in The Watchman. The Watchman is a dream. He's a mahogany-coated Adonis. Like you he's a brilliant footballer. I like Sly too, Candice's sister. She's a MC, a girl rapper and she's bad at it too.

Jackie isn't too bad tonight. I found some flour and made us some fried dumplings. Jackie says she's going to cash her book tomorrow, go shopping and then see if she can get into supply teaching. My mother used to be a full-time teacher, that's where she met Anthony. Anthony has invited me and Delany to stay for the weekend. Maybe that's why Jackie's happy 'cos she talked to Anthony on the telephone. I haven't seen her this content in ages. Anyway, it's my birthday on Sunday and Anthony says he has a nice surprise for me. Sorry about the Premiership. I'm going to bed so that when I wake up tomorrow will be here. Write to you soon.

Love,

Shona Alicia Anderson

They hand Shona a spliff, telling her to lighten up and be cool. It's pure hash. There is an old woman on the bus pretending to be looking the other way. Shona chokes on the spliff almost retching. This makes Candice and Sly laugh. The bus surges past the school. Shona is a little worried. She has never missed school in her life. They get off the bus and take another one to town, along the university route, Oxford Road towards the city centre, Manchester. They start to talk about hobbies. Theirs are boys, clothes, music and sex. Shona tells them she loves football and reading. They all look at her like she's stupid. Football? How can a black girl like football for God's sake? They tell her to get real and get with the programme. Shona knows it's useless trying to tell them that football can be thrilling. Before she knows it Candice, Sly, and the rest are getting off the bus, shrieking like animals in a dense jungle, nearly leaving her. Shona has to beat down the closed doors before the driver will let her off, remonstrating with her at the same time. Shona gives him her index finger. She gets maximum respect from Candice for this.

They're standing outside a top sports store. 'Go in and clear what you can,' Candice orders.

'What? Steal?'

'No, bake a freakin' cake.'

'Why? Why do I have to steal?' Shona's voice has a crack in it like when she's gonna cry.

' 'Cos I say so and I'm the Don-ette. Shona, that's the test. Do it and you're in.'

Dear Andy Cole,

I told Candice and the crew what they could do with themselves. I've never lifted anything in my life. Even if I was cold and hungry I'd never steal. I know if you were me you would do the same thing wouldn't you? I just can't believe they wanted me to rob. Candice spat in my face 'cos I said I wouldn't do it. All I wanted was to be her friend, her sister even. Respecting and loving each other, sharing secrets and stuff. But I've got no friends. So the season's over now until August. I'm looking forward to the World Cup. I saw you on telly last night. You're looking good.

Yours always,

Shona

'What's up, Shona? We laid on this birthday treat for you.' Shona plays with her meal. Delany is watching her across the table with his huge brown eyes. He looks a lot like Anthony but being mixed-race he doesn't have Anthony's white skin. Unlike his sisters. And Stella. Anthony's wife. Stella is also watching Shona. Excusing herself, Shona runs to the guest room. Anthony knocks on the door and enters although Shona doesn't tell him to. He asks her what's wrong. Shona stays silent. He asks Shona if she and Delany would like to live with him, Stella and her sisters. Shona says nothing. He says he knows Jackie has a drink problem. He tells her he loves her but doesn't want to hurt Stella. Anthony tells her to think about living with him.

Dear Andy,

I can't leave Mum. How can we leave her? When I told her about Anthony's offer she went straight to the off licence and bought two bottles of wine. I went to her bedroom to try and talk to her but she slammed the door in my face. I know why she's crying. Anthony didn't ask her to live with him. Get rid of Stella and the two princesses. That's the deal, Jackie wants Anthony. It's like my mum's dying. It's like she's dying in front of me for love. I feel as if I'm in the middle of two people, people forcing me to make choices. I've got school tomorrow. I'm sweatin' it. How come you haven't written? I'd love to hear from you. Just to know someone out there is listening.

Shona

'Here she is. Miss motherfucker. We don't want you in our crew anyway. We elite.' Candice is blocking Shona's entrance to the school canteen. 'Get down on your knees, bitch, and beg me to forgive you.' Candice has the attention of Year 8 and 9. She commands respect and gets it. But Shona ain't getting on her knees for nobody but the Almighty. Candice is a bag full of shit but Shona is scared to tell her that. Instead she tries to edge past. Candice grabs her pullover. In an instant Shona turns, bringing her hand in a vicious slap across Candice's face. Candice stands there, flabbergasted. Slowly, confident outside, shaking inwardly, Shona walks away, finding a quiet place next to the window where she can stare out into the school fields. She can hear Candice boasting to her friends about what she's going to do to her after school. The fear's gone. Slightly. Backing out of the canteen, they all leave. Shona tries to eat the dry school fries but they're like wooden sticks. Suddenly she isn't hungry. Soon she notices enquiring, dark and sexy eyes stealing across. It's The Watchman. He smiles. Shona looks behind her. No, he's smiling at her. He rolls his eyes, smiles again and nods.

'Mind if I sit next to you?' Shona's voice is hoarse and creaky when she says no. 'I like your freestyle. Wanna flex with me?' Shona stares at him for a second. 'No, I ain't dealing with Candice no more. She's last year's news.' Why? 'I like you. I like the way you dealt with her. She's a vain bitch. But you, I've been watching. You, I have desired for a long time. You're smart, intelligent and beautiful. You got that shy, innocent thing going on. I like, baby, I like.' Is this a trick or dream? Shona thinks she's fat and ugly. 'Wanna meet up at my place, we'll go someplace. Flicks, McDonald's. Whatever.' At sixteen, The Watchman is two years older than Shona. He has a part-time job and says he wants a job in computers. His eyes are like light-brown saucers; his skin looks like smooth brown cocoa. His voice is deep and wavy.

Remembering her responsibilities, Shona tells him to meet her at hers later, her heart pumping wildly, making her dizzy and her knees weak. Shona takes the short cut home, avoiding the crew at the bus stop, legging it across Stockport Road.

Shona gives Delany some colouring to do, puts on a Barney video and tells him not to bother her. Jackie's in one of her drunken drowses in her bedroom. Shona takes The Watchman to her bedroom, when he knocks. Jodeci is rocking the groove, seductively, through Sony speakers. It occurs to her that The Watchman is as nervous as she is. He makes chit-chat but soon gets down to what he wants. Shona tells him she isn't ready for that so soon. They haven't been anywhere yet. She asks him if he's sure if he's over Candice. He tells her Candice was under him. They both laugh.

'What matters to me, Shona, is inside of you. Not how your hair is or what label you're wearing. Just you. Natural.' He stares hard at Shona, before taking her coy face in his hands and kissing her softly.

Dear Andy,

Second to you I've found the love of my life. He's everything I've ever wanted. He says he'll take me to see United next season. He's already bought me the latest away kit. We have so much fun and so much in common. He makes my life flow. Jackie hasn't drunk anything for two days but she's like that. She can go weeks before hitting it. Right now I hate Arsenal. The Watchman and I cried for Man U. You deserve better Andy. Anthony's coming around to take Jackie out for a meal. He says Stella has left him and he wants Jackie back. Everyone is happy. I'm happy for Jackie. This time next week The Watchman and I will have been together for ten days.

Shona

Shona knows there's something wrong before she steps out of the toilet cubicle. It's too quiet. It's the last period. In fifteen minutes time school will be over. Shona unlocks the toilet door to find them waiting for her, Sly, Candice, Frankie and the dumb-looking one with the mad spidery plaits and the twitch.

'I wanna talk to you,' Candice says grabbing her arm. 'I hear, whore, that you're checkin' my man.' Shona tries to tell her, her man says they're finished but Candice drags her roughly. Someone pushes her. Someone ties something on her face, a blindfold over her eyes. They pull her out of the toilets, up steps. Where? The fire-escape. Hollow wrought iron steps. Outside past the playground. The forbidden area concealed at the back of the school. What the hell are they going to do to her? Suddenly, Shona starts to scream hysterically, starts to lash out. She hears the panic in Candice's normally clear voice.

'Shona. No. Don't. Watch out.' Shona feels the wind rushing. Feels the scream in her ears. Feels a strange sort of weightlessness. Then nothing.

Jackie picks up the early morning mail from her doorstep. There are the usual bills. There's a letter addressed to Shona. Flipping it over curiously she reads the address and emblem on the back. Manchester United Football Club. Tearing the envelope hurriedly she starts to read the letter.

Dear Shona,

I'm sorry to take so long to write back to you but you know with football, training and everything. It was nice to hear from you. You sound and look like a nice girl (thanks for the photo). I read some of your letters with sadness and then joy. I truly hope everything is all right with you and your family. I want you to know that although things might be hard at the moment they do get better as time goes by. So stick with it and don't be defeated. I'm sure you'll shine through. You sound like a girl with spirit, which is what we both have.

Jackie can't bring herself to read the letter as the tears sting her eyes and smear the ink.

All my love, Andy Cole

He has sent a signed photograph. Two complimentary match tickets fall from the envelope to the floor.

Dear Colin
Dave Haslam

4th September 1990

Dear Colin,

This is just a quick fax to confirm the details we agreed at our meeting regarding my proposal for a club night at the Boardwalk. The night will be called Freedom, and my responsibilities will include DJ-ing, booking the guest DJs, sorting flyers, mailing out press releases, dealing out membership cards, and keeping everyone vibed-up about the night. As well as a fee you will be paying me a cut of the door once my costs and your club costs have been met. All systems go for the 1st December.

11th October 1990

Dear Colin,

Tomorrow I'm in Paris DJ-ing and I'm over there again next week at a three-day festival headlined by James, the Charlatans, and John Cale. It's very brave of the promoter to put me on before John Cale. I intend to play something very acid house, something cheap and Italian I think.

13th December 1990

Dear Colin,

Two Saturdays gone and so far so good with Freedom, but before this week we need to find somewhere to affix the smoke machine permanently or someone will make off with it.

4th March 1991

Dear Colin,

Freedom was wonderful. The queue reached Warrington by 10.30. With the guest list and a well-worked one-out-one-in system, we had 833 people in on Saturday. Not bad when the official capacity is 440. A massive night, it has to be said.

5th December 1991

Dear Colin,

Saturday went well. Jason bought some satsumas from the barrows on Church Street (108 for £7). We gave them away, with whistles, drink tokens etc. There's a bit of a problem with the exhibition of photographs from the club, though. We've had a call from a girl who comes to Freedom without the knowledge of her husband. She appears in one of the photographs, on the dance floor, and she's concerned that somebody might see it and cause her trouble. She was very tearful.

10th February 1992

Dear Colin,

The Todd Terry special is confirmed. He's costing £800, but it's his first DJ slot in Manchester so I think it's worth it. He also wants a twin and a single hotel room which I can get at Sacha's for £105. Sacha's is that new hotel at the back of Piccadilly. I thought Todd Terry might appreciate it; it's got a huge stuffed polar bear in the lobby.

17th February 1992
Dear Colin,
I'm glad you liked my revamped ideas for Yellow. Although town is quiet on a Friday at the moment, musically – with Elliot and Jason as co-DJs – we're on to a good thing. We'll appeal to an older, soulier crowd than Freedom. It'll make a good Friday/Saturday double header at the club.

17th April 1992
Dear Colin,
We needed 448 to break even on the M-People gig and by the end of the night we'd had 597 through the doors, so it's time to celebrate.

11th April 1993
Dear Colin,
Last week at Yellow a guy who'd been turned away tried to climb in through a 2nd floor window. I don't know how he had got up there. Most of the customers were cheering and encouraging him to come in, and the doormen were telling him to go back out. The drop either side is pretty high, and he was left dangling halfway in and halfway out for a good five minutes. Finally he got himself into the club, but the doormen grabbed him and threw him out of the front door. I didn't see it happen; this is just a report. In fact, I thought the crowd were cheering my records, but I was wrong.

6th September 1993

Dear Colin,

I worked on Friday which was good, sold out early etc. Then
I was in Berlin on Saturday at E-Werk playing 2 til 6 after
Paul van Dyk. As I left the club it was light, but there were
still people coming in. I got straight into a taxi to the airport
for the 7.30 flight home, and unsurprisingly fell asleep on
the plane. Record of the night; THK 'France'.

9th November 1994

Dear Colin,

Paul Oakenfold rang today to see if I was interested in
DJ-ing on the PJ Harvey tour; which, it became clear,
wasn't going to be my cup of tea. He kept going on about
'the old days', but then don't we all?

5th December 1994

Dear Colin,

The Freedom 4th Birthday was a great success. We've got a
very enthusiastic bunch of regulars, and that's sustained
the night really. The music on Saturday went down a storm;
the odd piano classic – 'Last Rhythm', 'Electric Choc', 'Rich
In Paradise' – plus some new Danny Tenaglia-style stuff.
I'm that much better at DJ-ing now that I can hardly believe
I did four hundred Haçienda nights only half knowing what I
was doing, busking it.

9th January 1995

Dear Colin,

Paul Ince was in on Friday, apparently United's next home
game is Monday evening. As a consequence of Sky TV's power
over football schedules footballers now get to go out on Fridays.

1st March 1995

Dear Colin,

Pete Tong is now confirmed for August. My only worry is a slow deterioration in the quality of our clientele. Clubs seem to get a honeymoon period, but then a bunch of roughnecks attach themselves to the night and it goes downhill from there. At Freedom it's mostly nasty white kids who are killing the spirit of the night. I can't imagine seriously heavy gangsters are interested in hanging around the Boardwalk picking fights with students. So who are these wannabes? They think they're Al Pacino, but how come they've never got girlfriends?

13th March 1995

Dear Colin,

I agree with you that the competition on a Friday is harder now than when we started. Headfunk is doing well at the moment, and there's talk of yet more bars. The Yellow 3rd Birthday with the Hooch and Wear It Out fashion show should do well for us, though. Please could you remind your staff to clean the dressing rooms? They need to be clean, lockable, with working toilets, chairs, and – if possible – mirrors.

21st June 1995

Dear Colin,

The police raided Home, Equinox, and Cheerleaders on Saturday – stopping the music and searching for drugs. Is that it, I wonder, or are we next?

4th August 1995

Dear Colin,
The Pete Tong posters are up. I saw six in a row opposite
Whitworth Park, one under Mancunian Way, two at the
Great Western Street end of Rusholme, and one near Owens
Park; all on just a mile stretch of Oxford Road. There's one
right opposite the Canal Bar on Whitworth Street, and one
on the corner opposite Atlas; two very good sites. Should be
a great night.

21st August 1995

Dear Colin,
We got a huge audience for Tong, with queues round the
corner all night. Tim Booth and Graeme Le Saux came
down. Add Le Saux's name to the list of footballers in the
club over the last year; Ian Wright, Paul Ince, Ryan Giggs,
Andy Cole, Roy Keane, Terry Phelan, Nicky Summerbee. Are
footballers the new pop stars, or are DJs the new pop
stars? Is comedy the new rock & roll? Is Bristol the new
Manchester?

6th November 1995

Dear Colin,
The earlier we make a start on New Year's Eve the better, so
your usual help with sponsorship would be appreciated. I
think we've done well holding it together with all the
pressure on the door at the moment and the number of new
clubs opening all the time. But I was looking at the figures;
our security costs have gone up from £170 to £650 in five
years. Says it all really.

11th December 1995

Dear Colin,

It's been a bad end to the year. Yellow on Friday was excellent, but Freedom was a near disaster. When I'm playing the records and the crowd is good, the atmosphere can be brilliant, and it feels like the best job in the world, but we've started attracting more and more shady characters. It's the same all over town, a depressing vibe; the Haçienda's reputation as unsafe is really harming the club. A couple more Saturdays like the one we've just had, and it'll all be over for Freedom too.

We're in a no-win situation. I understand the theory that we take the conflict out of the situation and avoid going to war with the gangs to minimize the risk of trouble, violence, running battles, but, unfortunately, once an element have infiltrated the club this softly softly approach has the effect of giving them status 'above the law'. Every week I see these lads wrecking the night, including harassing women, smoking spliffs, throwing beer over each other, provoking other customers etc., and there's apparently nothing that can be done, except wait for them to drift off to some other place.

4th February 1996

Dear Colin,

Freedom is still bothering me. I'm there trying to do my thing, but I find it demoralizing. Yellow is great though. We get people travelling from Liverpool, North Wales, Cumbria, and over the Pennines. Lemn Sissay tells me he recently did a poetry gig in Sunderland, and he met a guy there who wouldn't shut up about Yellow. He said it was the highlight of his recent weekend in Manchester. Last week we could have let in a thousand paying customers.

18th February 1996

Dear Colin,

Oakenfold is confirmed as a guest DJ next month.
According to the contract not only does he have to have a
flight up to Manchester from London, a hotel room for
himself and a colleague, a selection of drinks, and three
decks, but we have to pick him up at the airport and escort
him to the club. It must be something that happens when
you've made your first million; you find it hard to hail a
taxi.

21st March 1996

Dear Colin,

It's clear that Freedom is never going to recover from the
gang problems. It's frustrating for me. Those guys are
nothing to do with me. Yet, month by month they've
deterred our good customers, and they're right in my face;
literally. I've been punched, and spat at.

22nd March 1996

Dear Colin,

I didn't mean to imply that door problems were the only
reason. My decision is also down to my desire to end
Freedom on a high. It's not perfect, but it's still busy and I
still love getting on the decks. I don't want to see Freedom
dwindle away, me playing to thirty people.

   I know you're right to point out that when thousands of
people come through the door week in and week out then
it's unlikely that we will be getting 100% party people with
good attitudes, and I accept that it's not solely a Boardwalk
problem, or a club problem. The other week someone I
know got beaten up by some guys while he was walking

past Marks & Spencer on a Tuesday afternoon. It's not to do with clubs, it's to do with . . . What exactly?

27th May 1996

Dear Colin,
The last Freedom sold out early and Robert Owens was brilliant, the perfect guest DJ for the event. Excellent.

10th June 1996

Dear Colin,
Friday was lively. One of Sefton's mates jumped off the balcony.

13th June 1996

Dear Colin,
Thanks for keeping me up-to-date on the figures. Please can we meet soon to sort out some cheques.

17th June 1996

Dear Colin,
It was chaos on Saturday with the IRA bomb. Kiss 102 did well giving out information, passing on police advice not to come into town. I was actually DJ-ing at the Cotton Club in Stalybridge with Erik Rug, safely out of town. There was still a stunned, muted atmosphere out there, though.

28th June 1996

Dear Colin,
For three weeks now I've been asking somebody in the office to leave full details of Yellow on the outgoing message on the Boardwalk ansaphone, but there's still nothing but a bland 'there's no one here right now' type message. An

unhelpful message like that doesn't encourage people to
come down and try the night, does it?

2nd July 1996

Dear Colin,
The Haçienda are expected to have a new-look Saturday in
September promoted by Paul Cons; there are all sorts of
rumours about what form this will take.

4th October 1996

Dear Colin,
On Wednesday I was interviewed in the back of a Mercedes
by Jenny Ross for a programme on Granada about clubbing
in Manchester. I plugged Yellow endlessly, but the director
kept telling me to be 'frothier'. Frothier; that's so Nineties
isn't it?

11th October 1997

Dear Colin,
Cons has asked me to do Freak at the Haçienda every
Saturday from the beginning of November. On a Yellow
vibe.

21st February 1997

Dear Colin,
For the Yellow 5th Birthday tonight we have Andy Madhatter
DJ-ing, plus a live PA by Veba. She's got a great track out
called 'Spellbound'; have you heard it?

4th March 1997

Dear Colin,
Midweek blues everywhere. Despite his busy weekends, last

week Cons only got 60 at South for Sleuth. Kaleida is doing OK at the weekend too, apparently. Only holds 250 though.

31st March 1997

Dear Colin,
Lo-and-behold all day Friday the outgoing message was 'This is the Boardwalk, on Wednesday the 26th March . . .', going on about some local band or other playing.

14th April 1997

Will you be able to come to the Haçienda 15th Birthday on Sunday May 24th? Sasha, Graeme Park and Alistair Whitehead upstairs, Laurent Garnier in the Fifth Man, and I'm doing the VIP room.

21st April 1997

Dear Colin,
I have two tickets reserved for you for the Haçienda birthday on Sunday May 24th.

27th May 1997

Dear Colin,
I was looking out for you at the Haçienda, but I had heard from other people that they had waited 40 minutes to get in. I don't blame you for giving up and going home.

16th June 1997

Dear Colin,
Repercussion in Castlefield was great, despite the rain. I did the Duke's stage from 9 until 10pm between Marc Littlemore and Darren Partington. I ended up with just the

kind of mad mixture I like; a crowd of nutty e-heads with
their tops off and Yellow girls dancing in the drizzle to
Mantronix.

17th June 1997
Dear Colin,
Paul Cons has now also taken over the running of Friday
nights at the Haçienda. This weekend they got less than
300 payers. He's unhappy. He says he'd prefer to get a
thousand pounds out of the bank every week and set fire to
it on Whitworth Street.

25th June 1997
Dear Colin,
It's that time again to sort out the cheques. When can we
meet?

4th July 1997
Dear Colin,
Sorry I've not been in touch this week but the Haçienda
closure has kept me busy. Today it's front page of the
Evening News and headlines on Granada. Earlier a Key 103
newsman arrived in a van with a big aerial on the roof and
interviewed me at home, then I did a phone interview with
Kiss, then this afternoon a car from Granada picked me up
from home to do a short interview with Patrick Snell outside
the Haçienda. Soundbite: 'The Haçienda is Manchester's
greatest cultural asset . . .' Thing is, I don't have any real
information. I don't know the whole story. In the taxi back
the driver said: 'It's obvious where the money has gone;
they've been milked by the gangsters.'

6th October 1997

Dear Colin,

Me hosting and promoting the night as well as DJ-ing is one of the strengths of Yellow (as it was for Freedom too). It keeps me close to the audience. It's got to be preferable to the new breed: marketing graduates looking for the commercial angle, flicking through Mixmag for the latest DJ everyone's booking. A lot of the decent nights in town at the moment have got a similar DIY spirit; the things Mark Rae does, or the Unabombers.

15th October 1997

Dear Colin,

Did the first of four programmes for MCR FM yesterday. Played stuff like Dub Syndicate, Joyce Sims, Sunburst Band, MC Solaar 'Qui Seme Le Vent'. Generally I don't like doing radio. Every time I open my mouth I feel like DLT.

3rd November 1997

Dear Colin,

Last night I DJ-ed at Chris Joyce's wedding party at Mash & Air, and one of the guests was Adrian Sherwood. He got on the dance floor for 'Good Times'.

18th November 1997

Dear Colin,

At previous meetings with the Council, licensees, promoters etc. it was amazing how bad their relationship with the police had become; they just didn't seem to be trusted. But at today's meeting the police seemed willing to listen. Maybe they're more relaxed now the Haç has gone. The problem will be when they all move on to new posts and we're given a new set of officers to get to know.

Also, it's hard to put measures in place when the situation is so unpredictable. We can get one-off nights when it looks bad, and then for six or seven weeks it's all quiet on the gangster front. Major measures just aren't appropriate. Most trouble in town isn't gangster-related, anyway; it's just mindless battles in the chip shop queue. These things go in phases. It only takes one tragic incident to increase the fear, but, I don't know, go anywhere – Redcar, Warrington, Reading – and there'll be lads scrapping.

26th January 1998

Dear Colin,
On Friday, before the club was open, the magistrates came into the club to be briefed by Phil Owen and to watch Saxon, the sniffer dog, in action. Apparently he goes round empty clubs and can pick out 'drug hot spots' (whatever they are). Anyway, he didn't sniff anything out at all in the Boardwalk. The magistrates watched expectantly, and perhaps we should have planted something somewhere to give them all a thrill.

30th January 1998

Dear Colin,
Tonight we have six Irish journalists on a North West Tourist Board junket from Dublin coming to Yellow. Unfortunately it's been suggested that they eat at Sticky Fingers beforehand; what kind of advert for Manchester is that?

2nd February 1998

Dear Colin,

I know I'm always whining and you all think I'm obsessed by the state of the girls' toilets, but one girl I know actually shudders when I talk to her about them. Your plans to improve them will trigger widespread rejoicing.

2nd March 1998

Dear Colin,

I think faxing is useful because it orders my thoughts, and writing stuff down usually gets a response. Also I like putting everything on record, so it doesn't get lost.

23rd March 1998

Dear Colin,

I get the odd annoying request (like 'Have you got anything we know?' and 'Have you got anything good?') but I had a weird one in Glasgow on Saturday, in the back room at the Tunnel. This guy was yelling at me over the top of the DJ box, but I couldn't make out what he was saying. I thought he was complimenting me, so I said 'Yeah, thanks.' But he kept on shouting at me, still smiling. He stood there, I played another record. He'd been there about six or seven minutes when he held out his hand. I went to shake it, but he carried on shouting and gave me a five-pound note. I realized what he was saying: 'Bottle of Bud, bottle of Bud.' He thought I was a barman. He'd been watching me DJ-ing for nearly ten minutes, and he thought I was serving drinks.

24th April 1998

Dear Colin,

There's a TV crew coming in to film Yellow tonight for a programme on the club scene. Apparently they've got to be in and out by midnight because the crew charges exorbitant overtime rates. I hope we're busy because I've told the guy we're always packed. It'll be embarrassing if no one's in.

26th May 1998

Dear Colin,

The Boardwalk's outgoing message hasn't been carrying any details of Yellow for four weeks; apparently nobody knows how to use the new machine.

6th July 1998

Dear Colin,

I went out on Saturday to Golden which had Sasha on and it was packed. John says he's seen a cheque in an envelope for me.

20th July 1998

Dear Colin,

Golden are leaving Sankey's Soap; this Saturday, July 25th, is the last one. Word is, this will spell the end of Sankey's. Another club closure. Not good is it?

25th September 1998

Dear Colin,

I still think we should work towards improving the look of the club. As things get even more of a struggle in town, it's probably the one thing letting us down at the moment. It's a shame because the door problems have eased considerably. The work you and I and Charlie and the others have done to dissuade the undesirables has worked well. In fact, the only trouble we seem to get now are 'domestics' – ex-girlfriends slugging it out etc.

23rd November 1998

Dear Colin,
On Saturday I was in Dublin DJ-ing at a PR party for Guinness held in a grand country house in the Wicklow Hills. I was told that Ireland's VIP set would be there, but there was no sign of Boyzone or the Edge. Or the Corrs. Nice buffet though.

4th January 1999

Dear Colin,
We've both had success, and I hope you've had as much fun as I have. Despite my gripes about the refurbishment, all the money hassles, all the roughnecks, I'm hooked. Maybe we all are. This New Year in Manchester we had all the usual clubs and bars plus the Arena, Granada Studios, G-Mex. How many people did those three big events alone bring into the city: 20,000 people. More? Before I did my set at Granada I was at Cream, and Liverpool hadn't got any of those big events. Cream was good but Manchester does it better.

8th January 1999

Dear Colin,
I was hoping you could find the time write the last few cheques. Are you available this week?

Dear Colin,

Yellow has had a good seven years. It'll be strange leaving
the Boardwalk. John says he'll miss my faxes, which I can't
believe. There's a mixture of excitement and sadness about
the last night next month. So many friendships will end
when Yellow ends. I'm sure it will be momentous; the crowd
will make the night swing. Lots of great records planned,
but not much else required, although I'll maybe get some
balloons to let loose at 12.30. You know; those huge wobbly
yellow ones.

Billy Micklehurst's Run
A Tale of the 1970s
Tim Willocks

In the winter, Billy Micklehurst used to say, when the nights were bitter and long and you woke up before first light with your hair frozen fast to your collar, and when the hostels and dosshouses were crammed to the doors with the fallen – or when you just weren't in the mood for the company of the living – then Billy, in his raggedy suit and his laceless shoes and with his shoulders hunched against the wind, would make the long march from the nether world between Deansgate and the river, through the concrete bunkers of Hulme and the splendoured decay of Moss Side, and past all manner of things upon the way, until he found the sanctuary he craved in the great necropolis of Southern Cemetery.

There were over a million graves in Southern Cemetery, said Billy. He knew this to be true for he had counted every tombstone himself – each and every one, he swore – and had read by moonlight the names and valedictions on more than just a few of them. Furthermore – and this next revelation he prefaced with a backward glance over either hunched shoulder, as if to exclude the unwelcome presence of eavesdroppers and spies – he claimed to be familiar with the still earthbound spirits of certain of those long entombed and poetically memorialized dead. The identities of these still-present dead he refused to reveal – to anyone, not even me – because, Billy said, they had entrusted him with some small but precious part of their soul, and it would have been a breach of that trust to identify those spirits who had elected him their guardian and saviour in this world.

Billy went to the cemetery because the vents from the crematorium gave off heat long into the night, and so if you slept on the vents you could curl up warm as toast. See, said Billy, burning bodies wasn't like burning wood or coal. No, burned bodies were like a kind of atomic power station. Even when the ashes were cold they gave off an invisible power that you couldn't feel with your hands but which warmed your bones to the core. It was the spirits, see, fighting to escape from the earth. At this point – as if those very spirits were even now dancing in front of him – Billy's eyes would strain out from their sockets with a terror more pure and true than any I would ever see again. For, he explained, some of the spirits never did escape. They were trapped, for all eternity, in the Southern Cemetery. And later, towards dawn, when the warmth from the vents had faded, their ghosts would wake Billy from his sleep and torment him with their anguish.

The ghosts were real, he swore to God. He could see them as plain as he could see me. And solid flesh and blood they were too, not wispy and faint like they always were in the films. They were of all sizes and all ages – from withered old ladies who'd died alone, and big strong lads with their bodies smashed by cars, to a tiny little toddler boy scarred with pox. And they came from all times past, too – maybe fresh from just last week, or maybe from a hundred years ago or more.

Billy's eyes would roll with an awful pity and his hands would flutter like broken wings. Because the most horrible thing of all was that none of them knew why they'd been left behind. They weren't bad people – and there'd been plenty of them put under out there, you could mark Billy's word; people who'd done all manner of terrible things. But how bad could a little toddler be? No, they were just people, that's all, who didn't know why they couldn't get out, nor why out of all the living there was only Billy Micklehurst to stand up in the dark and witness their suffering.

You see, they were counting on Billy Micklehurst to set them all free. And the source of Billy's torment was this: he did not know how this might ever be done.

To look at, Billy could have been ten years either side of fifty. Decades on the road, and unqualified gallons of Mann's brown, Yates's blobs and methylated spirits had forged his bone, skin and inner organs into an indestructible wreck. His face was remarkable for its eyes and its teeth. The eyes managed to be simultaneously both deep-set and ferociously protuberant; and whilst his lower jaw boasted a full set of yellowing stumps, his upper, scurvy ravaged gums could only field two – one canine and one incisor – which wobbled precariously and stuck out over his lip when he closed his mouth. Despite these handicaps he was quite a dapper fellow, in his way: his hair was still as black as oil and always slicked back in a greasy skein from his wide, scar-speckled brow. He always wore a suit – usually grey and double-breasted – its subtle pinstripe blotched with multicoloured stains of obscure and unsavoury origin. His shoes were rarely laced, as laces always broke and cost a fortune; and in summer – and many years before this habit became *de rigueur* amongst the self-consciously fashionable – he often appeared without socks to reveal feet as white as bathroom china and threaded with delicate threads of blue. His shirts tended toward the thread-bare and filthy, but were invariably brightened by a scarlet silk scarf with a gold-tasselled fringe, which he wore cravat-style around his throat.

He said – on several occasions; and always with some considerable pride – that the scarf had been given to him in 1963 by 'a woman of means in Leicestershire', who herself claimed to have once slept with David Niven, during the war.

The first time I met Billy, in July 1976, he was perched like a vigilant gargoyle on a bench in St Ann's churchyard, elbows on his knees, fingers laced together, brooding on the time-polished paving stones at his feet and occasionally glancing up to sneer at the pedestrians emerging from the King Street passageway. I was seventeen years old and looking for somewhere to eat my dinner, and thought the little yard an exotic place to do so. It did cross my mind not to sit down beside the gargoyle and to find somewhere else to eat, but since this idea seemed both discourteous and cowardly I took my place on the bench a couple of feet distant from him. At this point – in this holy spot, and instilled as I was with the strictures, good and bad, of Roman Catholicism – the paper bag in my hand which contained a cheese and tomato sandwich and some salt and vinegar crisps suddenly seemed like an instrument of torture. The man had to be starving. He smelled like he was starving. Yet at the same time I didn't want to impugn his dignity by effectively saying: 'Here, have a sandwich, you poor old bleeder.' So I didn't open the bag. As I sat staring into space, pondering this unexpected moral conundrum, the gargoyle – elbows on his knees and fingers laced together – slowly rotated his head and looked up at me.

I looked back at him, into the deep-set yet protuberant eyes that had beheld a universe I would never know. I couldn't think of anything to say. He had lived life incarnate; and all I'd done was go to school and take exams. I just looked at him.

He said, 'I'm Billy Micklehurst. And I don't give a fuck.'

I raised my paper bag, as if it were an offering to a pagan idol, and said, 'Do you fancy a sandwich?'

Billy squinted dubiously at the bag and said, of the sandwich within, 'What's on it?'

I said, 'Cheese and tomato. I've got some crisps too if you like. Salt and vinegar.'

Billy said, 'Go on, then.' I produced the sandwich and Billy took it. When I offered him the crisps he shook his head. 'Crisps give me wind.'

He necked the sandwich down in huge bites that left strips of crust sticking out from between his gums and which he shoved home with the back of his hand, whilst proclaiming, with grateful references to Christ, just how good a sandwich it was. In seconds it was gone, and it seemed to me that because it had found its perfect resting place inside Billy's gut it was possibly the most perfect sandwich ever made. Billy pulled out a soiled rag and wiped butter, tomato seeds and slavver from his chin. With a magician's flourish, he snapped the rag free of debris and replaced it in his breast pocket.

'God bless you, Ginger,' said Billy. He made a gesture with his hand that appeared to take in the whole world. 'They're all over the place,' he warned. 'So don't you let 'em get their bloody hands on you.'

'Who?' I said.

'Them as 'll try to drag you down, and all manner of other things better left unmentioned,' said Billy. He added: 'You take my word for it.'

And with that Billy got up from the bench and walked away.

That summer I seemed to run into Billy all the time. Sometimes he would be engaged in ferocious arguments with a ragged gathering of his brethren, waving his arms and shaking his fists and turning to spit in the gutter with disgust. On one occasion, this time in St Ann's Square proper, I saw him waltzing – with a surprising elegance and perfection of form – up and down the pavement outside Sherratt and Hughes with a can of Hofmeister held in either hand and a beatific grin on his face. On another I saw him standing rigid and mute at the exit to Victoria railway station. I smiled and said hello and asked how he was keeping, but Billy stared at me with a lack of recognition so complete that I might have been a creature from a distant galaxy. The very next morning he hailed me from the churchyard bench like an old friend, and offered me a drink of what smelled like Domestos, without the slightest memory of our encounter of the previous day.

Sometimes I'd walk round Ancoats with him and he'd show me the gutted factories and warehouses where a man without ties to bind him down might fashion himself a lair. On Sundays, sometimes, I'd go with him to the Mass organized by the St Vincent de Paul society, in an abandoned church in the blitzlands east of the Erwell, where scores of men like Billy, and a handful of women too, would gather to hear readings from the Gospels and take communion in order to pay for the hot tea and sandwiches that followed hard on the last 'Amen'. You see, Manchester was 'a good town for dossers', said Billy.

A good town. Much better than most. Occasionally Billy left for weeks at a time and headed south, 'on matters of some importance best left unmentioned, now that they've been settled'; but he always came back, because Manchester was his town, and a good one. Why, Billy used to say, even the coppers were a soft lot in Manchester.

And so, in my imagination, and by way of Billy's tales and guided tours, another town arose more concrete and vivid than the one I thought I knew: a dark city. A ghost city. A city of outcasts stacked tall with broken majesty: an architecture of loss more monumental by far than the teeming triangle of shops and offices staked out by the train stations and unknowingly invested by the grandeur of its forgotten past. Billy's dark city was an epic whose purpose, conception and construction were far beyond the means – or dreams – of modern men, and had been built by a race whose like would never be seen again: vast and blackened red brick hulks where generations uncelebrated and unnamed had toiled their lives away; crumbling Florentine confections which boasted of a long-vanished wealth both vainglorious and austere; wind- and weed-blown docks stacked from stones so large they might have graced the tombs of Memphian kings; vacant temples to insurance and exchange, storage and manufac- ture, exploitation and greed; scum-festooned canals, rusting incinerators, factory pulleys weather-welded to their chains; the silent geometry of railway arches and cobbles where feet no longer stepped; the Sharp Street Ragged School with its red and faded sign; and the chimneys slender and impossibly tall that would never smoke again. And all of it empty, van- quished, derelict, redundant and despised – by all except Billy, whose heart ached for its beauty and who knew that, like himself, this dark city's glory would soon be done and gone.

It was winter, February-winter, and bitter, and I hadn't seen Billy for months, when one evening I ran into him in Shudehill. He was matted and unshaven, sockless for all that the night was cold, and trembling from head to toe as he clung to a lamppost in a pool of yellow light and wept. He saw me approach and wrenched one hand free in a desperate invitation.

'Ginger,' Billy cried. 'Ginger! The game's up for Billy! The word's out! They're after me!' He paused and hissed and slavver spilled from his lips. 'They're on my back!'

I took him in the Turk's Head and bought him whiskey and beer, and Billy's trembles abated, though not the anguish and terror in his eyes. He stared into his glass, a man beset with demons in a world only he could see, and which he inhabited alone.

'I will tell you,' said Billy, 'they'll not let me get away this time. This time I'll swing, and that's a fact. You mark my words.'

The tears returned to his eyes and Billy swabbed his face with the red silk scarf, whose gold-tasselled fringe was grey with dirt. He seemed shattered with confusion and grief. 'And there's nowt that anyone can do,' Billy whispered, as if even he, who could believe in ghosts, could hardly believe this. 'Nowt at all.'

At that time I had little idea what alcohol could do to the brain, nor any concept of the blind horror of psychosis. I didn't know that Billy's mind was the neurological equivalent of the derelict landscape he inhabited. The streets of his memory and hallucinated perceptions were randomly gutted and crumbling, bombed down and burnt out, shrouded in darkness, filled with rubble and infested with starving rats. The contents of his skull were like the scrambled fragments of innumerable jigsaw puzzles – soaked in meths, blowtorched by hardship, ravaged by malnutrition and disease – and assembled and constantly reassembled with shaking hands into fantastic pictures, distorted and yet punishingly real. Amidst those bits of puzzle forged from delusion, psychosis, and a brain-damaged imagination propelled into dominions awful and unknown, there were without doubt great slabs of real memory, real events, real crime, atrocity and suffering. Yet which was which – which was real, which imagined and which the malformed offspring of the two – no one would ever know, least of all Billy himself. For Billy, all these things were as concrete as the table he sat at.

The game was up for Billy. They were after him. And he would swing.

Despite my ignorance, I did know that Billy was ill – very ill – and offered to get him up to the Royal Infirmary for a check-up and a rest; some clean sheets; a quick wash and brush-up, that's all. Billy lurched to his feet with alarm. He stared at me as if I were suddenly revealed to be one of 'They'. Then he turned, abruptly, and stalked off through the door.

I caught up with him outside but Billy would have none of it. If he went to the Royal he was dead. The word was out for Billy Micklehurst. They were already on his back. The minute he lay down in that hospital bed 'they'd 'ave me like that' – he snapped his fingers – and the next I'd hear of Billy his bones would be floating in the Bridgewater. No. It was now or never. He had to make his run while he still had the chance.

I didn't know what to do, and for all I knew Billy experienced these episodes all the time and always managed to escape their clutches, so I shoved a five-pound note in his pocket, which Billy seemed not to register at all, and told him to take care of himself.

'God bless you, Ginger,' said Billy. And with that he disappeared into the night.

Standing there, I wished I had the guts to go with him. But it was dark and cold, and I was too sensible or scared or both. I didn't know if I would've lasted the night, even if he did. I assured myself that Billy's indestructibility would see him through to dance another day with a beatific smile on his face. But this wasn't to be the case.

Three days later, in St Ann's churchyard, one of Billy's fellow travellers, who introduced himself as 'Brady', and whom I recognized and who knew me to be of Billy's acquaintance, collared me at the passageway to King Street.

'Billy's dead,' said Brady. 'I thought you'd want to know. He strung himself up from a cross in Southern Cemetery, with that fancy red scarf he always wore. You know.'

Billy Micklehurst – the indestructible man – had killed himself. It seemed impossible and yet inevitable. Had he made his run to the graveyard with that bleak purpose in mind? Or had the ghosts of anguish woken him from his sleep and driven him to die alone in a vortex of isolation and fear? Whatever the sequence or intent, impenetrable despair had made hanging himself from a tombstone a more alluring prospect than the pain of the next day's dawning.

I told Brady I was sorry.

Brady nodded, and agreed that it was a right shame. But Brady walked the hard road too and he pointed out that these things happened, and that, after all, Billy Micklehurst had lasted a lot longer than most. And so we parted in the church-yard and left it at that.

I found out from the police that it was true. Billy had hanged himself from a cross; no foul play was suspected. No one claimed his body and they buried him in a pauper's grave in Longsight, which in the end is as good a resting place as any other. Billy had lived his life the way he'd wanted to and the city – like all cities – had much darker tales than Billy's to tell. Yet I thought of him: every time I strolled through St Ann's Square, or up Shudehill, or passed through Ancoats on the 236. I couldn't get him out of my mind. So one night the following summer, after I'd been out late in Chorlton, I walked through Southern Cemetery to see if Billy's ghosts were still around.

They weren't, as far as I could see, though it was an eerie spot to be sure. I thought of Billy, encircled by the ghosts he could not free, and wished for some supernatural event or revelation of the kind I never believed in. No such event took place. So I imagined it instead. I imagined Billy's spirit arising – indestructible – from his pauper's grave in Longsight, and swooping down from the heavens like a raggedy Pied Piper to rally the earthbound dead who'd never done wrong. They all saw him coming and they cried out his name – 'Billy!' they cried, 'We're 'ere! We're 'ere!' – and Billy laughed and rolled his eyes and brandished the scarlet scarf from Leicester-shire in his fist. And this time – now that he too was free, and had made good his run – the ghosts were able to cast off their bonds and follow him. They circled the necropolis once, with Billy laughing in the van, then he led them into infinity and they were gone.

No such exodus happened – or, at any rate, I wasn't there

to see it – but it cheered me to think that it did; and it still does. So to this day, when I'm blue – when the game is up, and the word is out, and they're on my back – then I think of Billy Micklehurst, and the last run he made, and Billy helps free me from torment too.

Keeping on the Right Side of the Law
Val McDermid

Just imagine trying to get a straight job when you've been a villain all your life. Even supposing I could bullshit my way round an application form, how the fuck do I blag my way through an interview when the only experience I've got of interviews, I've always had a brief sitting next to me reminding the thickhead dickheads on the other side of the table that I'm not obliged to answer? I mean, it's not a technique that's going to score points with the personnel manager, is it?

You can imagine it, can't you? 'Mr Finnieston, your application form was a little vague as to dates. Can you give us a more accurate picture of your career structure to date?'

Well, yeah. I started out with burglary when I was eight. My two older brothers figured I was little enough to get in toilet windows, so they taught me how to hold the glass firm with rubber suckers then cut round the edge with a glass cutter. I'd take out the window and pass it down to them, slide in through the gap and open the back door for them. Then they'd clean out the telly, the video and the stereo while I kept watch out the back.

All good things have to come to an end, though, and by the time I was eleven, I'd got too big for the toilet windows and besides, I wanted a bigger cut than those greedy thieving bastards would give me. That's when I started doing cars. They called me Sparky on account of I'd go out with a spark plug tied on to a piece of cord. You whirl the plug around like a cowboy with a lasso, and when it's going fast enough, you just flick the wrist and bingo, the driver's window shatters like one of them fake windows they use in the films. Hardly makes a sound. Inside a minute and I'd have the stereo out. I sold them round the pubs for a fiver a time. In a good night, I could earn a fifty, just like that, no hassle.

But I've always been ambitious, and that was my downfall. One of my mates showed me how to hot-wire the ignition so I could have it away on my toes with the car as well as the sounds. By then, one of my brothers was doing a bit of work for a bloke who had a second-hand car pitch down Strangeways and a quiet little back street garage where his team ringed stolen cars and turned them out with a whole new identity to sell on to mug punters who knew no better.

Only, he wasn't as clever as he thought he was, and one night I rolled up with a Ford Escort and drove right into the middle of a raid. It was wall-to-wall Old Bill that night, and I ended up in a different part of Strangeways, behind bars. Of course, I was too young to do proper time, and my brief got me out of there and into a juvenile detention centre faster than you could say 'of previous good character'.

It's true, what they say about the nick. You do learn how to be a better criminal, just so long as you do what it tells you in all them American self-help books in the prison library. You want to be successful, then hang out with successful people and do what they do. Only, of course, anybody who's banged up is, by definition, not half as fucking successful as they should be.

Anyway, I watched and listened and learned and I made some good mates that first time inside. And when I came out, I was ready for bigger and better things. Back then, banks and post offices were still a nice little earner. They hadn't learned about shatterproof glass and grilles and all that bollocks. You just ran in, waved a shooter around, jumped the counter and cleaned the place out. You could be in and out in five minutes, with enough in your sports bag to see you clear for the next few months.

I loved it.

It was a clean way to earn a living. Well, mostly it was. OK, a couple of times we ran into one of them have-a-go heroes. You'd think it was their money, honest to God you would. Now, I've always believed you should be able to do a job, in and out, and nobody gets hurt. But if some dickhead is standing between me and the out, and it's me or him, I'm not going to stand there and ask him politely to move aside, am I? No, fuck it, you've got to show them who's in charge. One shot into the ceiling, and if they're still standing there, well, it's their own fault, isn't it? You've got to be professional, haven't you? You've got to show you mean business.

And I must have been good at it, because I only ever got a tug the once, and they couldn't pin a thing on me. Yeah, OK, I did end up doing a three stretch around about then, but that was for what you might call extra-curricular activities. When I found out Johnny the Hat was giving one to my brother's wife, well, I had to make an example of him didn't I? I mean, family's family. She might be a slag and a dog, but anybody that thinks they can fuck with my family is going to find out different. You'd think Johnny would have had the sense not to tell the Dibble who put him in the hospital, but some people haven't got the brains they were born with. They had him in witness protection before the trial, but of course all that ended after I went down. And when I was getting through my three with visits from the family, I had the satisfaction of knowing that Johnny's family were visiting his grave. Like I say, families have got to stick together.

By the time I got out, things had changed. The banks and building societies had wised up and sharpened up their act and the only people trying to rob them were amateurs and fucking eejits.

Luckily, I'd met Tommy inside. Honest to God, it was like it was written in the fucking stars. I knew all about robbing and burgling, and Tommy knew all there was to know about antiques. What he also knew was that half the museums and stately homes of England – not to mention our neighbours in Europe – had alarm systems that were an embarrassment.

I put together a dream team, and Tommy set up the fencing operation, and we were in business. We raped so many private collections I lost count. The MO was simple. We'd spend the summer on research trips. We'd case each place once. Then we'd go back three weeks later to case it again, leaving enough time for the security vids to be wiped of our previous visit. We'd figure out the weak points and draw up the plans. Then we'd wait till the winter, when most of them were closed up for the season, with nothing more than a skeleton staff.

We'd pick a cold, wet miserable night, preferably with a bit of wind. That way, any noise we made got swallowed up in the weather. Then we'd go in, seven-pound sledges straight through the vulnerable door or window, straight to the cabinets that held the stuff we'd identified as worth nicking. Here's a tip, by the way. Even if they've got toughened glass in the cases, chances are it's still only got a wooden frame. Smack that on the corner with a three-pound club hammer and the whole thing falls to bits and you're in.

Mostly, we were off the estate and miles away before the local bizzies even rolled up. Nobody ever got hurt, except in the pocket.

They were the best years of my life. Better than sex, that moment when you're in, you do the business and you're out again. The rush is purer than you'll ever get from any drug. Not that I know about that from personal experience, because I've never done drugs and I never will. I hate drug dealers more than I hate coppers. I've removed my fair share of them from my patch over the years. Now they know not to come peddling their shit on my streets. But a couple of the guys I work with, they like their Charlie or whizz when they're not working, and they swear that they've never had a high like they get when they're doing the business.

We did some crackers. A museum in France where they'd spent two million quid on their state-of-the-art security system. They had a grand opening do where they were shouting their mouths off about how their museum was burglarproof. We did it that very night. We rigged up pulleys from the building across the street, wound ourselves across like we were the SAS and went straight in through the skylight. They said we got away with stuff worth half-a-million quid. Not that we made anything like that off it. I think I cleared 15k that night, after expenses. Still, who dares wins, eh?

We only ever took stuff we already knew we had a market for. Well, mostly. One time, I fell in love with this Rembrandt. I just loved that picture. It was a self-portrait and just looking at it, you knew the geezer like he was one of your mates. It was hanging on this Duke's wall, right next to the cases of silver we'd earmarked. On the night, on the spur of the moment, I lifted the Rembrandt an' all.

Tommy went fucking ape. He said we'd never shift that, that we'd never find a buyer. I told him I didn't give a shit, it wasn't for sale anyway. He thought I'd completely lost the plot when I said I was taking it home. I had it on the bedroom wall for six months. But it wasn't right. A council house in Wythenshawe just doesn't go with a Rembrandt. So one night, I wrapped it up in a tarpaulin and left it in a field next to the Duke's gaff. I rang the local radio station phone-in from a call-box and told them where they could find the Rembrandt. I hated giving it up, mind you, and I wouldn't have done if I'd had a nicer house.

But that's not the sort of tale you can tell a personnel manager, is it?

'And why are you seeking a change of employment, Mr Finnieston?'

Well, it's down to Kim, innit?

I've known Kimmy since we were at school together. She was a looker then, and time hasn't taken that away from her. I always fancied her, but never got round to asking her out. By the time I was back in circulation after my first stretch, she'd taken up with Danny McGann, and before I worked up the bottle to make a move, bingo, they were married.

I ran into her again about a year ago. She was on a girls' night out in Rothwell's, a gaggle of daft women acting like they were still teenagers. Just seeing her made me feel like a teenager an' all. I sent a bottle of champagne over to their table, and of course, Kimmy came over to thank me for it. She always had good manners.

Any road, it turned out her and Danny weren't exactly happy families any more. He was working away a lot, leaving her with the two girls, which wasn't exactly a piece of cake. Mind you, she's done well for herself. She's got a really good job, managing a travel agency. A lot of responsibility and a lot of respect from her bosses. We started seeing each other, and I felt like I'd come up on the lottery.

The only drawback is that after a few months, she tells me she can't be doing with the villainy. She's got a proposition for me. If I go straight, she'll kick Danny into touch and move in with me.

So that's why I'm trying to figure out a way to make an honest living. You can see that convincing a bunch of suits they should give me a job isn't easy. 'Thank you very much, Mr Finnieston, but I'm afraid you don't quite fit our present requirements.'

The only way anybody's ever going to give me a job is if I monster them into it, and somehow, I don't think the straight world works like that. You can't go around personnel offices saying, 'I know where you live. So gizza job or the Labrador gets it.'

This is where I'm up to when I meet my mate Chrissie for a drink. You wouldn't think it to look at her, but Chrissie writes them hard-as-nails cop dramas for the telly. She looks more like one of them bleeding-heart social workers, with her wholemeal jumpers and jeans. But Chrissie's dead sound, her and her girlfriend both. The girlfriend's a brief, but in spite of that, she's straight. That's probably because she doesn't do criminal stuff, just divorces and child custody and all that bollocks.

So I'm having a pint with Chrissie in one of them trendy bars in Chorlton, all wooden floors and hard chairs and fifty different beers, none of them ones you've ever heard of except Guinness. And I'm telling her about my little problem. Halfway down the second pint, she gets that look in her eyes, the dreamy one that tells me something I've said has set the wheels in motion inside her head. Usually, I see the results six months later on the telly. I love that. Sitting down with Kimmy and going, 'See that? I told Chrissie about that scam. Course, she's softened it up a bit, but it's my tale.'

'I've got an idea,' Chrissie says.

'What? You're going to write a series about some poor fucker trying to go straight?' I say.

'No, a job. Well, sort of a job.' She knocks back the rest of her pint and grabs her coat. 'Leave it with me. I'll get back to you. Stay lucky.' And she's off, leaving me surrounded by the well-meaning like the last covered wagon hemmed in by the Apaches.

A week goes by, with me trying to talk my way into setting up a little business doing one-day hall sales. But everybody I approach thinks I'm up to something. They can't believe I want to do anything the straight way, so all I get offered is fifty kinds of bent gear. I am sick as a pig by the time I get the call from Chrissie.

This time, we meet round her house. Me, Chrissie and the girlfriend, Sarah the solicitor. We settled down with our bottles of Belgian pop and Sarah kicks off. 'How would you like to work on a freelance basis for a consortium of solicitors?' she asks.

I can't help myself. I just burst out laughing. 'Do what?' I go.

'Just hear me out. I spend a lot of my time dealing with women who are being screwed over by the men in their life. Some of them have been battered, some of them have been emotionally abused, some of them are being harassed by their exes. Sometimes, it's just that they're trying to get a square deal for themselves and their kids, only the bloke knows how to play the system and they end up with nothing, while he laughs all the way to the bank. For most of these women, the law either can't sort it out or it won't. I even had a case where two coppers called to a domestic gave evidence in court against the woman, saying she was completely out of control and irrational and all the bloke was doing was exerting reasonable force to protect himself.'

'Bastards,' I say. 'So what's this got to do with me.'

'People doing my job get really frustrated,' Sarah says. 'There's a bunch of us get together for a drink now and again, and we've been talking for a long time about how we've stopped believing the law has all the answers. Most of these blokes are bullies and cowards. Their women wouldn't see them for dust if they had anybody to stand up for them. So what we're proposing is that we'd pay you to sort these bastards out.'

I can't believe what I'm hearing. A brief offering me readies to go round and heavy the kind of toerags I'd gladly sort out as a favour? There has to be a catch. 'You're not telling me the Legal Aid would pay for that, are you?' I say.

Sarah grins. 'Behave, Terry. I'm talking a strictly unofficial arrangement. I thought you could go and explain the error of their ways to these blokes. Introduce them to your baseball bat. Tell them if they don't behave, you'll be visiting them again in a less friendly mode. Tell them that they'll be getting a bill for incidental legal expenses incurred on their partners' behalf and if they don't come up with the cash pronto monto, you'll be coming round to make a collection. I'm sure they'll respond very positively to your approaches.'

'You want me to go round and teach them a lesson?' I'm still convinced this is a wind-up.

'That's about the size of it.'

'And you'll pay me?'

'We thought a basic rate of £250 a job. Plus bonuses in cases where the divorce settlement proved suitably substantial. A bit like a lawyer's contingency fee. No win, no fee.'

I can't quite get my head round this idea. 'So it would work how? You'd bell me and tell me where to do the business?'

Sarah shakes her head. 'It would all go through Chrissie. She'll give you the details, then she'll bill the legal firms for miscellaneous services, and pass the fees on to you. After this meeting, we'll never talk about this again face to face. And you'll never have contact with the solicitors you'd be acting for. Chrissie's the cut-out on both sides.'

'What do you think, Tel?' Chrissie asks, eager as a virgin in the back seat.

'You could tell Kimmy you were doing process serving,' Sarah chips in.

That's the clincher. So I say OK.

That was six months ago. Now I'm on Chrissie's books as her research assistant. I pay tax and National Insurance, which was a bit of a facer for the social security, who could not get their heads round the idea of me as a proper citizen. I do two or three jobs a week, and everything's sweet. Sarah's sorting out Kimmy's divorce, and we're getting married as soon as all that's sorted.

I tell you, this is the life. I'm doing the right thing and I get paid for it. If I'd known going straight could be this much fun, I'd have done it years ago.

Acts of Vengeance: One Two Three Four
Gareth Creer

Dawn. Because of somebody I know too well, tonight I will snuff out the life of a stranger. And whilst I know I am responsible for the loss of at least one life in my past, I do not consider myself to be a murderer.

I watch the unmoving and naked outline of the somebody I have learned to love and who I willed to love me in return. Angela is standing on the balcony, overlooking the canal in the heart of the city. She is in shadow and I cannot see the complex truths of her; the curves and lumps and detail hair of her; the moles and tiny scars of her, and the other ravages that map the stories of each change that has been visited on her. I know her completely, I think. And I know I am responsible, that I must make amends. I can see the prints of my fingers with their still burning touch on her buttocks – a pure white that lies. She draws her arms W-shaped across her breasts.

Last week, you could have watched the early parts of my progress from here, high in the city, as I sped to save her from emergency services. I would have disappeared from your view, and gone fast motoring down Oxford Road, through the canyons of university, and disappearing into badlands, charting myself to her latest troubles.

Sounds of a new day come in from the Gay Village below. Delivery vans clutch and grind; harmless banter between people leaving early for work and coming in late from play. I swing my legs from between the sheets and feel the chill of early morning.

'I love you, Jimmy,' says Angela.

'I love you too,' I motion with a changing expression on my face.

'I'm sorry for what has happened. I will get better.'

And I take her face into the hollow of my neck and shoulder. I do it to hide the expanse of doubt I can feel spreading through the soundscape of the shapes my face makes.

I love the city, living right in its soft heart, where we can step straight into its beat, feel it pulse around us. Like we're in a womb. Me an orphan. She an orphan and the living half of twins that are half dead.

Morning. We've come to Metz for coffee and Angela is moded for flit and chat. Her sadness has stayed high in the city behind closed doors, not given the light of day. I know that some of the people she's talking to may have purveyed some of the something she hides behind; a thing that dilutes her past. Changes its flavour. Some of them will even know the man whose prescriptions create substitute pains that have taken her into a new world without alternative. And now it is him making demands on her. Somebody has to break the circle – from the outside.

I have to believe in the saving of individual souls. And Angela is the living half of the complete good and bad yinyang whole of a person whose better half could not survive the arc I meteored into her fates. Lisa was the less destructive, split-atom twin part of Angela. I loved her from the first time I saw her until she died – when she and I were both fifteen. It was my fault. So you can understand that I must save Angela the only way I know I can. Whatever it takes.

'Come and sit with us, JimmyMack,' shouts Angela.

'No, I'm all right,' I signal. She understands. Metz, like many things, is venned into our separate circles. She chatters. I read. But that is understandable. There is nothing unhealthy in this aspect of our relationship. If anything, we are twined too tight.

I first met Lisa when we were in the same Home. Not a home at all, but a place I was sent to: when all the families Foster had been driven to distraction by my soundlessness; when it was decided that I had elected to be the way I am. Mute.

The first night in my first unfostered, institutional home, I woke in white brushed cotton. I could smell disinfectant. I got down off the bed, walked into an echo sound of radio tunes. There was a girl in a corridor. She carried a radio and she smiled at me, the smile of an angel – as if I hadn't woken. She said to me, 'What's your name?'

Silence.

'Are you shy?'

I pointed at my throat.

'Are you deaf and dumb?'

I shook my head. Deafandumb, like it's one word, one possible state of affliction.

'I like this song,' she said. 'I'll call you JimmyMack. Do you mind?' She took me down some stairs, sat me down and gave me cereal in a big kitchen. And with my new name came glimpses, samples of a new and better life.

I saw her later that day, on a swing. I stood by her, waiting for another kindness. She looked the other way, as if she couldn't see me. I went up close to her so I could feel the warm waft of air as she cut arcs around me. I put my hand out so she could take me to what we had to do next. She jumped off the swing and said, 'You're the dumb one, aren't you.'

I nodded and smiled. She spat at me in the face, ran away shouting 'Dum-bo Dum-bo Dum-bo' and I didn't realize until that evening at supper, she was Angela. They were exactly alike and as different as can be.

Angela comes to my table with a here-today glisten in her eye. She wants to set up the visitation from the man who treats her like meat, who I will later receive without human rights. 'Yes,' I nod, 'yes I will help. It is still on.' We're in above our heads. But I message 'yes, yes' with an earnest nod of my head. I send her signs that give her the gist but not the nuance of what I mean. 'I will settle up with this man. He can come to our place. He should bring enough stuff to keep you going for at least a month, because I'm going to take you away, I'm going to help bring you off it. I'm going to save you.' And in doing so, I will save myself.

'What? A month's worth of gear?'

I nod.

'Oh Jimmy, I don't deserve you.'

But what I don't signal to her, is that she deserves better than anything I can give her, which is necessarily tainted. She deserves a new lease of her whole life.

'I'll go then, set it up. OK?'

'OK. See you in the Piccadilly,' I mute with a lofty point and an eating mime. She nods, but my suggestion puts sad corners on her smile and she goes off with a slow coil step, like I've drained life from her.

Afternoon. It's Charlie Bubbles up here, at the top of the Piccadilly Hotel. Have you seen the movie? It is homecoming. It is retrospective. It is good things that can fuck you up. Me and Lisa came here, in our best togs, going up and down in lifts and pretending to be residents. We would look across the gardens, above the street-level signage dross to the city's past: great ornate blocks of unwashed Victorian endeavour, created from nothing by the fruits of foreign crops, in a foreign time.

And if, like me, you have honed your senses, one by one, so individually they are far greater than the division of their collective powers, you can hear the playground bustle, the Chinatown hustle, the gearbox grind of Deansgate. You can even strain for the empty-life sounds of women in silk rustling their porcelain chink in Kendals.

It will be the longest day of the year, watershedding us to Christmas and winter. You can see the heat haze in the streets. It could be a beautiful day, if it wasn't also to be an end and beginning of something planned and not planned.

I'm looking at Lewiss's, a vast and tiered cake of a department store, where we used to go at Christmas time, watch the rich kids, wishing we were them. And watch the rich kids looking at us, wishing they were us, running amok. Fancy free.

Ten years ago, I came to Lewiss's. It had been thirty days since she had last stolen into my room. Thirty days since our last monoversation, and by the time I came to Lewiss's that Saturday, I had started to receive visions of first draft sketches of more positive options for a new lease of life. Perhaps no more than a lease.

I'd had blinding images of an inversion of myself.

Wear the badness on the outside, start feeling good about yourself. Show them something to respect, something they can be scared of. It's what people want, need. And my inside had been made harder than the surface anyway. Scar tissue all around my heart and soul – what made me live and breathe. As they said, I was just a dumb fuck anyway. Hide that. Turn it in on itself. Feel good about yourself.

That Saturday at Lewiss's, I was ripe for a fearless launch into a new and dangerous life, one that Lisa would be powerless to resist. She was in a doorway at the back of the store – as quiet a place as you could find to get up to no good. She was with a man I recognized, from the schoolgates. I approached them, unseen. I saw Lisa flinch and go into a cower stoop. He raised his arm and she let out a tiny yelp that she strangled for herself before anyone noticed. I was close, her sobbing came into my fields. 'No, no, please,' she said in a clammy groan, 'I'm sorry, I'm sorry.'

He was bigger than me. He had lanky hair, greasy, and a tattoo on both forearms, 'Mum' on one, 'City' on the other. I caught Lisa's eye. And her's mine. She shook her head. But I didn't go back. I checked left and right, saw I was on my own. He raised his hand again. I tried to shout, forgetting my limitations in the surge of my blood and nerves that merged and frayed: that made me think the inevitable would visit me in punches and kicks and maybe worse, with nothing gained.

But nothing to lose either.

I grabbed his shoulder, tugged at him so he came round to face me, off balance and effing and jeffing at me. He swung at me and I dived under the curve of his fist, into his belly. I clutched tight to limit the swinging of his punches and kicks.

He got me on the floor, twisting me round with superior

strength and knowhow. He pushed the air from my chest, put his knees on my arms. He sat on me, smiled, spat in my face.

'Who's your boyfriend then, eh?' he said to Lisa.

'Let him go. Please Steve. He's no harm.'

'He fancy you? Do you?' he said, looking back down at me. 'Do you?'

'He can't speak. He's mute.'

'He can, look.' He grabbed my face in his smelly hand: chip fat and worse, a smell I didn't know. I know it now, a smell her sister has too.

He forced my mouth open with salt, grit fingers. He grabbed my tongue with his nails, hurting on the soft underside you never use and making me want to scream an impossible scream. 'Look, here's his tongue.'

'Leave him, Steve. Please.'

'Does he use this tongue on you? Eh? You slag.' He was turned away from me. I gathered air in through my mouth, gagging on the taste of his hand in my mouth. I gnashed down, I gnashed down as fucking hard as fuck on his hand. He tried to pull it away. But too late, I had him in a five-knuckle bite, feeling bone jarring on my teeth.

I opened my mouth and his fingers dropped away, trailing behind his body that slumped off my chest. I started choking, choking on a taste I knew. Everyone's blood must taste the same. Funny that. Fingers don't. Maybe we're all the same on the inside. He was groaning, with Lisa kneeling next to him. Not caring about me. Or him. I know now she was tending to her own safety. I roared inside at him and at her and at myself and I kicked him and kicked him and kicked him until Lisa had tired of pleading and until he had stopped groaning and until I became myself again.

*

Except I was never myself again after that. And since then, I've been disabled by the conviction that I can do anything to anybody. Because I've offered myself up and been rejected by comeuppance, I have that card to play until the decks turn against me.

I hear the sound of my name coming at me from the bar, like a noise from another dimension. It jolts me.

'It's all arranged, Jimmy. He's coming to the Place at ten, tonight,' says Angela.

What's that, I point. Her face is bruised.

'Oh, nothing. You know what they're like. They didn't understand what I was saying. They thought I was . . . oh, you know what they're like. It was my fault. A misunderstanding. It's going to be all right, Jimmy.' And she smiles, as if she believes I can solve all her problems. With her half-lid dazed and bruised face, she smiles like her lips are butterfly wings, dying under their own weight. She tries again, but she can't do it.

'I don't know why you come here, Jimmy. You shouldn't do this. I miss her too. She was my sister. But it's just us now, Jimmy. Isn't it?'

And I count as a single blessing on the finger of one hand, the impediment that silences my thought that no, it can never be just us.

What happened after I fatally inverted myself that afternoon outside Lewiss's, was that Steve took out all the shame of his beating at the feet and mouth of a mute, by beating Lisa to within an inch of her life. Except he miscalculated. So I exacted my First Act of Vengeance.

Evening. I'm sitting in the apartment, lofty and with the sound of happy drinking swirling up from the Village. There's a technobeat mixing in, from the open windows of Manto.

I have had a change of plan. I have decided to finesse what I must do into a perfect and long-term solution. I've been bumping into reminders all day. They say you can be anonymous in the city, but things and people you know are in the carbon ether of the place: nowhere and everywhere. You can see your future reflect back at you in shop windows when you're not looking. I have seen, today, that there is no substance — no abuse of that particular kind — at the source of Angela's problems.

You might chart a material rise in my fortunes since I changed myself. But nothing good has come of it. There has been more loss than profit. What I must do, is adjust imbalance.

My First Act of Vengeance led directly to the Second Act, when I was summoned to the home of a policeman. Corrupt and broken; a smalltime copper deserted by a wife in favour of a smalltime criminal, Silverpiece said he could introduce me to a man who would give me an alibi. He could save me from the consequences of the hotblood coldlight vengeance I had visited on the lover of my truelove. And then he tasked me to do something for him. To be honest, once I had heard his story, I would have done it anyway, without pro quo or quids.

As it was, I shifted up a league the day after I delivered to Silverpiece a harmless-looking package, a small carton which I'd wrapped in brown paper. The parcel was light. I remember carrying it to his house. I waited for him to answer, and with the sound of sobbing coming young and ceaseless, unhealing from a bedroom window, I was appalled at how light that box was. Its mass bore no relation to the significance of what it contained, the weight of burdens it has wrought on my life and Silverpiece's. Because in that box that I held was the wonton scrotum of the man who had raped the daughter of a single parent and policeman. One and the same and with no faith in the power of law. No faith at all.

'JimmyMack, I'm scared,' says Angela coming in from the balcony. She looks brand new. She has blown her hair, going auburn in the evening sun and tumbling on her shoulders. She looks nothing like her sister. I have tried to love her, but I can't. I can only destroy her. 'Oh Jimmy, I'm so scared,' she says. 'What if he . . . what if he's just coming for the money. He said some terrible things.'

I know. I take her by the arm, lead her into the room. She trails fresh scent, not cheap. When she's like this it makes you wonder why she can be the other way she sometimes is. The opposite. But I know why. It is because of me.

I sit her next to me on the bed, I turn her eggshell shoulders so she faces me, and I try to press into her that, it's over. It's all about to end. I'm going to make it so you don't have any badness left around you.

Twilight. We have made love, and now she is preparing for a new life. And me too. I have the airline ticket, and the cash. All she will have to do is secrete her medications, and start anew, unburdened by our joint past. I will send her into the city, when the time comes. She will discover the secret codes to a kind of re-birth, later. The means for a whole life can fit into the bottom of a decently proportioned handbag.

She will return later to see blue lights flashing by the apartment block. There will be scene-of tape, barring entrance to the Village. She will have to take flight, and she will be spared the sight of the ending of one half of a bad life, and the beginning of opportunities for a better half of a new one.

She kisses me, says goodbye, slams the door. And with her liptaste fading to nothing I take my shotgun from the cupboard. I sit in the window and watch the city scroll like closing credits. I dismantle and clean. No mistake. Remantle. Barrels: one two. Acts of Vengeance: three four. The second barrel, fourth act, to be exercised on barely a person at all, merely the illusion of a me that really died a long time ago.

When the Rachmaninov is Over
Charlotte Cory

'Nno . . .' Helen stuttered. It all seemed clear. 'I don't have any questions.' Except, of course, what am I to do with the rest of my life? She clutched absent-mindedly at the Victorian jet brooch she had pinned to her throat that morning. I must get a grip, she thought. I probably ought to have some questions, then at least Mr Verender would know I have been listening.

Her husband's solicitor, Hugh Verender – who had also been her husband's colleague since James too had been, until last week, a solicitor in these same offices – glanced over the top of his half-moon spectacles. He smiled kindly. 'You must be sure to let me know if I can be of any assistance . . .'

Helen nodded and murmured her thanks. She wondered how many times James had been in exactly this situation, awkwardly trying to explain things to the newly widowed wives of clients. Ex-clients. Clients do not come more 'ex' than when you sit across the desk from their pale-faced widows, explaining that they will be perfectly comfortably off so long as they do nothing foolish or rash.

'And don't let yourself get talked into anything hasty,' Verender was now saying. 'Nothing that might eat into the capital.' He shuddered visibly. And, if she *were* to contemplate anything of that sort, to be *sure* to come here immediately and consult him first. In fact, she was to feel free to consult him at any time, about anything. He would always be here. He waved his hand expansively round the room so that Helen's eyes travelled round the room also, examining the room where Hugh Verender would always be. Then she eyed the man. If anything, he was possibly a little *older* than her husband had been. She wondered if James had assured widows in his time that he would always be there to advise. They were to feel free to consult him at any time, about anything. And where was he now, she'd like to know? She sighed. As far as all those other widows were concerned, it would probably not make a lot of difference. Another man sitting behind James's desk, ready to offer any necessary assistance, might even make a welcome change. A fresh face. A new start. Had James thought of that?

Helen realized she had missed what Mr Verender was saying but, when she attended again to his voice, she gathered that, rather incredibly, he had been inviting her to dine. With him and his wife next Saturday. In Timperley. She stared at the man and hastily shook her head. She and James had never dined with the Verenders. The association had been strictly one of business and, although the men had worked together, the wives had only encountered each other on a few unmemorable occasions when they had been politely friendly.

'Well, the offer's there,' Mr Verender went on. 'You have only to telephone and let us know. I'm sure Margaret would be very glad to see you.'

I'm sure she wouldn't, Helen thought. 'Very kind!' she said, rather more sharply than she'd intended. She tried to remember what Margaret Verender looked like, and she wondered if the woman knew that at this moment her husband was inviting his dead colleague's wife – widow – to dinner. Next Saturday. At their home in Timperley.

'Any time,' Verender repeated. 'You have only to . . .'

It occurred to Helen that James had probably done *this exact same thing*. Issued distracted widows with offers of meals at her own table – which thankfully they had never taken up, so she had never known. She wondered what *else* there might be she had not known? She felt like laughing. You would think there must be something but in these long dull days since James's death, there had been nothing at all untoward. None of those sorts of thing you read about sometimes – a film in a camera which, when she got it developed, turned out to contain pictures of some unknown fancy woman, a mistress he had been keeping (and keeping hidden from her) for twenty years. Or a dry-cleaning ticket, or the return half of a train ticket, or an unexplained hotel bill that leads, by this means and that, to unravelling a mystery. Then strange disclosure. Helen sighed. The camera had had no film in it and when she had emptied his clothes from the wardrobe she checked the pockets very carefully, but there had been nothing. Nothing. James had been as boring in death as he had been in life. She sighed.

Hugh Verender was now telling her how very sensibly James had settled his affairs. Her future well-being completely taken care of. Verender had also been able to carry out all his instructions in accordance with the wishes of the deceased since James had written everything down in great detail apparently. Even the hymns he wished to have sung. 'So considerate,' Verender was remarking appreciatively. 'So typical . . .'

So bloody typical! Helen thought. But if a solicitor couldn't order his own affairs after all those years of advising others . . . She almost felt angry. James was not even going to allow her the luxury of going to pieces. Wistfully she pictured herself sitting by the war memorial in St Peter's Square swigging gin. Her companions, last November's sodden red paper poppies, a crowd of scratchy scrawny pigeons and a few eager-eyed *Big Issue* vendors – the ones James always managed to skilfully side-step. Helen had a vision of Verender and his tedious wife Margaret driving past, staring at her through the window of their shiny car. 'It can't possibly be!' they would say to each other. Not James's widow, not after he had settled his affairs so sensibly. They'd be on their way to a concert at the Bridgewater Hall but later, when the Rachmaninov was over, they would make a point of returning this way. By then, though, she'd be asleep under the bushes in another part of the square so they would not see her and they would drive home to Timperley and, over a nightcap in their kitchen, laugh together at the mistake they had made. Not James's widow. Ha, bloody haa!

It was Helen who now felt like laughing. She was struggling to suppress small whoops which Mr Verender fortunately took for the onset of delayed tears. He feared hysteria and showed her hurriedly to the door. 'If I can be of *any* assistance,' Hugh repeated, grateful for once that another client was waiting in the waiting room. 'Any assistance at all.'

Helen glanced furtively round the outer office as she left. She smiled at the girls behind their typewriters. She herself had been James's secretary before he married her. 'You've known me long enough,' he had said rather gruffly that gusty afternoon when they had left these premises together and gone round the corner to the registry office. 'At least you know what you are getting.'

At the time, standing there in her new cream suit and matching hat, she had smiled and patted his arm. She had anticipated no surprises. And, in all the years since, there had been none. Until, that is, his sudden death last week.

'Thank you so much for everything you have done,' she called back up the stairs to Hugh as she ran from the airless building. The laughter welling up inside her burst out at last and people turned in alarm as an otherwise respectable woman went amongst them, laughing to herself for no discernible reason. There was only one thing for it, Helen thought as she pulled herself together. A good strong cup of coffee. She headed briskly down Deansgate towards Kendals, sober now and happy to be lost in the throng on the pavement where nobody knew. Nobody cared. She must have walked this street dozens of times on her own in the past, so why should this walking along by herself now be so different? And yet it was. She was not walking away from him so that she could walk back to him. Or he could join her later. He was no longer . . . But couldn't she pretend? Would it be so very difficult to go on as if nothing had happened. As if James was still back there in the room beside Hugh's, answering the telephone, advising anxious clients.

As she entered Kendals on the corner, the man ahead of her let the door swing back in her face so that she only just caught it before it knocked her off balance. She would be perfectly comfortable, so long as she did not do anything rash or foolish. That probably included pretending. She fetched coffee from the counter and went to sit at one of the little round tables on her own. How often she had sat drinking cups of coffee waiting for him. James always delayed by some business or other, had never kept very good time. She had not minded, not having anything better to do than to sit about waiting for him. What bliss that had been, she thought. If only she were sitting here now, waiting for James to join her. It might have been different if there had been children, there would be things to do, grandchildren even, but by the time they had gone to the registry office that gusty afternoon there had been no question.

She got out her handkerchief and meekly sniffed. Such a very ordinary fate, she thought. So entirely uninteresting to anyone, even to herself. She glanced around at all the couples – and everyone else in the café did seem suddenly to be in a couple. She had never noticed before. Not when she herself had been one half of a couple waiting for the other to arrive at any minute. It'll happen to all of you one day, she thought as she looked from one table to the next. Don't think it won't, because it will. Sooner than you think – and then where will you be? Sitting and sipping and sniffing at a little round table on your own, wishing that you were waiting for someone who only a week ago used to annoy you by continually keeping you waiting . . .

'Mind if I?' The girl had pulled out the chair opposite and sat down at the table before Helen could say or do anything. 'And would you start talking to me,' the girl said. 'Make it look as if we're together, or somethin'.'

Helen drew herself stiffly upright.

'Pretend you're my mother and we're out shopping,' the girl went on.

Helen quickly shifted her handbag towards herself.

'Look, what do you say to this?' The girl now produced a lilac sweater from a plastic carrier bag and held it towards Helen who was incapable of saying anything. 'Do you think it will match that skirt I bought last week?'

'How should I . . .'

'You don't like it, do you? I can tell.' The girl sounded genuinely disappointed. 'Maybe I'd better take it back.'

'I didn't . . .' Helen glanced at her watch.

'Talk to me will you?' the girl hissed. She swivelled her eyes. 'Don't look now, but there's a man over there's been following me. I want him to think I'm with you – then he'll go away.'

Helen glanced quickly about, but could not see any man the girl might be referring to. Everyone appeared to be in fairly ordinary couples but there was an urgency in the girl's voice which made Helen comply. After all, she had nothing better to do. Nowhere else to go. Except home – but home was a quiet and empty house. It occurred to her in a flash that the lilac jumper was most likely stolen. She said so.

The girl laughed. A laugh that was more of a cheerful snort. 'Course it is,' she said. 'Anyway he's gone now, thanks to you. Security bloke from the shop. Security my eye – he was in the class below me at school. Full of hisself in a uniform.'

Helen regarded the young woman calmly. 'I suppose that makes me an accessory after the fact,' she said without expression.

The girl grinned. She had a great bob of unkempt hair the colour and texture of coconut matting. It was not, Helen reflected, entirely unattractive. 'You on your own then?' the girl asked. Her manner was alarmingly direct but that was the way these days. James would have called it a *lack* of manners, but Helen wasn't sure. It was different from when they were young. The girl would probably have felt it ruder *not* to show interest, which in a way was rather nice.

'My husband died last week,' Helen confided. 'I'm on my own.'

'Sounds nasty,' the girl remarked with a frown.

'It is,' Helen admitted.

'Still,' the girl went on chattily, 'means you can do whatever you want now.'

Helen stared at her companion.

'Have some fun at long last.'

Helen opened her mouth to say something but the girl was laughing. 'Whenever anyone ditches me, that's what I always tell myself: "You can do whatever you like now, Angie!" Always helps.'

'James did not *ditch* me!' Helen did not know whether she was outraged, or amused.

'Course he didn't,' the girl said soothingly. 'But yer know what I mean.'

Helen certainly did *not know* what this young lady meant so she pushed back her chair to stand up. She felt suddenly weak so instead she went on sitting there, taking petulant sips at her coffee and wondering how James would have coped. He would surely have asked this 'Angie' to go. At once. Or he'd have clicked his fingers and summoned the manager to make a complaint. I did not come here to be insulted over a cup of coffee! he would have barked, and action would immediately have been taken. You'll have to stand up for yourself when I'm not around, James had once said. Helen frowned. Perhaps James would have given the girl five pounds to go away. He often took the line of least resistance. Like when he had married her. She had been such a bad secretary that in the early years of her marriage she had wondered if James had not made her his wife as a means of getting someone more efficient into the office. She had been released from her typewriter, and from typing his letters, to sit about all day doing nothing. So it had often seemed to her, but Helen could be sure of nothing any more. She had not slept for nearly a week now. She fingered the Victorian jet brooch at her throat. Was it really only a week? A week tomorrow – the night she had heard him calling faintly from the kitchen where he had gone to make their cocoa and she had found him slumped on the floor, cocoa powder all over the place. The doctor had come, and then the ambulance that had taken its time and not rung its bell to get through the traffic because by then speed, that had always been so much 'of the essence', no longer mattered. The doctor had given her a sedative. It's shock, she had told herself. It's so shocking. She remembered the cocoa powder scattered everywhere. The girl was saying now with renewed energy, 'You've got to help me. That's my boss over there. He's turned up to see I'm doing me job. Talk to me.'

Helen blinked. 'What do you want me to say?' she asked stupidly. She thought she was still meant to be pretending to be the girl's mother and as the girl's mother she probably ought to tell her to return the stolen property to the shop. 'I don't think that lilac sweater . . .'

The girl smiled. 'Never mind that now!' she said, and bent down and retrieved something else from yet another plastic carrier bag. It appeared to be a box of soap powder except that the box had no label or printing. 'It's a new brand. I've got to persuade you to try it,' she said. 'So if you would look as if I'm giving you the hard sell and you're listening.'

Helen bent forward obediently. 'That's a sample is it?' She touched the box with her finger. 'Of this brand-new brand?'

'Sort of.' The girl leant forward also. Helen gazed in admiration at the nose ring and the hair that was so ginger and so matted. 'I've been sent to find someone who'll let me come home with 'em and do all their washing. Show them like how wonderful this stuff is.'

'And is it?'

The girl shrugged. 'Shouldn't think it's a lot different from all the rest, but don't tell anyone I told you.'

Helen nodded. She thought about all James's clothes blocking the hallway at home. She had turned out the pockets and then crammed all his suits and shirts into black dustbin bags ready to take to the Oxfam shop. She knew she ought to have cleaned them first – especially the ones with cocoa down the front – but had been unable to bring herself to do so.

'So,' the girl smiled, 'have yer got a lot of things you want washing?'

'As a matter of fact . . .'

'Drink up then – the coffee here's crap – let's go!' The girl was on her feet and waiting for Helen, whose only thought was that at least this would save her from returning alone to the empty house. What James would have thought, allowing a total stranger to come into the house and do all his washing for him, she dreaded to think. Perhaps he would have laughed and said it was clever of her to get out of doing the task herself. More likely though he'd reckon the girl was in league with a team of burglars who would arrive as soon as Helen's back was turned and make off with everything valuable, stuffing it all into the black plastic bin bags.

Sure enough, the moment Helen disappeared into the kitchen to make a pot of tea she heard the girl in the hall on the telephone, giving out the address. 'My mates,' Angie explained casually when she joined Helen in the kitchen. 'They won't be long.'

The house was very quiet when Angie and her mates eventually left. Soon afterwards, though, the son was knocking on the door, claiming what was rightfully his. 'I never knew you existed,' Helen told the young man who had – quite unmistakably – James's nose and chin. He also had an official bit of paper which he waved in her face. 'You're welcome to anything you want, of course, but I'm afraid I've had burglars. There's not a lot of James's things left.' She gave the lad the Victorian jet brooch that had been James's mother's.

Later, sitting with last year's sodden poppies, the pigeons and the *Big Issue* vendors in St Peter's Square, Helen tried to recall the precise order of events as they had unfurled. They had come upon her so thick and fast.

Hugh and Margaret Verender stopped their car but explained that they did not have long as they were due at a concert in the Bridgewater Hall.

'Rachmaninov?' Helen asked.

'How did you guess?' Margaret smiled.

James, it seemed, had taken out a subscription for Helen. So considerate. So typical. She will leave your office, Hugh, and make her way to Kendals cafe for a cup of stewed coffee. She will sit there feeling sorry for herself so tell them to get cracking right away. Here he had chuckled. As well he might.

First, there was to be the washing powder stunt. In the event, the girl got confused and muddled up assignments. She had done the stolen jumper routine but Helen had been preoccupied and it hadn't seemed to matter. Let them into your house, let them loose on your washing, then they summon their film crew and while you're concentrating on grinning at the camera and saying with deadly seriousness that your dead husband's smalls have never been whiter, they start ransacking the place. There's nothing like a good old-fashioned burglary to clear out the cobwebs. James should know. He had dealt with enough pale-faced widows in his time.

They were apt to get too attached to things from the past, to find themselves nailed down by them as if the coffin lid had closed and buried them alive, along with their dead husbands. *Any horror*, but that.

Next, send along a long lost son waving a bit of paper and claiming his inheritance. For this, some fellow who resembles the deceased in some small particular is needed. Follow this immediately with the 'Congratulations, you've won a cruise!' letter. The boat departs next day and you find yourself bundled up and carted off round the world, sipping Martinis and being courted by widowers who assume that as a rich widow swanning about the world there must be plenty more cash where that came from. A fine romance, even a bit of fumbling sex in the night to take your mind off things. Then, when you get back home with him in tow and he sees that your wealth is tied up in a nice tidy house in a nice tidy suburb of Manchester which has, sad to say, burned down in your absence – faulty wiring and renewal of insurance policy understandably over-looked – he disappears pronto. And here you are, homeless amid the poppies, pigeons and *Big Issue* vendors in the drizzle in St Peter's Square.

'I thought we'd find you here,' Hugh said. Margaret started to ask him how he could possibly have known such a thing but Helen only smiled.

'I've got a nice blanket,' she told them. 'When it gets dark, I shall curl up under those bushes.'

'You can if you want to,' Hugh Verender said. He put his hand on Margaret's arm and sent her back to wait for him in the car. 'But now is the time to move on to the next stage of the operation.'

'Oh?' Helen offered Verender a sip from her gin bottle.

He politely declined. 'You didn't think James would let you end up like this!' He laughed. James, of all people! His deceased colleague had been clear in his instructions. James had not wanted his widow to sit about waiting for him after he had gone, the way she had sat about waiting for him while he was alive. He had decided she would be better off earning her living as part of that great troupe of actors people employ at considerable expense – at the cost of everything they own, in fact – to make life interesting for loved ones they leave behind. There are always plenty of parts, and plenty of people to play them. It's a scheme that finances itself but you only ever find out about it when it happens to you.

Helen felt confused. She put this down to the cold, and the gin.

'They should be along shortly to give you your first assignment,' Hugh Verender told her. 'You'll probably see that nice girl, Angie, again. And all the burglars who posed as a film crew. And that young man with James's nose and chin – he took some finding, I can tell you. Not to mention those jolly widowers that buzzed about you on the cruise. Should be fun – more fun than sitting here – and think of all the happiness you in your turn will now bring.' He broke off. His wife was waving impatiently to him from the car. 'Must go. We'll be late for the concert.'

Hugh Verender did not want Margaret to hear any of this and know what lay in store for her also, when *he* eventually passed on. It was only after a widow had sampled the gaping emptiness that she was likely to appreciate the arrangements that had been made for her. Not that this busy and growing troupe of actors confines its activities to brightening up the lot of the bereaved. By no means. You find them in many an office and in all kinds of public places. They pose as policemen and make arrests, as bouncers in nightclubs, as car-park attendants, librarians, telephonists, schoolteachers. They lose luggage in airports, drive lorries, operate trains. They invent useless gadgets, give out spurious weather forecasts, create new laws. They are everywhere and their brief is simple: to cause mayhem and disruption at every opportunity. You have only to look around you to spot someone who has been taken on under this ingenious scheme to make life a tad more interesting for their fellow citizens.

So it was that later that night when, the Rachmaninov over, Mr and Mrs Verender looked for Helen among the sodden paper poppies, pigeons and disconsolate *Big Issue* vendors in the darkness of St Peter's Square James's widow was nowhere to be seen.

'I wonder where she got to?' Margaret remarked as they stood in their kitchen in Timperley and she handed Hugh his night-cap.

'I wouldn't worry,' Hugh Verender said, glancing briefly at his wife over the top of his half-moon spectacles. Then he tipped back his head, and drained the glass. 'I dare say you'll meet her again.'

The Best of Mates
Shelagh Delaney

Vincent and Ishbel Howard had lived on the housing estate since it was built by a zealous and idealistic Labour council in 1946. After the little two-up-two-down terraced house, whose front door opened straight on to the pavement, the largess of the new house, with its back and front gardens, three bedrooms, bathroom, kitchen, dining-room and living-room, almost overwhelmed them. They had no idea how they were going to furnish it all.

Eventually they moved in with their double bed, tallboy, a pre-war three-piece suite, a stove, a drop-leaf dining table and two chairs, four grandfather clocks and a piano neither of them could play. The presence of the piano was justified by the possible musicality of one of their, as yet unborn, children. The piano was cherished. It was tuned up twice a year. Its rosewood casing glowed and the silver candlesticks, set either side of the music stand above the keyboard, shone in the dark. Apart from the biannual caress of the piano tuner, though, it remained silent. There were no children.

Vincent and Ishbel's brother, Bob, had been in the army.

They'd served in the same regiment and spent the same years in the same Japanese prisoner of war camp, building the Burma railway. When Bob and his wife, Norah, were allocated one of the new council houses everyone thought it was the least a grateful city could do for them. Vincent, Ishbel, Bob and Norah were all that was left of what had been two large families. The bombing raids on the city had killed the rest. They took some comfort in being close neighbours.

The men were both engineers and worked for the same firm, Metropolitan Vickers, in Trafford Park, a huge industrial estate near the docks. They travelled to and from work together just as they'd walked to school when they were boys. They shared the same interest in renovating old clocks and gardening. They smoked the same pipe tobacco, John Cotton Empire Blend. They had the same sense of humour and never discussed God or politics. They were the best of mates.

Their wives were not. They kept their dislike for each other a secret; to admit that they couldn't stand the sight of each other would have jeopardized their husband's friendship and that, they felt, would have been cruel. Both marriages were childless and without ever talking about it, the women felt that their husbands' closeness filled that gap and diffused the yearning.

It didn't do much for them though that Ishbel blamed her persistent feeling of depression on the strain of maintaining the totally bogus camaraderie with her sister-in-law. Her mystified and slightly irritated doctor prescribed a new tablet for her, Valium, which did seem to cloak, if not cure, the desolation inside her and, in view of his success, the doctor gave her a repeat prescription that went on repeating itself for the next four decades.

Norah, who despised all forms of medication, believing that

the body would always heal itself, died rather quickly after a bout of chronic indigestion turned out to be a massive stomach cancer. During her last days in Hope Hospital she clutched Ishbel's hand and said: 'I'd rather die than be a drug addict.'

After his wife's death Bob spent more time with Vincent and Ishbel. He ate with them every day after work. He had dinner with them every Saturday and Sunday. Knowing how sweet her brother's tooth was, Ishbel made sure his cake and biscuit tins were never empty.

He never said thank you, although he conspicuously enjoyed his food. Everyone knows that actions speak louder than words and why, therefore, should he state the obvious? Even Ishbel's husband started to take the three beautiful meals, plus snacks, that she put on their table every day for granted. Ishbel craved appreciation.

When she was fourteen years old she'd been put into service as kitchen maid at a big house in Didsbury. The cook she skivvied for there had been a slave driver, an artist and a great teacher. When Ishbel left to get married the cook cried. They weren't sentimental wedding tears. They were tears of rage, frustration and disgust that this girl, who had such a perfect feeling for food, was going to spend the rest of her life cooking for little Vincent Howard, whom she thought of as the runt of her mother's litter.

When the men retired they went into the clock-mending business in a small but successful way. Their ad in *Exchange & Mart* established their reputation with antique dealers and collectors who spurned the modern timepiece. One of the empty bedrooms became a workshop and they made more money from their old clocks than they'd made from a lifetime's work with Metrovicks.

Bob spent his money on holidays. He started to enjoy travelling and even went back to Burma to visit the site of the prison camp he'd spent so many years in. It was a privilege Vincent wouldn't share with him. Vincent didn't like leaving home. Ishbel was too timid to travel alone so they'd stayed where they were, spending a lot of money in the Pendle Inn on Friday nights, drinking their favourite malt whisky and playing dominoes. Very few of the original housing estate settlers were still alive and some had moved away. Ishbel, Vincent and Bob were regarded by the newcomers sometimes gently, sometimes contemptuously, as three ancient relics.

When Vincent was eighty-eight he lost the use of his legs. No one knew why. He was examined, tested, studied and scanned by the head of every department in Hope Hospital but his legs had simply given up. He was a medical mystery. He was also a bloody nuisance as far as Ishbel was concerned. In a quiet but ruthless way he became completely dependent on her.

The dining-room had to be turned into a bedroom for him and because the only bathroom was upstairs, the social services provided him with a commode.

The commode was the stuff of nightmare to Ishbel. She had horrible dreams about it. The thought of touching it turned her stomach over. She wondered why her husband's bowels and bladder hadn't stopped working instead of his legs.

He wouldn't let anyone else deal with the commode, not even Bob. Ishbel understood her husband's shame but she also hated him for it. Emptying it and disinfecting it, she often wondered if she would have felt the same revulsion changing a baby's shitty nappy.

Not having children had been a tragedy for Ishbel. It might have been a tragedy for Vincent, but they'd never talked about it. She'd envied her friends and neighbours as their children were born and grew up and had children of their own. But lately as she endured the antics of the present younger generation on the estate, she sometimes thought her barrenness had been a blessing. These children were like devils sent to torment, steal and decimate. When she'd first moved in she'd planted a couple of crab apples on the patch of land outside her home and in spite of everything one had taken root. But these children were determined to destroy it. So far it had survived several attempts to bring it down with a chopper and Bob, or herself, often had to dash out of the house with buckets of water and blankets to put out the flames of yet another attempt to burn it down. But it survived and bloomed and fruited abundantly every year.

Vincent didn't set foot outside his home for the last five years of his life. He refused to use a wheelchair. Every morning Ishbel helped him wash and shave and dragged him – because just as he was getting weaker and older so was she – into the front room where he'd sit beside the fire all day, reading the newspaper, enjoying long pipe-smoking silences with his pal, Bob. Bob looked after the garden now that Vincent couldn't. The clock business ended and only the original grandfather clocks that they'd brought to the house with them in the beginning remained.

Ishbel went shopping every afternoon. It was her only form of excursion. She would have liked to take day-trips to Blackpool, or even London, but her husband didn't like her to be too far away from his side for too long. So she went shopping instead and sat in the cafes in the precinct, day-dreaming about life without Vincent.

She was surprised at how upset she was when he died. He'd gone into hospital for yet another investigation into the uselessness of his lower limbs and, in much the same way as his legs had stopped working, so did his heart. It was short, sharp and brutal.

Bob was heartbroken. He'd lost his best pal. For the first time in his life he offered his arm to his sister as they climbed out of the big black car that drove them to the church. She took it, thinking that she couldn't remember ever touching her brother before. It was a simple, perfunctory service. None of them believed in God.

The crab-apple tree outside Ishbel's garden gate was in full fruit. After the funeral, brother and sister sat in her front room and looked at it. They were alone. All their friends and the few neighbours who were not strangers to them had gone home. It was getting late. The summer sun, which had been hot that day, was going down.

'Pity that piano never got used,' Bob said suddenly.

'Yes,' Ishbel replied. 'We should have got rid of it years ago. It's getting dark.'

'I'll draw the curtains,' Bob said.

As he moved toward the window, she switched on a small reading lamp which stood on a shelf beside Vincent's empty chair. It was hard to think that she would never see him again. They hadn't talked much about anything that had really made a difference to their lives. They hadn't been brought up like that. She'd known he'd missed the children they both looked forward to having when the war was over, but it had never been said. Would it make any difference if it had, she wondered? And they'd never talked about his time in the prison camp. That was something he'd only shared with Bob. Too terrible to dwell on, she supposed.

Brother and sister sat either side of the fire. They didn't turn the television on. The silence was pleasant.

Suddenly the front of the house seemed to come under

attack from what sounded like machine-gun fire. The windows and the walls were being pelted with God knows what missiles.

Bob got to his feet, told her to stay where she was and opened the front door. For a moment the bombardment stopped. The group of children, who had been hurling the crab apples they'd stripped from the tree, were surprised and silent for a moment as they came face to face with the old man. But he barely had time to close the front door on them before they laughed and started the broadside again.

Bob returned to the living-room and sat down opposite his frightened sister. 'Kids,' he said, 'just kids as usual.' They both looked white and suddenly frail in the darkening room.

'What are they throwing?'

'Crab apples.'

'They must have stripped the tree,' Ishbel said, and, as the bombardment stopped as suddenly as it had started, she felt her heart break.

The Funeral
from 'Making Angels', a Novel in Progress
Michael Schmidt

It was just another blue day. I had not brought a formal suit
– I hadn't worn a suit since my wedding day – so my mother
chose one of my father's. A maid shortened the legs and
sleeves with a brisk needle, ironed new creases into place,
laid out a black tie and a blinding shirt, also his, on the
bed. I wore my own underwear at least, though bleached and
pressed and strangely soft against the flesh, and my shoes,
expertly polished in the plaza the day before. My mother and
I sat at breakfast on the terrace in a kind of lazy silence,
knowing that the day was spoken for and that – at least until
the service was over – we belonged to others, a joint venture,
our grief and bereavement on show.

'Don't have more coffee, dear.'

'It might keep me awake.'

'It will kill you. Your father always drank too much coffee.'

'QED. He's dead. He was eighty, but that's another
matter.'

'Eighty-two.'

'A detail.'

'You'll need the toilet halfway through the service.'

'It will get sweated off. If not I'll go behind a pew.'

'You look so like him in that suit. He used to wear that suit when he went to see Don Gonzalo Camarena. You remember him – the broker. Then he got too thin for it. You look as he did way back then, when you were still a boy.' She shivered. 'But he was always older. I doubt you'll ever be as old as he was, even if you live as long.'

'I don't have a clear memory of what he was like in those years. I never saw him in focus except in the last few weeks. All I recall is my nurse, Doña Constanza, and the parrot, and the odd revolutionary friend.'

'The less said about him, the better.'

'So we will never talk about it?'

'It's better not to. It's more than twenty years ago. You've outgrown the ugly times. You got an education, you got married, you might have had children.'

'I got divorced.'

'But you got over those early years.'

'I don't seem to forget them, but I've managed to forget my father, except the end, especially that last night. When I think of it I see his grey eyes. He was not confused, he didn't feel for me. He was full of revulsion, he looked at me as though I had done something terrible.'

'You *had* done something, and it *did* seem terrible.'

'But not in the way you mean. It would have been nice if just for a moment he had tried to get into my skin.'

'He was sixty-two years old! He was older than the century, remember that. You can't expect an old man to entertain what all his life he knew to be an evil.'

'You were better about it, but you never even tried to stop him when he hatched his plan to send me away. That last night stays with me, and when we bury him, it's that man I'll be burying. He's the only father I remember.'

'That's a shame. He could be magnificent. Much of the time he was – well, brilliant. Even in the last years when it was all over between us, I still looked up to him.'

She remained calm for a woman in mourning. I watched her face, its parched complacency as her eyes wandered over the papyrus and pirul, the sea-blue gloria where a humming-bird hovered on electric wings, drinking a drop of dew or honey. My mother took the images in freshly, innocently, from her new vantage point of widowhood. She looked almost young, still to be corrupted by expectation and disappoint-ment. To prick her calm torpor I remarked, 'You must feel very alone now.'

'Not really,' she said vaguely. Then, focusing, 'I have you here.'

'I mean, without your husband, after all these years.'

'It is a lot of years.'

'Have you cried a lot?'

'Not yet.'

'Will you?'

'I expect so, when the time comes.' For no reason she glanced at her watch.

'When will that be?'

'Oh, perhaps when you go back to England, if you do go back, or when I move out of this house, if I do move, or you move me; or when the cat dies.' The cat lay on its weathered yellow back beside the pots of geraniums.

'Aren't you going to mourn for him?'

'I did that years ago, when he started changing. They all warned me that he would, when I first decided to marry a man so much older than I was. They said that time would pass, but when you're in love – have you ever been in love? you may be one day – when you are you think time will not dare to pass. You live in the hourly process of your love, you can't imagine that a flower hardens into fruit, and at the heart the pip, the dreadful seed of memory.' Was this my mother the bridge-player, the formal blue-haired wife? She was a stranger. I almost began to love her.

'I think I know what you mean.'

'But you're divorced, you can't know what I mean at all.'

'I remember being in love, and I remember how I thought I could stop time.'

'Next time, make sure you stop it. Have your love and then end it, before it ends. Don't give it the choice,' she said, and I knew that my father's death released her, that now she had a chance to become less unhappy, though she was too old to be happy, ever. Was I too old as well?

'How many years ago did you mourn him?' I asked.

'Five or six. He became a hollow sort of person. He was magnificent, as I said, but no longer a man. He turned all venerable, his eyes watered, he drooled and dripped in ways no plumber could repair. He still made gestures, but he couldn't desire me any more. Or I wasn't desirable. We started drifting our separate ways. He ran the city and the state of Allende from his study and I played bridge and went out to galleries. We stopped going to the capital. We never had guests here, except the awful mayor and his lot, and I never let them dine. No, the last few years have not been very full ones. Not a life at all, in fact. The years to come may be less unkind. In any case, they'll be less heavy going. It's just me that's going on alone.' She sipped her tea, then glanced at her watch again. This time the hour registered. 'Goodness! The car will arrive in an hour. I must get ready.'

In an hour the car did arrive. She wasn't ready. Had my father been there, she would have been. This tardiness – five or ten minutes – was her first real taste of freedom.

Traffic climbed the familiar hill to the plaza, with a roaring of exhausted engines and fumes billowing from trucks and buses. We sat cut off from the mêlée, in a bubble of quiet. We were in a car appropriate to the occasion, the mayor's black limousine, like a patent-leather shoe wandering among sandals. Our long-nosed, patrician chauffeur had also been loaned to us by the mayor, our own driver being judged not up to driving the old Cadillac.

My mother, quite suddenly, decided to accept the mayor's offer the night before. He came to pay his respects for a third time, just after dinner, and on this occasion was admitted. She was calculating – a kind of protection, perhaps, or part of a bargain she was at work on. Also, she'd been drinking and drink helped her relent. His savage servility was gratified. Five minutes late for the car, and scheming: she had learned something in those closing years with the old man. But what, and how far could she go?

People watched us, then remembered the day and the occasion. Through tinted glass they could not see the widow swathed in dark blue, with a perky little hat and veil that made her look twenty years younger, or the son in his hand-me-down mourning, who travelled home all the way from Europe to wave his father off. Invisible, we sparked curiosity and resentment. Some turned to follow the car through the crawling traffic, around the barren plaza, into Calle Hidalgo.

'I wish you'd had your hair cut. You look so awfully ragged and professorial.'

'I certainly look too old to be your son,' I said gallantly, but it sounded ironic. She pursed her lips and studied her patent shoes.

We came to the crenellated cathedral wall, to the tall arched gate, and drew to a hushed stop. Then the door was opened and the storm of noise and heat burst in upon us. Flashbulbs popped, we were at the heart of the whirlpool. This ceremony was for church and state. The grief – had there been grief – did not belong to us, we were actors in the civic drama.

The mayor took my mother's arm and pulled her into the noise, greeting me as she adjusted her dress. Verdusco was so deep in mourning he looked like a fat shadow. And with him I recognized – thickened in the middle and thinned on top by years of relative prosperity – Javier, the editor of *El Heraldo*, and Paco the lieutenant, my former schoolmates. Behind them, a little way off, stood Francisco, properly solemn in his episcopal vestments the way, my father would have said, 'a bishop ought to look'. A cordon of armed police stood between us – the walk-on protagonists – and our audience that filled the street and courtyard. Here in full view of the city we endured a series of grievous embraces – the trick was to make the widow cry. How warmly the editor and the lieutenant embraced me, too, and Verdusco found it hard to keep his hand from my shoulder. 'At your service, always at your service,' he said in a voice different from the one he used the day before, over coffee. This was his public tone, the one he employed when a tenement collapsed on a family or a child was run over by a truck, to comfort the bereaved and injured and express for all to hear his unambiguous humanity. The editor and the lieutenant were less practised, but they did their best, following the mayor's protocol.

The bishop came forward, offered his arm to my mother, and we followed him into the courtyard. The sun blazed on the watching heads, every man had removed his hat as a sign of respect, but the eyes were not uniformly respectful. A figure far back began to gesticulate and shout. Instantly a policeman was at his side and he vanished under the tide of faces. I wanted to be with them, not on this side of the police cordon.

The police ploughed a way for us. At the main door we stopped for a moment beside a large black and gold object. Verdusco, the editor and the lieutenant positioned themselves at three of the corners. 'There, that's your station,' they said, gesturing to the front. Then I knew it was my father's coffin, and I was to be a pall-bearer. He was dead indeed. The shock of his proximity, even sealed within the wood and satin, made me shudder, not at his death but at his life and the power it still had over me and all these men.

It was hot. Even the bishop had begun to perspire. (Verdusco was awash, what with the sun, with nerves and excitement, his thick mourning, clutching at his breast to make certain he still had the important speech beside his heart.) Only my mother seemed comfortable and cool, absent from the event, communing with herself. The cross hove into view, the choir materialized from among the police and milling crowd, the giant organ coughed, and a desolate moan of music reached us. The procession began. Two anonymous strong men took the middle positions on the box and we heaved the weight together. Trudging behind the cross I carried my father, my left cheek pressed against the shining surface, my shoulder straining under the gravity of his death. From bright sunlight we stepped into airless shadow.

Inside were the people who mattered, the nave filled with well-brushed and scented bodies. It never occurred to me that my father could have had so many acquaintances. At eighty, after years of isolation, a man had a right to a little anonymity at death. But not Don Carlos. This was his best hour, the ironic climax of his long existence, when everyone paid a last debt in public and in the cheapest way. Flowers and sympathy. Swaying slightly, Verdusco gasping under the weight, we reached the holy end, set down the box before the altar, below the absent gaze of the madonna, and found our seats in the front row.

I stood beside my mother. I knelt beside my mother. The occasion was to be grand and so it had to be long. If the bishop had not arranged the full pomp, Verdusco would have seen to it. Solemnities commenced, the choir addressed Gregorian chants to the coffin, to the ceiling, no longer to the saints: to emptiness. The choir itself, in its ordered gowns, strove bravely, and the master waved his hands, forcing the voices to keep a kind of discipline, but with strange aleatoric syncopations, with lengthenings and shortenings, as though Pope Gregory had foreseen the samba. Hymns were attempted but in the end all was surrendered to the organ with its sonorous flats.

The bishop spoke. He had a large tenor voice and a remarkable directness of delivery, as if he was accustomed to more rustic congregations. He described his humble pride at helping to bring so distinguished a convert into the true church just in time, when death was tightening a fist around the old man's heart. And what a soul he had been, the bishop said, what power he had wielded, what good he had done to the community. He laid it on thick, my mother and I exchanged a guarded glance. But his purpose was not only to ingratiate himself with the bereaved. It was to affirm, without mentioning the madonna (whose headless form rose before us like a damaged mannequin) or the rumours, that a man of my father's character would not have been party to such a desecration. About corruption, about La Charca, he said nothing. He ended by recommending the widow and the son to the true God's protection. There was another hymn. Then Verdusco's oration began. Javier, the editor, leaned forward and whispered in my ear, 'You may like to know that we are printing the whole speech in tomorrow's edition. And there will be photographs.'

Outside, my mother and I stood together to receive more condolences, while the coffin was humped out and adjusted in the hearse. First we had to endure Verdusco, Javier and Paco once again, and then an endless file of people with more or less claim on the deceased, men and women who embraced us, shook our hands, wept, and tried to see just how we took the grief. My mother did not weep. She had decided not to. After Verdusco's speech – familiar, vulgar, sentimental – she at least would remain outside their frame. No, she was not sorry. No, she would not use the little handkerchief she held in her left hand. I did not weep either. Now the service was over I felt a lightness. We would soon plant the old devil and begin our own lives.

At the graveyard high above the town, just off the winding road to Pilar, the congregation was more modest: fifty official people gathered to watch the coffin lowered. The wall of the graveyard was lined with curious uninvited locals, mainly children. Here the air was cooler, the ruddy soil coarse and mined with ants. And below was the city in all its smoggy intricacy, spilling out of its valley on to the adjoining hills. Beyond it the zig-zag road to La Charca. The bishop spoke again, this time only the ritual, the coffin was inched into the hole and we threw our fistfuls of dirt on the lid of the old man's box. I felt for a moment – sadness, that he was going to be left alone after this pomp, that he would never see light again. Then the bishop mentioned 'the resurrection and the light' and I cursed the old dead hypocrite from my heart. We stood in silence as men with shovels covered in the hole and laid cut turf over it. Concentrating there, those who had God prayed and those without Him examined their fingernails. There was a sudden flash miles away on the road towards La Charca, and then the huge roar of an explosion and a plume of smoke. It was in the middle of nowhere: no house, no factory, no barracks, just on the bare hillside.

Our prayers concluded with that cordite amen. 'The guer-rillas!' said the lieutenant in a big voice, hurrying to his military car and speeding off into the city.

'They can't keep quiet even on a day like this,' said Javier sourly. making a note of the time in his pocket book.

'Especially on a day like this,' said Verdusco, hoarse from his oration, and alarmed.

'They can't be all that terrible,' I suggested. 'If they'd wished, they could have killed us all up here. Instead, they issue their noisy little reminder from a distance. That's a sort of respect, surely, like a twenty-one-gun salute from a single barrel.'

Javier was not amused. 'You can't make sense of them. They do things like this, just for effect.' But the mayor trembled and looked nervously towards his car, his second car because my mother and I still had use of the limousine. 'You'll need protection going down,' he said.

'Nonsense,' I insisted, and my mother added like an echo, 'Nonsense.'

Smoke from the explosion climbed higher and higher, a tall column of golden dust, rising until it seemed to support the underside of a single white cloud adrift in the sky which at this altitude, and above the smog, was unreally blue. Then the cloud was transfixed by the rising dust. Then it moved on, crossing the next border and the next, in its unrooted liberty.

'Time to get back, I suppose,' said my mother, as if reluctant to leave the cool heights. So we got into the limousine and our severe Charon piloted us down into town, retracing our path to the world of the living, through the city to our home. Our home was altered for good.

'A long day,' I said to break the silence.

'A long, dull day. A long dull morning, anyway.' She took from her black bag a pack of cigarettes. She had not smoked since I returned from England, but with her unstained fingers she drew a cigarette from the pack, tapped it, then rummaged and found her cigarette holder. She flicked a tiny gold lighter and 'lit the fuse'. She was gathering herself. She was entering again the form she had seemed to abandon in the morning, so that the ceremony might occur without pain or resistance.

'What did you make of the service?' I asked.

'I need to bathe. All that sympathy has made my hands and face sticky.'

'Did you enjoy the service? Were you moved?'

'By the mayor's speech, to tears.'

'You can weep again in the morning. Javier says he's running the "full text" in *El Heraldo*.'

'How can they do it, stand up and lie through their teeth? And in what they call the house of God! Assuming he could live in such a frowsty old barn as that.'

'I thought the bishop spoke well.'

'He's famous for it. He brought the crowd to heel when the icon was shot. I wish they'd dispose of her – it's gruesome having that headless thing sort of watching you, especially at a funeral. He could chuck her out. He turned out all the other old saints. But he's got an angel's tongue. He got your father to abandon his most fervent hatreds. He enchanted his soul. Why, he *found* his soul, which no one else had ever tried before. What an Orpheus that bishop is. And what a profitable soul to charm – I suspect there will be money in it. Your father spoke with his lawyer for a long time after the bishop's second visit. I wish I could like Francisco. I know he was kind to you.'

'I went to see him yesterday.'

'You never told me.'

'You weren't very curious when I got home.' I checked my tone. 'You had other things on your mind. I also talked to my brother for a long time in the plaza.'

'I beg your pardon?'

'Verdusco, the mayor. He told me he had become Don Carlos's stepson. That puts him in a strange relationship to you as well. Will he be in the will, do you think?'

'Stepson! That maggot?'

'He says he belongs to the family. He wants me to stay and become his next stepfather. Did my father give him money?'

'Money, help, ideas – every idea he's had, even the bad ones. Your father applied oil to the great machine, he wangled him his eminence. Your father was his patron, and he was your father's puppy.'

'What for?'

'Your father could never get his hands on quite enough to fill them. What big hands he had! He would fill them up with land, and with industrial projects, and with speculative deals, and he was always wanting more. He found in the mayor somebody like himself in greed and much closer to the sources of power than he could ever be at his age, and being a foreigner. The Golden Gringo, that was your father's nickname.'

'I'm not like that. I don't enjoy power, I don't need money.

I've forgotten this place.' For years after I left I missed it every day and every night. I would have died to get home. Then I forgot it. And just when I forgot, my father wrote his first letter to me, asking me home, if, that is, I thought I was now 'cured'.

'He never could come to terms with your complaint.'

'It's how I was. I got that way because I spent my life down here, alone, with a gardener boy for company and an Indian woman as my stand-in mother.'

'It wasn't your whole life. It was just a long convalescence.'

'The illness was rheumatic fever. It ended when I was eight. You finally packed me off when I was sixteen.'

'What you contracted afterwards was more serious. I wonder, did you ever talk to Francisco about it?'

'Why should I have done?'

'I've always thought he was a little that way, you know, what with the church and everything.'

'I don't know.'

'And you went to see him yesterday, your first full day at home.'

'Because a man takes vows of chastity, it doesn't mean he's got a complaint. Perhaps he's holy, or maybe he's a secret fornicator and keeps unbridled nuns in the vestry.'

'It's just the way he always behaved. Even way back then, so dreamy, studious, whenever he came to see you you'd both just vanish into the house. His older brothers were more normal.'

'Maybe he had a fixation on his mother.'

'He was strange. He didn't have many friends apart from you.'

'I had few friends apart from him. You seem to think he was odd because he wouldn't join Verdusco's gang.'

'Oh, that and other things. Maybe they just didn't want that sort of fellow. And what about you? You haven't told me about you. Why did you go to the bishop? Were you looking for more ghosts?'

'I wanted to stop the absurdity of a cathedral funeral for a man who didn't believe in God. I had no other reason. No other reason at all. He was glad to see me. We talked for a while about the work he's doing. Then he told me of the conversion – Verdusco had mentioned it, and that was that. I'd failed in my mission.'

'How long did you stay with him?'

'An hour, two hours, what does it matter?'

'A slow-speaking bishop he must be, to spend an hour or two to sort out something you've told me in a matter of minutes.'

I turned away, looking out of the window at the old houses along the city street and my reflection scraping on their surfaces. We were halfway home.

'Your father said the bishop was writing a report on happenings out La Charca way. Did he talk about that?'

'It's one of his obsessions.' She looked at me with the puzzled distrust I'd seen in her eyes years ago, when I tried to explain to her what I felt, and she gave it the wrong inflection, the wrong name in her mind.

'You must stay, stay a month at least, to sort things out. Talk to Verdusco and the others, see what kind of thing they have in mind. And there's the will.'

'I only want to talk to one person while I'm here. That's Doña Constanza.'

'I'll send word for her to come. We can send the driver out to fetch her.'

'No, she doesn't work for you any more. I'll go see her

in her own house. I'd like to take her something – money perhaps.'

'It's not safe to go to La Charca any more. You saw that explosion this afternoon.'

'Spectacular!'

'Not so amusing when a bomb like that blows up a barracks, or a police station.'

'But it didn't. It made a pillar of dust, a vertical road for the soul of the dear-departed to ride to heaven.'

'You'll have to take the driver.'

'I know the road to La Charca. I'll take the Beetle and be as secret as a worm. Don't worry. I'll go see her soon. When is the lawyer?'

'Day after tomorrow.'

'My flight's five days away.'

'You've reserved it?'

'I told you I had.'

'Your mind is made up?' She fixed me with a hard stare, as though my father's spirit had found her again. It frightened me. I knew I was leaving so soon only for effect, and the only person there would be an effect on would be her.

'My mind's made up like a bed.'

'Sleep on it,' she smiled, and with a kind of merriment we found the gates of the Green Island folding open; we braked in a place of enchantment from which the ogre had been driven for good. The chauffeur stood respectfully by the gates and as the engine died we were greeted with birdsong, chirring insects, and the irregular gargling of the yellow fountain.

Teenage Godzilla
Henry Normal

Alopecia Myhill had been convinced since the age of seven
that he and much of Greater Manchester were nothing more
than a figment of someone else's imagination. Accidentally
mentioning this in conversation one day the situation was
soon brought to the attention of the Greater Manchester con-
stabulary when local shopkeepers, seeking to capitalize on the
idea, refused to pay the water rates. Following the laid-down
procedure, Alopecia was immediately taken in for questioning
and, in an effort to persuade him of the inconsistency of his
reasoning, six of Sergeant Crocker's boys brought home to
him the stark realism of personal, as opposed to abstract,
pain by the strategic use of six knotted wet towels. Asked later
at his trial how he pleaded, Alopecia replied 'Guilty but entirely
fictional'. Alopecia was found guilty as charged, despite the
weight of evidence in his defence from three wise men, a group
of shepherds, the Angel Gabriel and a donkey, all of whom
complained they were in the wrong story. Alopecia was then
ordered to be taken from the court to a place of detention,
there to remain in custody until he agreed to recognize the

existence of the universe as perceived by Her Majesty's Court, that is, at all times, including the Greater Manchester Water Authority.

It was in prison Alopecia met the Reverend Gomez Dowdy, former chairman of EXIT jailed for opening the first home for the infirm, the easily tripped and for people who mess about with electric sockets. He introduced Alopecia to Professor Herman Steckler, pioneer of the Italian plan to invent a bomb that kills people and destroys property but leaves suits unmarked. Steckler had been imprisoned in the early sixties, MI5's suspicions having been aroused when his name appeared on a second application lodged under the Town and Country Planning Act of 1956 to bomb Warrington Runcorn. At his trial he asked for twenty-seven other new towns to be taken into consideration. Finally Alopecia met the third member of the Reverend's team, Gustav Minsk, notable Scotch dissident and inventor of the only digital watch that answers in-laws' questions whilst you're watching TV and says nice things about the deceased at funerals. Now, with the inclusion of Alopecia, the Reverend felt confident they would again be the leading contenders to take on the management of the British Space Project. He was sure that this time the EEC would not reject out of hand his plan to wood-panel the ozone layer. By the time Alopecia was released on probation some four years later with a degree in advanced sarcasm he had, to all intents and purposes, lost touch with reality.

He had paid the price for daring to think differently. But, rather than having been induced to conform, he now felt himself rebelling against the limitations that society had struggled to enforce upon him and chose instead to place his trust only in his Skeletor Master of the Evil Horde bubble bath and toothbrush holder. It was at this point he found himself changing, adapting, metamorphosing, undergoing a strange and terrifying rebirth as the Teenage Godzilla – a minor B-movie character with all the screen presence of Gummo Marx, trapped since the dawn of time in the surreal Victorian novel *The Cheese Roll of Dorian Gray*. Sadly within only six months of his change in identity, Alopecia Myhill died, but did however manage somehow to live on out of spite for a further three years by questioning the validity of any certificate issued by the same Government that could no longer expect the slightest credibility to be given to its own war reports.

Between Ourselves
Sherry Ashworth

Hannah glanced left before turning into Scholes Lane, and glimpsed her aunt's profile as she did so. Renie looked grim.

'Sod this,' she said, opening her handbag and fumbling for her packet of cigarettes. 'You don't mind if I smoke?'

'Not if you light one for me as well.' Hannah relished saying that; she enjoyed a frank relationship with her aunt. Her mother would have never given her a cigarette; her mother didn't even know she smoked. Or that she had stopped eating Kosher. It was hard work being a nice Jewish girl, especially when you'd started at university.

Renie pulled hard and long at her Silk Cut, and when she removed it from her lips the filter was smeared with lipstick. Heaton Park stretched away on their left. Hannah slowed as the morning traffic was heavy.

'Will you get into trouble if we're late?'

'They wouldn't notice,' Renie said. 'The way those nurses leave you hanging around. And all that bloody form filling. As if they didn't know me by now.'

Renie had been in and out of hospital all her life. She suffered from Crohn's disease. When Hannah was small she'd thought it was called crone's disease, something you got if you were old and single. Like Aunty Renie. She'd reckoned that married women like her mum didn't get it. Only this time, it wasn't her intestines the doctors were after. She was going into Crumpsall Hospital to have her womb removed. Hannah had been assured by her mother that it wasn't serious. Since it was almost Passover and her mother was busily spring-cleaning, she'd offered to take Renie in. Home from university, she had little to occupy her and she liked driving her mother's Volvo.

So Hannah had picked up Renie from her flat, and watched her pack her gingham nightie, her Oil of Ulay, her large-print library books and her puzzle magazine into her old brown suitcase. Hannah had carried it downstairs and thought it was a pity that Renie hadn't been given a souvenir sticker for each hospital stay. That would have brightened its drab exterior.

Renie would have liked that. She enjoyed boasting about her numerous operations, and it didn't take much to get her to unzip her skirt and parade her scars. She was shameless, Hannah thought, and proud with it. She inhaled on Renie's Silk Cut. The hysterectomy wouldn't bother her – it would be just another trophy.

Hannah checked herself. She ought to know better, especially since her subject was psychology, and her tutor had said she had an instinctive knack for understanding people. Losing a womb was different from any other sort of operation. It had undoubted emotional and metaphorical significance. Without it, one was a woman on the outside only. Hannah tried to empathize with her aunt and imagine how she would feel, wombless. It would be so inhibiting, especially when one had sex.

She glanced at her aunt again as they waited at the traffic

lights by Crumpsall Lane. Renie had given her face a cursory dusting of powder, but her blue eyeshadow had settled in the creases of her eyelids. She'd brown-pencilled the curve of her brows so that they looked like commas on their sides. She was attractive, in a brassy kind of way. She'd had plenty of boyfriends – not all of them Jewish – and some of them had lasted quite a while. They were clearly masochists, enjoying being lashed by Renie's sharp tongue. Would Renie feel the same way about men now?

'Do you mind?' Hannah asked her, stubbing out her cigarette in the ash-tray as the lights turned green.

'Mind about what?'

'You know. Having your womb removed.'

Hannah felt good. She was giving Renie the opportunity to talk, to share. It was something she didn't often get to do, living alone. What's more, Renie was broigus* with half the family, including Hannah's father. She was a mistress of the art of not talking.

'It's one way of losing weight,' Renie said.

Hannah appreciated her aunt's plucky humour. She was tough, the toughest person Hannah knew. When she was small, and had nightmares, her mother just used to panic; when Renie was baby-sitting, her boisterous laughter blew away her fears like cannon-fire. The family thought Renie was a little common, a little too assimilated, and maybe she was, but Hannah didn't care.

Then not for the first time Hannah wondered if her aunt was a virgin. Despite her boyfriends, it was possible. This was a sombre thought; it seemed such a waste to lose one's womb without having used it, so to speak. Could she ask Renie about

* *broigus* not on speaking terms

her sexual status? Hannah devoutly wished that there was a way of telling if someone was a virgin just by looking at her face.

Or perhaps not. She reflected that there would be ructions at home if her mother ever found out about her and Luke. It was bad enough to have a boyfriend who wasn't Jewish; worse still, much, much worse, to lose one's virginity to him. Still, Hannah had thought this through, and decided that it wasn't fair to force her mother to face up to her new incarnation as a non-virgin. It would be selfish of her. Her mother needed to think of her as a nice Jewish girl, which was what she was, on the outside. Good daughters ought to protect their mothers. Besides which, one's mother and one's sex life ought to be kept as far apart as Manchester and Mars.

They were driving down Crumpsall Lane now and the sky was heavy with soiled white clouds. On either side of them were large, brick buildings, some claiming to be hotels, and others council nursing homes. One quasi-tenement announced, intriguingly, 'luxury accommodation'. They passed Victoria Wine and the Battered Cod. A prison-like Edwardian school building loomed at them. Crumpsall was not the place to be on Monday morning, and especially not when you were facing a hysterectomy. Hannah was desperate to cheer herself up.

'Aunty? Are you still a virgin?' There. It was out.

Renie chuckled to herself. 'Chance'd be a fine thing.' She took another cigarette, this time without offering Hannah. 'No, to tell you the truth, I chickened out. My last fella wanted to go all the way, and I thought, the hell with it, who am I saving myself for? But to tell you the truth, it was all a bit disgusting. One look at him without his Y-fronts, and I sent him packing.' She took another long drag. 'And what about you?'

Hannah could not stop her face turning pink with embarrassment. Had her aunt guessed? Ought she to brazen it out, or tell the truth? Just then, Hannah ached to show Renie how mature she was. She was conscious of the symmetry of the moment, too. Renie was about to bid farewell to her womanhood; Hannah's had just begun. Two women on the threshold; the symbolism quivered in the air.

'Promise you won't tell Mum?' Hannah said.

Renie's eyes glittered with interest. Hannah knew she loved it when she confided in her.

'Course I won't,' she said.

'Between ourselves, I've slept with Luke.'

Renie's pencilled eyebrows arched in mock surprise.

'Get away with you!'

Hannah smiled to herself as she cruised around the hospital car-park, looking for a space. She felt utterly at one with her aunt. She linked arms with her as they made their way to the main entrance. The world was cruel to Renie, but Hannah vowed she never would be. She thought with contempt of her parents discussing Renie last night, and saying that they suspected all her operations were beginning to affect her mind. Hannah thought she was more sane than they were.

She squeezed Renie's arm as they entered the hospital.

Hannah's mother was peeling the potatoes for the Friday night dinner. Even though her thumb and forefinger were stubby and lined, her hand moved with an accustomed grace over the pitted potato, deftly removing its skin with surgical precision. Hannah was mesmerized by the steady rhythm of her fingers and the glint of the blade of the knife. This was her last Shabbos at home before returning to university. Forty-eight hours before she would be reunited with Luke. She would miss the challah and chicken, it was true, but at college there were other consolations.

Her mother's hair was pulled back in an untidy French plait and her apron was tied loosely over her ample hips. Everything about her was soft and yielding. Hannah observed her lovingly. Her mother cried easily: at the end of films, romantic novels, and whenever she heard bad news. Being a psychology under-graduate, Hannah had analysed this. Her mother was the youngest in her family and had been babied by everyone. She was a female Peter Pan. In her never-never land everyone was innocent and bad things never never happened. There was no sex, either. This childishness was what Hannah loved about her mother. She knew it was her responsibility to protect and shelter her.

'Have you asked Renie if she's eating with us?' her mother asked.

'I will,' Hannah said, not moving, still enjoying watching her mother handling potatoes.

'Because she didn't have much for lunch.'

Renie had come home a week ago from Crumpsall, minus one womb and plus a temper that crackled like fireworks. She wasn't able to look after herself and so she was convalescing with her sister, resenting it, and using her as a punch bag. Hannah had vacated her bedroom and was sleeping on the sofa in the lounge. This afternoon, however, the sofa was Renie's. She was lying on it in a state, watching afternoon TV.

'Shall I go and ask Renie if she wants a full meal?' Hannah asked.

'In a moment,' her mother said.

She swiftly halved, then quartered a potato.

'Renie told me you were sleeping with Luke.'

Hannah was winded, staggered by the enormity of her aunt's

treason. Only she didn't have time to think about that right now. The most important thing was that her mother shouldn't find out the truth.

'She told you that?' Hannah sounded convincingly incredulous.

'This morning.'

'Surely you didn't believe her! I mean, it was you who said that she wasn't in touch with reality these days. Too many operations – they must have affected her mind.' Hannah didn't know where to direct her eyes. 'It must be hard to come to terms with the loss of your womb, you know. Perhaps she's jealous.' She was floundering, but floundering to some purpose, she hoped.

'Jealous,' her mother mused.

'Jealous, or imagining things. I'll go and see what she wants for dinner.'

Once out of the kitchen, Hannah realized her legs were trembling. She felt as if she'd just leapt across a precipice. Then her relief gave way to a tidal wave of wrath. Renie had betrayed a confidence. It was intolerable. Hannah was determined to confront her immediately.

Filled with righteous anger, and making a choice selection from her arsenal of satirical phrases and stinging retorts, she pushed open the door of the lounge, and opened her mouth. She paused. Renie was lying on the sofa, asleep and slack-jawed. She was still in her pink towelling dressing-gown, which had fallen apart to reveal shockingly white calves with varicose veins like thick cords. The soles of her tartan slippers were coming away from their base. There was an acrid smell of stale cigarette smoke and the sharper scent of eau-de-Cologne with a twist of misery.

Hannah's anger dissolved as she stood there, shamefaced.

Inspired by nothing but selfishness, she had been about to savage her aunt as viciously as the surgeon at Crumpsall. The greater betrayal was hers; she had implied that her aunt was senile, purely to protect herself. If her father thought she was senile, he'd get her into sheltered accommodation in no time, to save him the trouble of doing all her odd jobs and only getting complaints in return. It was Renie, poor Renie, who had the most to lose, if Hannah persisted in her story that her aunt had lost her marbles.

Renie came to and smiled at Hannah; she looked comical because she hadn't bothered to put her teeth in.

'I've come to ask if you want any supper?' Hannah said meekly.

'Might as well,' she replied, reaching for her teeth.

Hannah realized she might be a virgin no longer, but she couldn't call herself a woman until she stopped being such a coward. For Renie's sake she would have to hurt her mother. Brandishing her imaginary scalpel, Hannah prepared herself for a naivectomy on her unsuspecting parent. Taking a deep breath she walked back into the kitchen, then cleared her throat.

'Actually, it's true. I am sleeping with Luke.'

Silence.

After a few moments, Hannah dared to look at her. It was as bad as she feared. Tears were coursing down her cheeks.

'It's the onions,' she said, and wiped her eyes with the side of her hand. Hannah could smell them. Spanish onions.

'I said I'm sleeping with Luke. Renie was telling the truth.'

'No she wasn't. She never said a word. I pretended she did because I didn't know how to tell you what happened. You see, I found a packet of pills in your bedside table when I was clearing it out to get ready for Renie.'

Hannah was numb with shock.

'Well, at least you're being responsible about one thing.' Her mother gave a little laugh, undid her apron and eased herself on to the stool at the breakfast bar.

'Are you angry with me?' Hannah asked her.

'Angry? Why should I be angry? A little jealous, maybe. I wish they'd had the Pill in my day. You don't happen to have a cigarette on you, love? I'm gasping.'

Hannah stared at her, lost for words, and experienced one of those moments when the known world re-arranged itself like the pieces of a kaleidoscope. Renie had been loyal after all; that much was easy to accept. But her blustering feisty aunt had vanished, to be replaced by a vulnerable, ageing, lonely woman, who needed her protection. In fact she needed her protection far more than her mother did. Her mother was one tough cookie. She swallowed hard, and looked at her again. Nonchalantly, she had resumed her peeling operations.

What a devious, scheming, deceitful, manipulative, artful – Hannah's store of adjectives was exhausted. All these years spent treading around her mother's sensibilities had been so much wasted energy. Why, she was probably even cleverer than Hannah. And what did she mean by that remark about the Pill? Could it be that her mother wasn't a virgin when she was married? Unthinkable and utterly disgusting!

But fun. Hannah's mouth curled in a smile. She and her mother had some catching up to do.

'I've got some Silk Cut in my bag,' she offered, experimentally.

'I'll put the kettle on,' her mother said.

At that moment, Renie appeared in the doorway.

'And make me a drink too. Tea, and go easy on the sugar. I don't like it too sweet. And get me my ash-tray, Hannah.'

Renie found a place for herself at the breakfast bar, grimacing as she settled down.

Hannah stopped to kiss her as she left the kitchen. Out in the hall, she reflected that for all her excellent end of term report, she had a lot to learn about psychology, and particularly the psychology of aunts and mothers. She could see now that going to university and losing your virginity was only the beginning of growing up.

Yes. Just like her mother, and just like her aunt, she was desperate for a cigarette.

The Lightweight Trigger
A. N. Other

He shot her for the fifth time and then he rested. It wasn't that he was tired or anything like that. He wondered whether her habit of leaving something on the side of the plate had rubbed off on him. Didn't matter if she was still hungry. Apparently it was good manners to leave something. He seemed to remember his mother telling him this was an insult to Biafrans. But he liked the fact she'd been to finishing school. Liked it and hated it, but then wasn't that the problem all round.

He sat on the edge of the couch. His most pressing decision was whether to settle back into the cushions to review the situation or sit forward, and hunch up on it. Was this a scene to be watched on television or on a computer screen? At several points in the last few minutes he had been getting the impression that he was a voyeur, watching and commenting on the unfolding action. Not that there was much action. She was stone dead from the moment the first bullet went in right between her eyes.

Definitely a movie. He settled back into the deep cushions.

He put his arms up on to the back of the couch, the metal semi-automatic in his right hand seemed to lie quite naturally in his now relaxed grip. Yes, it was a movie. He was playing his part.

The first thing that he noticed was just how much blood there was. He'd always thought gore scenes were a little overdone. Props men getting carried away. None of it. They underestimate considerably. The pools, and there were several of them, were still pools despite having soaked and soaked into the deep-pile carpet. Can you remember the centre spot area of a football pitch in winter before they got proper drainage? It looked worse. And dark dark red, mixed with a black sheen on the wide liquid surfaces. Rossoneri patterns on his soft-pile floor.

The first bullet was not in fact as previously reported, right between her eyes. It was central on the vertical plane, yes, but it was slightly higher, at the very top of that little valley that sloped up from her elegant, significant nose to disappear into the flat mid-western plain of her forehead.

He could never have her. That was the simple fact. Yes, she would never leave him, but then she would never be totally with him; the only totality was how she was against him.

He'd gone on-line for the weapon. Those first forays into Amazon.com and risking his credit card for Professor Kolve's rare 'The play they called Corpus Christi' had unwittingly prepared him for this carefully planned delivery.

He found it at galleryofguns.com. That's the great thing about the net. You can get just what you want. He set the search engine for finish; he could choose from a whole drop-down list. Blue stainless steel. It had to be.

He chose the Colt Combat Commander. At $813, not the most expensive, but definitely a style object. A dear friend used to always buy straight silver and black BM 3 series 'cause it was the nearest he could get to driving in a Braun shaver. It was in the same area. Compact, a metal blue slide, black Hogue grip running up the handle and the coolest carbon fibre lightweight trigger, made with black woven metal and with a series of 3 perfect small circles cut out of the hi-tech composite in a smooth arc, very Formula 1, very Maclaren.

One of the selling points was the white-dot sights, but he had found those pretty irrelevant. When he swung the gun up and pointed it and squeezed, before her face even registered surprise, he had just pointed and squeezed until he felt the cool comfortable metal pump in his hand. No aiming, because that would have been like thinking and that was not the way forward.

Having not used the sights he found it surprising to see how dead centre that first bullet had entered. He had not planned the moment. And what did he do, he went for the brain. Interesting. Was that the bit he could never own, never conquer, never be safe with? He had avoided any imaginings of how this solution would turn out; none of your marksman's preparation. He had wanted it to be fresh. And when the moment came, it went up there. Like a Nato Fighting Falcon homing in on an Iraqi chemical factory, he had, when the moment arrived, gone straight for the seat of human emotions.

Though violent and apparently final, this had, of course, been the only solution. He had realized, more than a year ago, that he could not live with her and had decided to leave. It was shortly after that he realized that he could not live without her. Each day was another empty cola-tin that may or may not have cigarette butts in it, a thing and a life unworthy of examination, the sides waiting to be crushed, the sides closing in.

It was around this time that he shot her for the second time. The bullet went in with a small thud. Into her heart. This was romance, this was love, this was poetry, so get back to the script. How could he say what had happened except by inexact but understandable metaphor. It was the heart, the heart that loved him too much and not enough, and he should have shot there if he'd had any sense of what was fitting.

But was it fitting to fire straight into a dead body and see it twitch.

Marc Bolan sang gently in the back somewhere.

Maybe it was a literary impulse. He'd never got over watching Falstaff shooting the already dead Geordie back in Stratford in the 60s, pumping several loads of Elizabethan buckshot into a corpse. Tarentino, poke your eyes out.

And maybe he did it to see how it felt.

It felt calm.

The bullet in the heart had taken a perfect path through the upper slope of her left breast. The grey Armani suit material was developing a small enamel-red badge on that perfect upper slope. Her breasts. And where was sex in all this? Such amazing, soaking sex. And then the periods of dryness. The droughts and the storms. Was their problem, his problem, precisely unresolvable because of the shape of a woman's flesh, those parabolas that intoxicate; because he could not live in a world where she might live with someone else. Not having her, his willed intention, would then mean her being had by someone else; not his intention at all.

Was this real love, was it genetic imperative, or was it just lust über alles? He shot her in the other breast.

Freud says love is either desire for imitation or desire for possession; maybe this was just desire for symmetry.

He'd started thinking about sex now, all the love he would

never make with her, and he started to get angry. Why did she make him do this? He said it out loud. Why? But it wasn't real pleading; more like Oliver Hardy giving the same stuff to Stanley. Why did you make me hurt you and by the way I'm going to hurt you some more.

He knelt down now at her feet and began to pull apart her legs. This was less a movie than a poem. Inside his new friend he had a 45-calibre worm that would try that long-preserved virginity. He pushed the grey-blue muzzle under the hem of her skirt, but got no further before the rush of revulsion hit him and he threw himself back on to the floor. In the sudden thought of how much she would enjoy this he swallowed all the pleasure that had been and all the pleasure that would now never be and it took all the breath out of him. Raising himself on his elbows he turned and looked at the room, their furniture, their things, their pictures, and that framed Polaroid of them both, sitting close on a leatherette bench, heads leaning together, smiling, in the dressing-room of some strange club in Highbury from a couple of years ago. What an amazing couple. He took aim this time using the white-dot sites and the glass and plaster of the picture frame exploded across the room.

It was getting late.

The Combat Commander felt like a good pair of Armani shades; it sat so easily in his hand, a fashion statement that in both form and function said all that had to be said about the innermost recesses of his personality. He looked at his new communicator. Good buy. He pulled his finger back from the trigger and eased it on to what the manual identified as the upswept grip safety. The light from the kitchen picked out his signet ring, a little gold, a little diamond.

Hers had four pure diamonds, but obliquely set into the

sides of a great chunk of white gold, rising like an anvil from the shanks of the ring. Gloriously understated. The four jewels weren't hiding, they were just busy being diamonds.

It was everything they had been. Everything they still were. It had just been one of those dilemmas. He couldn't leave but he couldn't stay. Neither with her nor without her. In such cases, you can sometimes turn away, but when it's a ring like that, when it's a thing like that, you cannot turn away. You have to do one or the other, you can do neither, you can only change the universe. Termination comes into play.

'All that love and maths can do is prove that one and one make two.' Maths proved he had only used four bullets so far. He pressed the flat blue muzzle against the stiff bone of her third finger and it came away with a sharp explosion; with the afternotes of cartilage crunching.

It was almost complete. Satisfactory.

He noticed with some sadness that at this central moment in his life the great questions were not of morality or existence but of setting and style. For a minute or two now he had been busy trying to decide whether to place the gun to the side of his temples or shove the barrel into his mouth – on entirely presentational grounds.

Giving head to four inches of darkened steel had much to offer, not least the sexual innuendo. Whereas holding the gun at right angles to the head seemed to be saying 'watch me', it was involving others. It was involving her. Hey, watch this.

Was it like the decision over which way to jump off the Golden Gate. He could never understand why eight out of ten, taking the big short cut, actually jumped facing the lights and sounds of San Francisco. Maybe the two out of ten who looked out to the blackness of the Pacific when they started their last dance weren't blaming anyone. He wasn't blaming anyone.

He pulled his right hand up as if to drink from a glass, his new friend now upside down but exactly level and he pushed it into the roof of his mouth. Took a beat. Squeezed the trigger.

The concept of the six-gun had stayed with him since childhood. He had felt good that his holster, bought from a toy wholesalers on Deansgate, had a little leather thing that wrapped round his thigh and tied. As a child he took this stuff seriously; very professional. And the six-gun. He'd found galleryofguns through the Earp.com portal. You found six-guns in the Wild West. The web catalogue never explained that this particular party item, the excellent 35-oz Combat Commander, uses five-round magazines.

He dreams of 'Goto, l'Isle d'Amour'.

No Place Like It
Mark E. Smith

PONDERING at half-step on the gross arrogance, blatant incompetence and thievery of the white trash in their late twenties, and their shaven-headed middle class imitators, FRANK circumnavigated what seemed like endless sand-holes, foxholes, spastic-convenient kerb stones punctuated by upright, kicked-over, reddy-orange and white fences on his way through the doing up of the Manchester Victoria post-bomb development.

It had been a muggy, slowcoach taxi ride, due to the incompetent driver, who in his porn-stupefied brain had not turned left before the Cathedral, where FRANK had made an early exit.

The only thing he remembered was the three healthy kids who'd thrown two rocks at the passing vehicles near the Rialto in Higher Broughton.

He was getting the black illuminations again, i.e. *All Is Substance – You Have Contact With None*, or *There's Been Nothing on Granada For At Least Ten Minutes*, *Never Mind the Digital Testing*.

DELIVERING leaflets 22 hours a week was just about manageable, thought JOE, if it wasn't for those big over-powered cars making him jump every time he crossed the road – they made him remember the small metal splint in his upper right thigh from that time he'd ventured into Rusholme, pissed, and got half knocked over. He'd agreed with most of the shit on that political leaflet that other bloke he'd bumped into was giving out, apart from that repeated phrase – *It All Makes Sense, Doesn't It* QUESTION MARK.

The men in the yellow hats sniggered as he limped by, and it seemed that they'd deliberately sanded near him, sending vicious particles coupled with lime flowing through the muggy, close, damp Cheetham Hill mid-afternoon on to his forehead and into his eyes.

STEWART Mayerling sat down in the Low Rat Head pub near the bottom end of Oxford Road, trying to work out how his plans to distract and confuse his English Drama lecturer hadn't quite worked out. Mother was a teacher, and the attention/distraction games had always worked on her. The pager going off, mid-lesson, the showbiz titbit asides in the middle of *Hamlet*, my vegetarianism – how the jumped-up prole sneered at that, of course not understanding my code of internal hygiene, well advanced beyond that of mere travellers and their ilk, or polytechnic balding lecturers. For that matter – I think I'll head up to Victoria, skip the lecture.

THE MITRE Arms, adjacent to the Cathedral, and next to The Shambles was empty this afternoon. FRANK walks in, having well given up on getting past Marks & Spencer, and blanching at the apostrophe on the Finnegan's Wake pub sign, towards the station. Picking a table was fairly hard even though – only one large eight-seater occupied by JOE.

In walks STEWART.

'Is it OK to sit here?' he asks the seated two.
'Sure.'
'It's crap out there isn't it?' says JOE.
'Damn right it is.'
'Let's form a Party,' says FRANK . . .

THE END

The Afghan Coat
Heather Leach

Begin at the beginning, they say, and work your way through to the end. What they never tell you, those smart arses, is where the beginning actually is.

Time: 1976. Simon at Yvonne's door. Kofi answers.

> *Knock knock*. Who's there? It's a man, Mam. What's he want?
> You, Mam, he wants
> you.

She's wearing dark red velvet trousers with gold stars, sleek as skin. A white cheesecloth shirt shows her small breasts, and he can plainly see the neat pink nipples, although he looks away. He's wearing the coat. The hatches are not yet battened down, so Yvonne's next-door neighbours come out to have a look. Olive on one side, fat Danny on the other. Olive pretends she's sweeping the front, and flaps her immaculate doormat against the balcony wall. Danny, long past respectable, stares without shame. The centre of his body is three times as wide as his shoulders so that his belly swings like a clown's hoop over his fat little feet. He wears a tight vest (tight clothes are all he has), and the slopes of his flesh are sharply outlined, fold on fold. Tomorrow he's off to Manchester Royal to have his teeth wired up, so today he eats what he likes. He smiles at Simon.

– I can eat what I like, he says, a Mars Bar in each hand.

Olive is wearing a bin bag overall and green rubber gloves. This is not quite what Simon had imagined.

Yvonne ignores Olive and Danny.

– Yes?

The rain's stopped for a minute and the sun's in her eyes.

Place: Charles Barry Crescent, Hulme. Sweet curve of balconies, huge white ships drifting on a sea of grass. The kitchens and walkways face south. The plan was that morning light would fall on to the housewives as they swept and chatted; and on to the children as they ran down the stairs to play. In one of the architect's drawings a woman leans over the balcony, her blonde hair flying as she waves at a boy and girl skipping under the full-leafed trees below. Another holds an infant in a bright doorway. She stretches out her arm, points: look! Raises the child, shows him his inheritance, this radiant city.

Dialogue:

– Are you Yvonne?

She puts a hand over her eyes, to see him better. A long narrow hand, he notices, bird bones with bitten fingernails.

– Who's asking?

– I'm Simon Mallon. John sent me. He said you needed help with the rubbish campaign.

– You'd better come in.

*

The Journey: To get here, he walks across half a mile of dogcrap grass, then up steps crowded with bin bags. Black bellies split, they ooze their half-digested guts down the stairwell. He catches himself sniffing guiltily, eagerly, as if smelling his own shit.

– You'd better come in.

He steps over the threshold, crosses an invisible line into the maisonette, and notes the moment with a particular thrill.

Archaeology: There was once a farm here. The map in the Central Library has that one black word: Newhulme, and beside it a tiny square mark floating in papery space. Under the cobbles and brickdust, below the rebuild and demolition strata, are dead fields and hedges, goosebones, sheepbones, farmer and farmer's wife bones: skulls, knuckles, tibia and fibia.

She sends the child to watch television and they sit in the kitchen. Olive and Danny are still out there, flapping and chomping, beyond the edges of the window frame.

– Go on, then.

– What?

– You said you'd come to help. What with?

– Ah. Well, John at community action said you'd signed a petition about the rubbish, you wrote your name and address on it, so we thought . . . we don't want to impose our views on the tenants, but, on the other hand, if there was any way we can help with . . . He is losing her interest, babbling away like a fool.

– Perhaps there might be some kind of meeting, I could . . .

As he talks, the coat behind him, resting in the corner where he'd left it, bends forward at the neck, and slowly slides down the wall like a well-behaved drunk.

– Where d'you pick him up?

– Sorry?

– Your mate over there.

– Who?

– The coat. The inside out sheep. It's fell over.

– Oh god, I know it's stupid. I got it in London.

– Carnaby Street?

– Well, that kind of thing. Portobello Road actually.

– Is that where you come from?

– Where, London?

– Yes.

– Well, sometimes, although Gloucestershire actually, I used to go between places . . .

Hard to explain his childhood, two houses, his mother in one, his father in the other, not separated, nothing so crude. No darling, Daddy and I get on fine. Bloody bourgeois hypocrisy. The white Afghan coat was one of those first-year sod everything extravagances, completely naff now he sees it in this little room – Sorry, do you want me to pick it up?

– No, leave it, it's like a bloody big dog guarding the door. I like it. I bet it's heavy on you though. D'you want a fag?

She holds out the packet to him across the table, eyebrows raised, sardonic but smiling, and he takes one, smiling back. The heating is on full blast and the windows are steaming over. They talk more about the petition, how to get the other tenants to do something, the state of the place. She gets up to make a cup of tea and he leans back in his chair, looking out at the view over the curved space to the back of the other block. He loves it all, the hopeless view, these hard chairs, the scuffed, pictureless walls.

– D'you want sugar?

– Two please.

She stirs it for him, as she's used to doing for Kofi, a gesture that neither of them notices.

– Thanks.

– Do you think he wants a cup?

She nods towards the coat which is on the floor now, arms folded across its lap, and he laughs. This is the other thing. This way of talking to you as if you were a human being instead of a machine. People are in touch with things more here, he thinks to himself. There's him coming in like a bureaucrat, and here she is making tea, and joking about the bloody coat. There's more heart to this kind of language, he thinks, none of that polite bullshit. Smoke slowly fills the small space over their heads.

Her point of view: Can you fancy a coat? From that first sight on the doorstep, she wants to touch it, to get a proper grip, inside and out. Just having it in the room makes things different. I opened the door and there it was. This is your life, Yvonne. Before and after the coat.

A hidden agenda: In one of the pockets, next to the Golden Virginia tin, and the A–Z, is Simon's other guidebook: *The Condition of the Working Class in England*, by Friedrich Engels.

History: Friedrich was scornful of many of the others: visitors, urban tourists, dilettantes. Most do-gooders were a particular waste of time, he ranted to Mary, writing their huge and useless reports, which gathered dust on government shelves. They came, they moaned, they mourned for the poor, the unemployed, disease, the moral decline. And then off they went to sit down at the dinner-table of some factory master, my dear Mr Greg, my dear Mrs Gaskell, will you take soup, beef, cake. None of them truly crossed the line as he had into those terrible regions where working men lived for all of their lives. That deep inner place, the warrens and calamitous hutches where he had been. He was a seeker not just of facts, but of reasons, fundaments. Beneath that chaotic surface there were intricate human mechanisms that he planned to lay bare.

There must have been one moment of doubt, surely, sitting at his desk, in the tiny bedroom in Dial Street, his careful notebook beside him. An afternoon perhaps, late, the light already fading, his anger burning steadily, yet contained like the small flames in the grate. A moment when he could not find a way through. He got up, agitated, fists clenched in frustration, glared about the room in which he could hardly move, his and Mary's bed almost filling the rest of the space. And she, reading below, caught the creak of the floorboard, a sound she knew well, looked up for a moment, then lowered her head to the book again. Friedrich gazed down at his own words and instead of the plain and obvious tower that he had hoped he was building suddenly saw only the heart of a Babel, undecipherable, ruinous. Ach! He threw down the pen.

What Mary did not do: She did not get up out of her chair by the fire when he came into the room, his hair sticking up in spikes, his face as pale as ashes. She did not go over to the sink and fill a kettle, nor did she get out a jar of biscuits, which she had baked in the difficult but interestingly old bread oven that morning. She had not blackleaded the oven before he was awake, nor donkey stoned the step, nor carefully and tenderly smoothed down his jacket, after picking it up from where he had thrown it down. She did not think to herself now or ever, that perhaps such a clever man might tire of her, simple mill girl that she was. This is certain, but the rest is vague: her hands, the colour of her eyes, the exact angle of her head as she read on by the whickering fire until the day was almost gone. She sat for a while in the dark, then rose and lit the candles. So much unwritten, laid down in the dust.

Friedrich dashed out on to the street, hatless, despite the ubiquitous rain and strode off into an area he had been warned not to enter alone. After a while he slowed down from his furious striding and looked around to see where exactly he was. Whole blocks of interlocked terraces, back to back, yard-less and waterless, built without plan except that of speed and profit, the side wall of one the front of another. There were pumps, privies and middens at intervals, side by side and stinking. He made notes, he wrote, he recorded. There are long narrow lanes, between which run contracted, crooked courts and passages, the entrances to which are so irregular that the explorer is caught in a blind alley at every few steps, or comes out where he least expects to, unless he knows every court and alley, exactly and separately. Friedrich the mapmaker, Friedrich the guide. He imagined the city laid out before him, its intricate spaces, both hidden and thrillingly open. His plan was to enter, not as the others did – overlooking, God-like, but from within. Sometimes, as they lay together in the dark, he said to Mary that it must be sweet to be nameless and faceless, without weight in the world. She could smell the smoke of foreign cities on his body: London; Bremen; Paris.

Simon knows that it is impossible to exactly retrace Friedrich's steps. There are no landmarks, no signs. Streets lie on streets, houses on houses. Even the old roads have gone, even their traces, the surface of the world scraped clean. How many layers down to the farmbones?

He's back the next day with his pockets full of leaflets. Yvonne wears a T-shirt now, but even so, he can see that she's wearing a bra. He tries not to think of her like that, but going along the balconies together, posting leaflets, he can't stop watching her, the tilt of her head as she turns to look out for him, her thin face, her long straight hair. They go back for a tea-break at her flat.

– Where's your little boy?

– Kofi, his name is. He's at my mam's. Thank god for a bit of peace. Do you want to come in here?

First the bra, now the best room. The more front she puts on, the closer he gets.

Each word is a turning, a possible path. Friedrich tramped for miles through the little streets, leant over Ducie Bridge, stared down into the filthy Irwell. 'Oh working men', he wrote, 'I saw you in your own homes, in your hateful and repulsive rookeries. I was an explorer, a traveller, yet I knew you intimately.'

What Yvonne thinks: That the coat has turned up just in time. Here it is at last, as if she'd been waiting years, flapping its hairy cuffs and its crack-creased elbows. Hiya girl, better late than never. She thinks that now there's just a small chance she might not have to be who she's turning into. That this coat is an opening, a possible door.

The balcony scene: They go up to the top floor. It's windy and they have to hold on to the leaflets, but still a few get loose. She runs after them, and he thinks how like a kid she is, the way she runs, the way she pulls silly faces. It starts raining again.

– We'd better go back, he says.

– Just a minute.

They've reached the far end of the block, and she stops to lean over.

– What?

– Look at the hills.

The cloud-thick light brings the Pennines into sharp relief, low dark walls round the edge of the city.

– I never knew about them until I came here.

He can't think of anything to say.

She shivers, Bloody hell, I'm freezing.

He moves around to get between her and the wind.

– We'd better go.

– No. Let's stop a minute longer, it's nice up here. Go on, give us a bit of your coat.

He opens it wide and she walks straight in.

She tells him to put it on the bed and lies down, naked, wrapping herself in its arms, burying her face into the fur, and he feels ludicrously jealous. He gets on to it with her, the two of them snuggling down like babies. Two little lambs, she says, suck suck.

What the coat promised Yvonne as she lay in its arms: Stick with me, girl and I'll get you out of this shit. It lied.

How the story went: Danny has his teeth wired, eats nothing but liquids and loses twelve stones in six months. As his body shrinks, his skin falls into flaps and loops. He makes his way down the stairs for the first time in a year, is caught interfering with a small girl in one of the useless garages, and is put away, where he gets even thinner. Olive after sweeping and dusting the whole of the balcony from one end to the other, starts on the garages which is how she finds Danny. Mary died and Karl wrote with only the briefest of sympathies, mixed in with his usual request for money.

My poor Mary, how she did love me, eulogized Friedrich, stung and reproachful. This suggestion of insult almost caused a rift between the two comrades, but was soon patched up. The class struggle continued. Karl died.

Friedrich died.

They are awkward, of course. Legs and arms in the wrong positions. He's too rushed, she pretends to like it more than she actually does. The bedroom's like a den, an inner room, he thinks, with dirty windows.

– I've fastened them shut to keep Kofi from falling out. You can't clean the outsides.

– I don't mind.

– Well I do, I'm sick of the sight of them. I'd like to see out, if there was anything worth looking at.

– What would you like to see?

He has his eyes shut, traversing her body, feeling his way.

– I don't know, somewhere with a better view.

She runs her hands over the coat's skin.

– Afghan-land. How about that?

He laughs, and they start again, slower this time. Better.

How it ends: He moves in. Margaret Thatcher says we must do something about those inner cities. He moves out. The Berlin Wall and then the crescents are pulled down on top of bricks, cobbles, and cowpats. A local committee thinks about putting up a plaque in the place where Friedrich and Mary lived, but can't decide on the exact spot. Yvonne doesn't go to Afghanistan. The coat stays, rotten but faithful.

The Day My Dad
Ran Away
Bill Naughton

Functional Penetration has not, so far as I know, to do with the
stratosphere, eugenics or jet propulsion, but is a term used
in sociology. It is a theory that holds that the best way for the
social scientist to find out the true facts about any group or
class is to go and live amongst them – as a social unit, so to
speak.

It was the carrying out of some similar notion, I imagine,
that brought a certain Professor Michelschweioz to the cotton
town where I lived as a youth. He was a Czech, a psychologist,
educated in Vienna of course, and he was engaged by a New
York trust to carry out a study of the Lancashire working class.

He rented a small house in an ordinary street, stacked the
room with fat books and the kitchen with fat sausages – salami
and wurst – and discovered, after a few months, that though
he had learnt nothing whatever about the people living round
him, they knew everything about him. It was then when he
called me in as a part-time assistant.

'Lancashire womens,' he told me at our first interview, 'iss
very septic. She iss not believing what I tell him.'

'Friday iss beings tomorrow,' he later explained, 'and I am wanting for you to observe.'

'Observe what?' I asked.

'Everyzink. Every little zink what iss happening in the home and factory of you iss social phenomena. Here is a notebook und pencil. Write all you are seeing and hearing.'

'Won't it look conspicuous, Professor?'

'Ah ha,' he said and smiled like a child, 'no! Dey remain in dee pocket. Watch!' and with one hand in his coat pocket he strolled round the room, his hand moving inside the pocket. Then he took out the book. 'See! I haf writing been int my pocket. Now listen: you are bringing your writings in tomorrow at eight o'clock. I am paying you two bobs. If it is very good I am maybe giving you half of the crown.'

When I woke up that Friday morning I tried to force my ear clear for taking in all impressions. I wanted to do my yogic breathing exercises in front of the window, but the scavenger's cart was only just disappearing, and I dared not open it. I hoped to do some abdominal exercises as a compensation, but my brother was fixing his Saturday-night trousers under the mattress – he liked me to give them a day and a night press – and so I couldn't do them on the bed. So I put my trousers on and went to the lavatory, to write down in my notebook all that I would normally have done. But then an instinct for truth caused me to cross it out and say nothing about the whole thing, hoping that something would happen over breakfast that I could write about.

I had my wash and the usual bother, because there were three of us round the tap, arguing about whose turn it was for the soap. I thought I might get something out of this, but I didn't. At breakfast there was nothing unusual. My sister was eating her banana sandwiches. She had a sort of fetish about bananas, and had to have them at every meal. Even at Sunday dinner, when we all sat down to roast beef, she insisted on her little plate of banana butties, and wouldn't touch the hot meal. My young brother (not the one with the trousers under the bed) had to have chips at every meal. My mother used to fry an enormous pan of chips at a time, and keep hotting them up to keep him going. He had them that morning. He stood them up around his plate like birthday candles, and kept blowing them down. Each one he blew over he ate. My older brother, the trousers one, was mad on fruit, and he had a habit of flicking his pips or stones at my younger brother's chips, and knocking them over. This always caused bother at mealtimes. It didn't worry me, because I had read somewhere that food went down properly only if you were standing and on the move while you ate, and so I used to keep walking round the table as I was eating. Sometimes I spilled my porridge on somebody, but I never stopped: I felt certain that if I didn't keep moving all the food would get lodged in my oesophagus and choke me.

My father was in a crabbed mood that morning over his newspapers. He used to get home from the mine about six-thirty in the morning, and before his breakfast he always read his three newspapers. Somehow his eye always wandered down to the tail-ends of the columns, where he would always find details of people's wills. They never failed to upset him. He simply couldn't stand the idea of people leaving money. Not only was he convinced that no honest man could ever possess more than would just keep him going, and would always be short if not heavily in debt, but he was infuriated by the mere idea of anyone having the presumption to actually possess so much money that they still had a lot over when they died. The very audacity of it – that a dead man should have more to his name than a living one, drove him frantic. Usually, if my mother spotted any big wills, especially those over a hundred thousand pounds, she would arrange for the paper to get a bit torn off, just to save any bother. But that morning he had spotted a brewer, of all people, leaving three-quarters of a million, and a bookmaker a neat sum of one hundred and seventy-two thousand. 'To hell's blue blazes with 'em!' he swore, while my mother kept blessing herself and saying prayers for their souls, trying to keep the odds even, so to speak, against his curses.

A diversion was created by my sister spotting my right hand. I was attempting to write notes in my pocket the way the professor had shown me.

'Look,' she cried, 'his arm keeps twitching. What's up with him?'

'St Vitus's dance!' shouted my trousers-under-the-bed brother, 'or,' he added ominously, 'locomotor ataxy.'

'Shut up!' I shouted.

'What's up?' asked my father.

'He's got St Vitus's dance.'

'Dance for us,' said my young brother, blowing over a chip and eating it.

There was a rat-tat at the door and a letter came, so that drew the scent off me. It was from my father's brother, Uncle Tom, to say that he was leaving Ireland to work for a few weeks at the hay, and that he would arrive at our house that very evening. That got us all excited, and I went to work feeling rather happy – especially as it was Friday and therefore pay day, and on top of everything I felt now that I had a purpose in life, since the professor had given me this assignment of observing people.

I was working at Mutt's Mill. In the weaving shed, learning to be a weaver, and I hated the job. I had two jacquard looms, and they seemed to go so fast that I couldn't keep up with them, though the women around me could keep four going and read *Peg's Paper* at the same time. Sometimes I simply couldn't suck the end of cotton through the shuttle hole. They call it 'kissing the shuttle', which should take about one-tenth of a second, but I used to be sucking and kissing away like Rudolph Valentino for minutes on end, until I had the shuttle halfway down my throat, and even then that little end of cotton wouldn't come through for me. The women all round used to come and help me – or else I'd have never earned a penny – and it was amazing to see how they'd put their faces near mine, and without even touching the shuttle that end of cotton would fairly leap out of the shuttle hole to their lips. But when the atmosphere got too much for me, I mean with my little alley crowded with weavers, all soft and round and womanly, pressing round me on all sides keeping my two looms going, then I'd escape to the men's convenience. On my way I used to grab a couple of heavy springs off the dump heap, and inside the cubicle I'd exercise until the sweat rolled off me. I was very fond of reading Jack London at that time, and I used to imagine I was Martin Eden, so much so that I used to call myself Martin to myself, and I'd say after a heavy bout of spring-pulling, 'You've had enough now, Martin, back to your looms.'

On that particular Friday it was rather trying to work all this in and the notebook as well. I rather liked the idea of writing inside my pocket, without anybody knowing about it, but I saw some of the weavers giving me queer looks, and opening their lips to each other – knowing well that I could never follow that lip-reading lingo. I soon realized that I couldn't get it all down in writing, so I devised a code with certain symbols. When anything happened which I felt should be noted for the professor – there was a fight between two weavers in the morning, and one of the overlookers went mad over his dinner and had to be taken to the asylum – I simply put A or B or C, and went on through the alphabet in that manner, relating each scene to a single letter. I thought the idea rather neat.

The awful news about my father came at five o'clock when my banana-eating sister suddenly appeared in my alley.

'What's up?' I asked. 'Where've you come from?' She worked at the other end of Mutt's Mill.

'You've got to come at once –' she said. 'Mum's had a heart attack.'

'What? – I've not got my wage yet.'

'She's not really had an attack,' whispered my sister, bending her face to my ear so that the other weavers couldn't see her lips, '– it's Dad.'

'What?'

'He's run away!'

'Eh? Who with?'

'Nobody, you fool. He's just done a bunk. Sent a telegram to say that he's gone for ever. Mum's in a terrible state.'

'What about?'

'He's not been home with his wages, you fool. You'll have to go an' catch him at Liverpool, if you can, an' get the wages off him.'

'But I can't go without drawing mine!'

'You can get them in the morning,' she said.

'No!' I was nearly crying. For forty-eight hours a week I worked – or at least attempted to – with a dumb mechanical efficiency, until in one brief moment of blinding illumination, when I held out my hand and received my packet at twenty-past five every Friday, the long ordeal was suddenly transfused with happy significance. Now I was going to be done out of it. And I was. In spite of all the bananas she ate – it couldn't be because of – she was very strong, and now she dragged me off home.

'What the heck do you keep twitching in your pocket about?' she asked as we dashed through the streets. I was just putting down letter O.

There was the telegram on the table when we got home.

Gone off for ever. Keep Notes. Michael.

'He must be in a terrible temper,' sobbed my mother, 'when he signs himself "Michael" instead of "Mick". And then him trying to pretend he put money inside the telegram – the divil out of hell.'

'Where did he send it from?' I asked.

'Liverpool,' she said, 'is the name on it. I want you to go off now and see if you can catch him before the boat sails.'

'Oh, I don't want to be responsible for bringing him back,' I said.

'Don't bother about that,' said my mother, 'but get his wages, or what's left of them. He went off at noon today to the pit to draw them, and as you know he should be back at three o'clock, but now it's after five, and the telegram here.'

'Did you have a row?' I asked.

'Of course,' said Mother, 'he had the usual one. A bit stiffer than usual.'

Just then I heard a motorbike in the street. 'Eggface!' I exclaimed.

'What about him?' asked my sister.

Ernest was his name, a bricklayer, with the most enormous hands I ever saw; he was keen on my sister, and used to come round our neighbourhood on his motorbike just to meet her coming home from work.

'*He* could go!' I said. 'He'd be there in less than half an hour. And he could bring the old chap back on the pillion – he could force him on. What about it?'

It was a desperate situation, and so they agreed to call in outside aid, especially as Eggface was on the dumb side, and wouldn't talk.

'It's my dad who's suffering from sort of loss of memory,' said my sister to him. 'He's gone off to Liverpool, an' he's probably wandering about. We don't want to call the police in – do you think you could perhaps try an' pick him up, Ernest?'

'Aye, lass,' said Ernest, 'I'd pick him up for you – but I've never *seen* him.'

'You can't mistake him,' I said. 'He's short and stiff-built with a black moustache. Talks to himself as he walks, and if you listen he'll be saying "To hell's blue blazes!" He nearly always says that. You could telephone us at Firclough's, the undertakers: Blitton 1919.'

'Would you like to come on the back?' he asked me.

'No thanks, not me,' I said. It was one of those 8 horse-power Indians, with a roar like a lion, and Ernest used to flatten it out all the time. 'Anyway, you have to bring him back.'

'Black moustache you said?' he asked, kicking it up, 'an' talks to himself? I'll get him. For you, love,' he added, looking at my sister. Like a shot he was gone. I ran back to the factory then to get my wages, but the gate had just closed, and the timekeeper said all the money had been locked up, so that I'd have to wait till next Friday, because they unlocked the safe only once a week. I never felt worse in my life.

Eggface must have gone like fury to Liverpool, for it was under the hour when Firclough's telephone rang and we were asked for. They were just paying out the bets when we rushed into the house. They were really bookmakers, who had a telephone put in on the pretext of needing it for the undertaking business.

'I've got him!' bawled Eggface, his voice loud enough to split an eardrum, 'but he's putting up a fight.' My sister and Mother were watching me, but they wouldn't take hold of the instrument, though they could hear plain enough. I could hear the muttering curses of my father: 'To hell's blazes with ye!' and so on.

'That's him!' I shouted, 'you've got the right man.'

'Right – I'll bring him back,' shouted Eggface. 'He'll not dare to make a leap off the bike, once I get him on it. Uoh . . .' he grunted, as though he had been hit. Then he hung up.

We thanked Mr Firclough, and then the three of us went out and back to our own house. When we went in the door there was my father sitting in the big rocking-chair, reading the evening paper, and just showering curses on some tobacco magnate who had just left four million pounds.

'Where the hell were you all?' he shouted.

'An' where were you?' asked my mother. 'You're soon back from Liverpool!'

'Liverpool?' he roared, '– who the devil was at Liverpool?'

'Then where did you send the telegram from?'

'Telegram!' he bellowed, '– are you out of your mind? What telegram?'

She picked up the telegram and showed it to him.

'"Gone for ever"!' he snorted. 'By hell, if I ever go you'll get no telegram! I'll go out that door, an' that'll be the last you'll ever see of me.'

'Then why were you late?'

'St Vitus's dance,' he said with a laugh. 'I saw the name against the probables, an' damme if it didn't win. Twenty-to-one. So I stayed behind and had a few extra pints with Martin Magee and one or two others.'

We all looked at each other. Then who had sent the telegram? And who, in heaven's name had Eggface got hold of – and was dragging back on his motorbike? And it was not to be long before we were to discover, for while we were standing there, unspeaking, there was a sudden roar of a motorbike at the front door. 'The Lord help us,' moaned my mother, putting her two hands to her temples.

Dare I go so far as to say who it was that actually leapt off the bike the moment it stopped, and started cursing at the top of his voice? Yes, I dare. *Uncle Tom* – that's who it was.

'Tom!' cried my mother. 'The blessings of God on you!'

'Arra phwat bleddy caper is this?' he shouted, ' – sending this mad hooligan to bring me here. God help me, I'm dead.'

Poor Eggface didn't know what it was all about, and he tried to explain that he'd seen this man with the black moustache strolling along the Goree Piazzas in Liverpool, muttering 'To hell's blue blazes!' and that he had admitted his name, but refused to come, and Eggface had shanghaied him.

Eggface now imagined he had been a dupe. My father thought there was some plot going on. My sister thought it had something to do with my St Vitus's dance. My mother thought she was going off her mind – and I was pretty sure she had done so. But the whole matter was cleared up by the arrival of Professor Michelschweioz.

'Ah, are you getting my telegram?' he asked.

'Oh, I'll come along with you now,' I said hurriedly, and off I went.

'What,' I asked him, 'was the meaning of "*gone for ever*"?'

'Lever,' he said. 'It iss my frient Doctor Lever I am going to see. "*Gone off for Lever*" is what I am writing. "*Keep notes*", for I zink I am no coming back tonight. For why do you ask?'

'Oh nothings,' I said.

'You are haffing the notes?' he asked when we got to the house.

'Yes,' I said, 'but you'd better copy them out in your own writing, while I tell you what happened.'

I then recited what looked to me like an ordinary day – but not the day that had just happened. However, I did tell him about the overlooker that went mad and had to be taken away, in which he appeared to be very interested, and asked for all the details. I told him how Ben, that was the man's name, had suddenly screeched over his dinnertime tomato sandwiches, 'Let me outa here! Let me out!' Ben, I explained, was a man of forty-seven, and had only been working there for thirty-five years. The older overlookers had sympathized about the case, and had told how those were the danger years – when a chap had been on the same job for thirty-five to forty years – but once he'd got over the forty he'd be all right.

'What is this O?' asked the professor, glancing at my notes.

'Oh, that's where I missed getting my wages,' I said.

'Ah,' he remarked, 'you are being too engrossed in your work, is that he?'

The family privacy had to be preserved at all costs, and so I agreed to this unspeakable suggestion: 'Yes,' I said, 'I forgot what day it was.'

The professor, I imagine, may have been working for two sides, because the notes of Ben's outburst went into a red notebook, and forgetting to draw my wage into a blue one.

He seemed immensely satisfied with my report: 'When we

are getting all the postulations, theories and correlations from this material, I zink there is enough for a book. For zis I zink I am payings you half the crown.'

I accepted the coin, and, feeling that I had made an immortal contribution to science, I squared my shoulders and set off home to face the row.

About the Authors

Andrea Ashworth was born in Manchester in 1969. She is a Junior Research Fellow at Jesus College, Oxford. Her first book, *Once in a House on Fire*, was her memoir of a troubled childhood set in Rusholme and Moss Side.

Sherry Ashworth's novels include *A Matter of Fat* (Crocus), *No Fear* (Sceptre), *Money Talks* (Coronet) and *The Best of Friends* (Coronet). She is a prolific journalist, an English teacher at the Bury High School for Girls and a mother of two.

Novelist, critic and former lead singer of the Factory-signed rap group Meatmouth, **Nicholas Blincoe**'s previous novels include *Acid Casuals*, *Jello Salad* and *Manchester Slingback*, which won this year's CWA Silver Dagger Award. He has also published a collection of short stories, *My Mother was a Bank Robber*.

David Bowker is author of the crime thrillers *The Death Prayer*, and *The Butcher of Glastonbury*, and the post-feminist comedy *The Secret Sexist*. His most recent novel is *From Stockport with Love*. He has been a columnist for *New Woman* magazine and *The Times*.

Michael Bracewell is the author of five works of fiction: *The Crypto-Amnesia Club* (Serpent's Tail, 1988); *Missing Margate* (1988); *Divine Concepts of Physical Beauty* (Secker, 1989); *The Conclave* (Secker, 1992) and *Saint Rachel* (Cape, 1995). His study of the English pop dream *England is Mine: Pop Life in Albion from Wilde to Goldie* was described as 'Surely the strangest and most beautiful book on pop music ever written.' Bracewell is also a prolific journalist.

Charlotte Cory has published three novels, *The Unforgiving*, *The Laughter of Fools* and *The Guest* (all Faber and Faber) and is currently working on her next novel, a contemporary Gulliver's Travels, as well as a non-fiction book about family, memory and Empire. She writes for various national newspapers and makes radiophonic poetry for BBC radio.

Gareth Creer was born in Salford in 1961 and brought up in Manchester. He went to Oxford and then into the City. In 1994 he abandoned his career to write full time, taking the Sheffield Hallam MA writing course. He is author of two novels *Skin and Bone* and *Cradle to Grave* (both Anchor books) and is currently working on his third.

At the age of nineteen **Shelagh Delaney** wrote *A Taste of Honey* (1958), which was immediately heralded as a classic of the kitchen sink drama. Two years later she enjoyed similar acclaim for her second play *The Lion in Love* (1960). She has since published a collection of short stories, *Sweetly Sings the Donkey*, and has written widely for TV, radio and cinema. Her screenplays include *The White Bus* (1966), *Charlie Bubbles* (1968), *Dance with a Stranger* (1985). Most recently she has adapted the Jessica Mitford novel *Hons and Rebels* for Working Title TV.

Richard Francis lectures in American Literature and Creative Writing at Manchester University, where he is also the deviser and convenor of an MA in Novel Writing. His novels include *Blackpool Vanishes*,

Swansong, The Land Where Lost Things Go, Taking Apart the Poco Poco, which won the 1995 Portico Prize, and most recently *Fat Hen*. He lives in Stockport with his wife and two children.

P-P Hartnett's club and street-style photography has featured in *The Sunday Times Magazine, The Independent, Attitude, Blue* and *Time Out* – among others – and exhibited in London, New York and Tokyo. He has written two novels and a book of short stories – *Call Me, I Want To Fuck You* and *Mmm Yeah* – all published by Pulp Books. He is currently editing Dennis Nilsen's autobiography.

Dave Haslam DJ-ed at the Haçienda during the 'Madchester' years. He has since played worldwide; from Detroit to Paris, Ibiza to Berlin. Through the 1990s he hosted Freedom and Yellow at the Boardwalk in Manchester. He has written for *The Face, NME, City Life* and *The Observer*. His book *Manchester, England* is published by Fourth Estate.

Jackie Kay was born in Edinburgh in 1961, grew up in Glasgow and moved to Manchester in 1995, where she lives with her son. She has published three collections of poetry: *The Adoption Papers*, which won the Saltire and Forward prizes, *Other Lovers*, which won a Somerset Maugham Award, and *Off Colour*. Her first novel *Trumpet* won the Guardian Fiction Prize. She is currently working on a collection of short stories.

Heather Leach has worked as a driver, post office worker, playleader, journalist, community worker and teacher. Her short stories have been read on Greater Manchester Radio and have appeared in various publications including *The Metropolitan, Northern Stories* and *The Big Issue*. She is currently working on her first novel.

Val McDermid has lived in Manchester since the seventies and worked as a journalist for sixteen years before quitting in 1991 to become a full-time writer. Her numerous crime novels include five Kate Branigan detective thrillers, a non-fiction book, *A Suitable Job* *for a Woman* which lifted the lid on female PIs, and two novels featuring the criminal pathologist Tony Hill – *The Wire in the Blood* and the 1995 CWA Gold Dagger winner *The Mermaids Singing*.

Livi Michael's *Under a Thin Moon* won the Arthur Welton Award for a First Novel; her second *Their Angel Reach* won the Faber Prize and the Society of Authors Award and was short-listed for the John Steinbeck and John Llewelyn-Rhys awards. Her third, *All the Dark Air*, was shortlisted for the Mind award.

Bill Naughton was author of the sixties plays *Spring and Port Wine*, *All in Good Time*, *He Was Gone When We Got There* and *Alfie* (which was filmed by Lewis Gilbert in 1966). He also wrote the novel *One Small Boy*, a three-part autobiography *On a Pig's Back*, *A Catholic Childhood* and *Neither Use Nor Ornament*, as well as the collection of short stories *Late Night on Watling Street*. He died in 1971.

Jeff Noon is the author of the psychedelic Mancunian fantasies *Vurt*, *Pollen*, *Automated Alice* and *Nymphomation* (Transworld). His play *Woundings* was first produced at Manchester's Royal Exchange Theatre and is presently being adapted in a film by Muse Productions. Last year he published his first collection of short stories, *Pixel Juice*.

Along with Lemn Sissay and Johnny Dangerously, **Henry Normal** was one of Manchester's most important stand-up poets of the early nineties. His poetry collections include *Do You Believe in Carpet World?*, *Is Love Science Fiction* and *Nude Modelling for the Afterlife*, and as a poet he hosted Channel Four's *Packet of Three* and Radio 4's *Encyclopaedia Poetica*. He has since gone on to become a BAFTA award-winning comedy writer, as a co-writer for *Paul Calf's Video Diaries*, *The Mrs Merton Show*, *Coogan's Run*, *The Royle Family* and *Mrs Merton and Malcolm*.

Jane Rogers is perhaps best known for her novel *Mr Wroe's Virgins* (Faber) which she adapted for television to great acclaim in 1993.

Her other novels include *Separate Tracks*, *Her Living Image*, which won the Somerset Maugham Award, *Promised Lands* (Faber) and *Island*. Her television play *Dawn and the Candidate* won a Samuel Beckett Award. She is a Fellow of the Royal Society of Literature and is currently editing the OUP's *Good Fiction Guide*.

Michael Schmidt is the founding editor of Carcanet Press and *PN Review* which have been based in Manchester since 1971. He is the editor of *Eleven British Poets* and *The Harvill Book of Twentieth Century Poetry in English* (1999), the author of *Reading Modern Poetry*, *Poets on Poets*, *The Lives of the Poets* and the forthcoming *Lives of the Novelists*, and Director of the Writing School at Manchester Metropolitan University. He has published two novels, *The Colonist* and *The Dresden Gate* and his *Selected Poems* were published by Smith/ Doorstop in 1997.

Karline Smith's short story *Ezekiel's Valley* (Afro-Caribbean Resource Centre) won the Vera Bell prize and was converted into the crime thriller *Moss Side Massive* (X-Press). A dramatized version of the book, *Taking it to the Max*, was shortlisted for the *New Writers' Showcase, Film Up North* and performed by Liverpool's Unity Theatre in 1995. She is presently working on her forthcoming novel *Balancing Acts*.

Mark E. Smith is the lead-singer and sole-surviving force behind Manchester's most prolific band, The Fall. Since the release of their first EP, 'The Bingo Master's Breakout' in 1978, The Fall have reflected and rejected over two decades of Manchester music, through punk, Mancabilly, Madchester and dance. They have produced twenty-two studio albums and over twenty compilations and live albums. In 1997 during a televised award ceremony the *NME* awarded Smith a special 'God-like Genius Award' and, true to form, he left it on the podium. This is his first piece of fiction.

Cath Staincliffe's first novel *Looking For Trouble* (published by local press Crocus) introduced us to crime fiction's first single-parent female detective, Sal Kilkenny, who has since starred in the novels *Go Not Gently* (Headline) and *Dead Wrong* (Headline), set in the aftermath of the IRA bomb. She is currently working on a fourth Sal Kilkenny novel while bringing up three kids.

Tim Willocks' first novel *Bad City Blues* (recently adapted for the screen) was followed by *Green River Rising*, which sold over 300,000 copies, and its sequel *Bloodstained Kings*. He continues to work as a doctor in a London clinic for drug casualties. Despite being born in Stalybridge, this is Willocks' first piece of fiction set in the city.